RUSH TO VICTORY

RUSH TO VICTORY

A Novel

BY
ROBERT E. SEIKEL

authorHOUSE®

AuthorHouse™
1663 Liberty Drive
Bloomington, IN 47403
www.authorhouse.com
Phone: 1-800-839-8640

This is a historical novel. Characters are fictitious except for the obvious true characters.

© 2012 Robert E. Seikel. All rights reserved.

No part of this book may be reproduced, stored in a retrieval system, or transmitted by any means without the written permission of the author.

Published by AuthorHouse   03/23/2012

ISBN: 978-1-4685-6061-9 (sc)
ISBN: 978-1-4685-6062-6 (hc)
ISBN: 978-1-4685-6063-3 (e)

Library of Congress Control Number: 2012904142

Illustration by Valen Richardson

This book is printed on acid-free paper.

Because of the dynamic nature of the Internet, any web addresses or links contained in this book may have changed since publication and may no longer be valid. The views expressed in this work are solely those of the author and do not necessarily reflect the views of the publisher, and the publisher hereby disclaims any responsibility for them.

CONTENTS

Chapter	Title	Page
1	Jim's First Patrol	1
2	Dutch Harbor	5
3	Rest and Relaxation	11
4	The Gilbert Islands	17
5	Work and Play	24
6	The Sea of Japan	32
Map	Sea of Japan	34
7	The Transition	47
8	The Change	55
9	Lifeguard Patrol	64
10	Home Again Safe	76
11	Mission Changed	88
12	The Marshall Islands	93
Map	South and Central Pacific Ocean	106
13	The Flight	107
14	The Hospital	112
15	The Recovery	118
16	The Recuperation	130
17	The Wedding	140
18	A New Assignment	148
19	Guam	159
20	A Time To Plan	179
21	A New Year	192
22	A New Station	203
Illustration	Janet	205
23	The Last Battle	212
24	Back to Pearl	222
25	Final Assignment	236
26	The Anniversary	240

CHAPTER 1
JIM'S FIRST PATROL

"WAKE UP MISTER Rush, it is 0130 and you have the 0200 watch." Seaman Henry Thomas said.

Jim Rush responded, "Okay, thanks Thomas. I'll get up in a minute."

Jim Rush could hear the diesel engines of the submarine and it reminded him of a heartbeat. In a way the throb of the engines were a heart beat. They provided oxygen and other essentials to keep them alive.

Jim muttered, "Just think four engines to keep us alive and going."

Jim could see that Jack, Don, and Al's bunks were empty. He knew they were on duty. Ensign George "Mac" MacDonald was still asleep. He hoped Mac did not oversleep because he was to relieve Jim at 0600 (6 a.m.).

Jim said, "Thomas make sure you wake Mister MacDonald up to relieve me at 0600."

Henry Thomas, "Aye, Aye, sir"

Henry Thomas left and Jim started dressing.

Jim muttered, "I think I'll sleep for a week on my next leave."

Jim dressed and went to the crew's galley. He would order breakfast and go to the officer's wardroom.

Jim entered the galley and Cook Seaman 2nd class Bill Schmitt greeted him. "Good morning Mister Rush. What do you want for breakfast?"

Jim, "Are the eggs real or powdered?"

Bill, "They are real. You know nothing is too good for an ensign."

Jim, "Yeah, sure. Okay give me two scrambled eggs, ham, and toast. Do you have any biscuits and gravy?"

Bill, "No sir, no biscuits yet. Here take this mug of coffee and I'll bring your chow to you in a few minutes."

Jim took the mug of coffee and went into the officer's wardroom. Jim sat drinking his coffee thinking about the day's work ahead of him. He recalled reporting to the skipper of the *Spearfish* about three weeks ago. Here he was on his first patrol. They had departed Pearl Harbor ten days ago.

Bill brought Jim his breakfast and Jim attack his breakfast with gusto. He thought I must be hungry. Jim liked the cooks on the *Spearfish*. He had got acquainted with them the day he reported aboard. He had formed up a detail to help them load some last minute supplies. The cooks appreciated this and had been friendly to Jim.

Jim liked the informality on a submarine. They were generally on a first name basis. They lived and worked in close quarters. The sub was 312 feet long and 26 feet wide. This was the outside measurement. It was smaller inside where the living quarters were located. It was probably 275 feet long and at its widest point with 16 feet inside for living space. They had to share bunks. There were two 12-hour shifts. When not in combat they had one-half the crew on duty while the other one-half was off duty. They generally dressed in work clothes. Dress was not so important.

The skipper insisted on cleanliness and when not on the sub all rules and regulations were to be followed. A skipper on a submarine has wide latitude in running his boat. Jim had heard that the skipper was one of the best and he believe it.

Jim finished his breakfast and went to the control room. The control room was in the center of the sub and was the brains of the operation. Jim entered the control room and saw Lieuantant Jack Jackson, the executive officer. Jack was in command on this shift.

There were ten men on duty in the control room and three more in the conning tower.

Jack, "Good morning Jim. Go on up to the conning tower and put on a heavy coat it is about 20 degrees outside."

Jim, "Good morning, Jack. Have we arrived at Dutch Harbor yet?"

Jack, "Not yet, but we should be arriving within the hour. Keep a close look out."

Jim climbed into the conning tower. Two enlisted men were already there. They were the lookouts for the crow' nest. Lieutenant (j. g.) Don Milton Phillips joined Jim in the conning tower. The skipper had a policy of two officers and two enlisted men on watch when they were on the surface.

Don to Jim, "Good morning Jim. Are you ready for a watch shift?"

Jim, "Yes, I am ready. Let's get our eyes use to the dark before we go out."

The watch crew spent about ten minutes in the special dimmed lights of the conning tower before opening the hatch to the bridge. Jim opened the hatch and could feel the cold December artic air.

They climbed out on the bridge.

Jim said, "Gosh! It's as dark as Dick's hatband. Why didn't we get a nice South Pacific patrol instead of the North Pole? Alaska is cold. Watch Crew, we relieve you."

They relieve the skipper, Lt. Commander Lawrence "Larry" Saxton, Ensign Al Valcheck, and two enlisted men.

Larry to Don and Jim, "If you need me I will be in the control room for the next hour. Keep a sharp eye."

Larry goes below and only Jim and Don are left on the bridge. The two enlisted men are in the crow's nest.

Don speaks, "We got Dutch Harbor, Alaska. We just got lucky I guess. You know they have a small sub base up here. Just thank your lucky stars we weren't assigned up here."

Don laughed.

Jim thought, "Don is okay he has good work ethic and takes things in stride. He is okay."

Jim said, "Don what are our orders?"

Don said, "I don't know. The skipper can open the special orders envelope upon our arrival. That is why we want to alert him when we spot Dutch Harbor."

Jim appearing through his binoculars blurted, "I see Dutch Harbor."

Don, "Check the TBT and see how far it is. Use the light and give them the password. We don't want our own people shooting at us."

Jim appeared through the TBT, Target Bearing Transmittal, a special pair of binoculars in a swinging mount designed especially for night surface attacks.

Jim to Don, "Range is 6,000 yards."

Don over the intercom, "Skipper we have Dutch Harbor in sight."

The skipper who had stopped in the control room replied, "Okay thanks. I'll go to my quarters now and see what orders we have."

Jim and Don directed the helmsman toward Dutch Harbor port. The *Spearfish* had a diagram of the minefield and the sonar and radar officer directed the helmsman through the minefield.

Before the *Spearfish* docked the skipper came on the intercom.

The skipper, "Attention all crew members. This is the Captain. I have read our orders and in summary here is our mission. We are directed to leave all but five of our torpedoes at Dutch Harbor. We are to transport personnel from the army's 7th Infantry Scout Company to a landing on the island of Attu. The Scout Company will be an advance party to help prepare the way for troops to land in the invasion of Attu. We are going on the offensive. I know we would rather be sinking Jap ships, but that is not our mission on this patrol. I will give you further orders when we dock. The reason we have to unload torpedoes is because of the weight. The army personnel will need the room."

Don to Jim, "I wonder if this means we be part of an invasion fleet?"

Jim, "I have a feeling there will be more of this kind of patrols. You and the rest of the crew have had two or three patrols under you belt. But this is my first patrol and I am a little disappointed."

Don, "We can't cry over spilled milk Jim. Let's take this patrol and do as good a job as we can do. Everything happens for the best. Oh, by the way happy New Year."

Jim, "That's right I forgot that tonight is New Year's Eve, isn't it?"

Don, "Yes."

Jim, "Happy new year's Don. The year 1943 should be better. Just think we have been in this war for a year. It kind of makes me home sick."

Don, "I know what you mean."

CHAPTER 2
DUTCH HARBOR

THE *SPEARFISH* DOCKED at one of the Dutch Harbor sub pins. A shore crew was waiting to come aboard to remove the torpedoes and service the sub even though it was 0530 (5:30 a.m.). The captain announced to the crew that they would be billeted in a barracks building and they would wait on the shore crew to complete their job.

The crew of the *Spearfish* soon found out that it would be two or three days or maybe a week before they sailed. The sailing date depended on the weather.

The officers and men of the *Spearfish* passed the time away by playing cards, writing letters, and "shooting the bull." The *Spearfish* officers were all billeted in a large room in an army barracks building. The building was cold and drafty. It had a coal furnace, but that didn't keep it warm.

Jim, Mac, Don, and Al, found themselves in a "bull session." Larry, the captain and skipper, and Jack, the XO, (Executive Officer) had gone to HQ for a briefing.

Mac to Jim, "Jim I did get up in time to relieve you on the watch, but we docked before 0600."

Jim laughing, "Yeah, I bet you were really disappointed."

Jim liked Mac. They had reported for duty aboard the *Spearfish* the same day. Mac was just a few months older than Jim.

Mac to Jim, "Jim, how did a landlocked guy like you come to be in the navy?"

Jim, "Well you see it was like this. I wanted to join the army air corps. I wanted to be a pilot. I had just finished my first semester in college. They were not deferring college students so I decided I would enlist and get the service of my choice. A couple of my old high school buddies talked me into going with them to enlist."

Al said, "You obviously did not go in the army air corps."

Jim, "We hitched a ride for Dale to Oklahoma City. We went to a state National Guard building. They had recruiting officers from every branch. Well we got in the army air corps line. There must have been 40 guys in that line. The navy line only had six or seven guys in line. We got tired of waiting in line so we moved over to the shorter line"

Don said, "But if you wanted to be a pilot why change lines?"

Jim, "Well we knew that the navy had airplanes and we could become a navy pilot. I didn't know then that the navy called them aviators. Any way we said we would apply for navy flight training."

Mac, "So naturally you wound up in the silent service."

Jim continued, "The navy recruiter signed us up and said we could put in for flight training after boot camp. After boot camp I found out I was not qualified for navy aviation. They had a height limit of 5 foot 10 inches tall and I was 6 foot 1"

Mac said, "Gosh, what a kicker. But why the sub service?"

Jim, "I put in for OCS and went there. Upon graduation as an ensign I volunteered for the submarine service and went to sub school. I had read where the submariner's get a higher pay for hazardous duty and promotions come faster in the sub service."

Al piped in, "I have heard that too Jim. That is about promotions in the sub service. I don't know if it is true or not."

Don said, "There is some truth in what you say Jim. Look at the top navy brass. Admiral King, Admiral Nimitz, and the president's military aide are all former submariners."

Mac said, "So Jim, you went in the navy because of a shorter line. You became a submariner because of pay and promotion. Was all this an accident?"

Jim, "Let's just say it was not all planned. Many times little things in life direct our future. Sometimes we make decisions based on minor facts that have a major impact."

Al said, "Jim what did your girl friend think of you going in the navy?"

Jim said, "My girl friend, Janet, and I mutually parted company when I joined the navy. So really I did not have a girl friend when I came in the navy. I did continue to carry Janet's picture. I didn't want to appear to be the only guy with no girl at home.

Jim continued, "You see, Janet had a semester of high school left, she was to graduate in May of 1942. We thought it best if we were free from the relationship. I knew she would have school activities to go to and would want to date. She had been my steady date for about six months."

Mac to Jim, "How did you meet Janet? I heard you say before she was from a different town."

Jim, "Janet and I were introduced by a preacher's wife at a combined church young people's social."

Jim continued, "Enough about me, what about you Mac? Why did you choose the navy and the sub service?"

Mac replied, "As you know my home is in North Carolina. I have always lived on the coast and use to watch ships come and go as a kid. But the real reason I'm in the navy is because of my Uncle Marion."

Jim to Mac, "So how did your uncle influence you?"

Mac continued, "My uncle was in the navy during World War I. He was on a destroyer. He stayed in the navy . . . a 20-year man he was. In 1926 or '27 he transferred into the submarine service. He used to talk about his sub service and tell me of all the ports he went to and some of the exciting things he did."

Don joined in, "Mac is your uncle still living? If he is I bet he is proud of you."

Mac replied, "Oh yes, Uncle Marion is still living. On December 8, 1941 he went with me to join the navy. He was too old for the navy, but they put him in the Seabees. He is on some island building run ways."

Jim to Mac, "So you joined the day after Pearl Harbor was bombed."

Mac, "Yes, I was among the first from Brunswick County to enlist."

About this time, the skipper and the XO returned.

Larry said, "Gather around men. Jack and I will brief you on our mission."

The group of officers pulled chairs close to the skipper and sat anxiously awaiting his words.

Larry continued, "Our boat and the *Tiger Shark* will take 215 army officers and enlisted men from here to Attu. They will be an advance party to clear the way for troops to land and take back the island."

Jack said, "This means we will transport about a hundred and seven or eight men on our boat. As you can see we will be crowded. Space and air will be a problem. You will have to help us work out how to house that many passengers for the trip."

Al to the skipper, "Sir, how long will this trip take?"

Larry relied, "I am not sure, but I would guess the trip would take about 50 hours."

Larry looking at Jim said, "Jim work out our route on the chart and give me the best route to Attu. Assume we will travel at night on the surface at about 20 knots. Assume we will travel submerged during the day traveling about 15 knots. As you know Attu is the western most in the Alaskan Aleutian Peninsular Islands."

Larry looking at Don, "Don I want you and Al to work out seating and sleeping arrangements. Keep in mind that we will probably feed the army personnel at least three meals."

Larry to Mac, "Mac I want you to brief the chiefs and the enlisted men on the boat. Explain to them that we will be very uncomfortable with a boat overloaded, but they will have to work with us and make the best of things."

Mac, "Aye, Aye, sir."

Larry to all, "Weather permitting, we plan to shove off tomorrow night at O 20-hundred. We can all report to the boat now. The shore crew has serviced the sub and it is ready. Check all instruments and Jack and Don will double-check the sonar and radar equipment. See you on board."

The meeting broke up. The officers packed their small carry-on bags and went to the sub.

The next evening the army personnel boarded the *Spearfish*. Each man had his rifle or other weapon, his cartridge belt, and his backpack. The sub was crowded. No one was used to such crowded conditions.

There was some grumbling among the army men. The *Spearfish's* crew did not comment about conditions. They had been instructed to be good host.

The four-army officers were housed with the submarine's officers in the officer's quarters. Cots were put up. But with one-half of the sub's officer on duty at all time, three bunks were available. The army enlisted men were "housed" in several areas including the navy enlisted men's quarters, the officer's wardroom, and the forward and bow torpedo rooms.

Jim being the navigation officer had worked out their route. The most direct route was 825 miles and the estimated travel time was 48 hours. The skipper approved the route. He did not want to follow the Alaskan peninsular as it added 300 miles to the trip.

Mac worked out a scheduled for the army personnel to take turns on the deck when the sub was on the surface. If the sea was too rough they could not go on deck.

After about 24 hours the oxygen in the sub became stale and a number of men were gasping. The army personnel would welcome action just to get off the sub. They reached Attu and waited until night.

The sub surfaced about midnight. The army personnel disembarked in rubber rafts that were specifically designed for this kind of a mission. You never saw a happier bunch of men than those army men getting off the sub. Within two hours the *Spearfish* had delivered her army personnel and headed back to Dutch Harbor.

When daylight came the skipper decided to stay on the surface. The lookout crew was told to keep a sharp eye and the sonar and radar operators were alerted. The skipper said that they had five torpedoes and if they spotted a target they would try to sink it. The only shipping they saw was Aleutian fishing boats as they got near Dutch Harbor.

The Dutch Harbor navy base would keep the 15 torpedoes the *Spearfish* gave them. The sub depot could use them. The station had about ten subs in their squadron and had an emergency repair dock. Within a year the sub base at Dutch Harbor would be closed and their operations moved back to Pearl Harbor.

The *Spearfish* set their course for Pearl Harbor. Ten days later they were docking at Pearl.

The skipper gave his usual talk to the officer's and men about what was expected of them. He cautioned them about their behavior while on shore and especially when on leave. It would be two or three weeks before they were assigned a new patrol.

This would be a two-week period of rest and relaxation.

CHAPTER 3
REST AND RELAXATION

THE NAVY HAD rented the plush, Royal Hawaiian Hotel on Waikiki Beach for a rest camp. The officers from the *Spearfish* would be billeted there for the next two weeks. Jim, Mac, Al, and Milt shared a suite. Jim and Mac felt lucky to get a rest after only one patrol.

On the second day their mail was delivered to the officers. Each had a stack of mail that had come in during the past 30 days. Jim, Mac, Al, and Milt were reading their letters.

Jim read his letters. His mother had written about the family and told Jim about his sister, Shirley and his brothers Joel and Noel. She told him his Dad had gone to work at the Midwest Air Depot. This would help the war effort. She told him that she had heard that Janet had entered nursing school at O.U. Jim was glad to hear all the news from home. He read his mother's letters over two or three times.

Jim had a letter from his maternal grandmother, a college friend, and one of his high school teacher's. He missed his grandmother's apricot fried pies and her wisdom and advice. One of his college friends had joined the army air corps and was stationed in England. One of his favorite high school teachers's asked him to write an article for the school paper.

Jim could see that Mac was sad with almost tears in his eyes after he read one of his letters.

Jim to Mac, "Mac, what's wrong? Did you get bad news from home?"

Mac hesitated and said, "Yes, Mary Jo has called off our engagement. She has fallen in love with someone else. I have been gone a year and she couldn't wait any longer."

Jim, "I am sorry Mac. I shouldn't have asked. That was very personal. Is there anything we can do or say to help?"

Mac, "No thanks. It's okay for you guys to know. I know you will understand how I feel."

Mac changing the subject, "My brother Tom has joined the paratroopers. My dad still works at the machine shop and my mother is doing volunteer war work. Gosh it's good to hear from the folks."

Don to the others, "Hey, Mildred, my wife, has taken a job in the Boeing plant in Seattle. She wanted to do something for the war effort. There is a shortage of men in the labor force so a lot of women have gone to work. My mom and dad are doing okay."

Al speaks, "Well Edith, my fiancée, is doing okay. She works in a 5 and 10-cent store. Edith is 19 and finished high school last June. I have two younger sisters and they are okay. My dad still works at the printing company. Chicago is busy in the war effort. They had a big bond rally at Soldier Field last week.

Each officer's moral was boosted by the mail from home. They spent the next hour replying to the letters they received.

Al to group, "Say what are we going to do? How about going swimming on Waikiki? Hey, the USO is sponsoring a dance today right here in the hotel ballroom. It starts at 7. Anyone want to go?

Mac, "Yeah, I think I will. I like to dance. Jim, how about coming along?"

Jim, "Yeah, okay why not? I'm not much on dancing but I'll watch you guys."

Don, "Not me, I think I'll take in a movie. *Casablanca* is showing at one of the down town theatres. Anyone want to go?"

Jim, "Thanks for the invitation Don, but I have seen the film. It is a good one."

Mac, "No Thanks, I'll go to the dance"

Al, "It is a good movie, I have seen it, but I'll go again with you Don."

All the men went swimming in Waikiki Beach before the evening meal.

That evening Jim and Mac attended the USO dance. The ballroom was crowded. There was hardly room to dance. Mac immediately spotted a red head and went over to her and asked her to dance. She accepted.

Jim stood against a wall and watch Mac dance. Jim thought Mac is a good dancer and the girl he has is a good dancer. They looked like they were having fun. Jim looked around to see what girls were available.

Jim saw one girl who had just finished a dance and was sitting down. Jim went over to where she was. He thought she was good looking and thought he would be lucky to meet her. Jim approached the good-looking brunette.

Jim to girl, "Hello, may I have this dance?"

To Jim's surprise the girl said, "Yes."

When the girl stood up Jim could see that she had a nice trim figure and she was about 5' 4" tall. They moved to the dance floor. He took her in his arms, but did not hold her too close. It was crowded with little real dancing going on, but it did give Jim an opportunity to hold a girl close. This had been the first time he had been this close to a girl in a year.

Jim to the girl while they danced, "My name is Jim Rush. I am from Oklahoma. What state are you from?"

The girl, "My name is Linda Gower and I am from Mississippi."

Jim and Linda danced two more dances. All the time they were talking. They decided to sit out the next dance and went to the hotel bar. Neither drank liquor, but they got a coke. They found a table and continued their conversation. Jim liked Linda; she was good looking, had a good personality, and was a good conservationist.

Jim to Linda, "Linda, how did you get to Hawaii? Are you civilian or military personnel? What is your job?"

Linda to Jim, "I was a first year school teacher in Grenda, Mississippi. The war broke out and I thought I had an opportunity to travel, for adventure, and enjoy life, I took a civil service test and the government hired me and I took a job at Eglin Field near Pensacola."

Jim, sincerely saying, "You have a good background, but how did you get here and what do you do?"

Linda, "I work in the AG's office and in the Special Orders Section. I supervise eight employees—civilian and military. I had a chance to transfer to Hawaii. We had a TWX in wanting someone with my job description and classification. I put in for it and got transferred here about a month ago. Our office takes personnel and match them to various jobs and transfer them all over the world."

Jim was fascinated with Linda's career. He thought Linda might be two or three years older than he.

Linda to Jim, "Jim, tell me about your job? Have you seen any action?"

Jim to Linda, "As you know I am in the sub service. I am the navigation officer, the assistant sonar officer, the assistant deck gun officer, and anything else the skipper assigns to me. I have just been on one patrol and we saw no action."

Jim told Linda about his family back home and how he got in the navy. Linda told Jim about her family and her childhood. They talked for an hour.

Linda, "Jim I think we had better be going it's getting late. The USO really doesn't want us to stay out too late. Of course, they cannot really enforce their rules on us volunteers."

Jim, "Linda, Can I call on you for a date? You are not engaged or going steady I hope?"

Linda, "You can call on me . . . here is my office telephone number . . . we don't have a phone in our apartment. No I am not engaged or going steady. If I were would that make a difference?"

Jim, "Only if you said it did."

Linda laughed, "You know I like you Jim you make me laugh."

Linda had written out her work telephone number on a slip of paper and handed it to Jim.

Jim and Linda took a base bus to Linda's apartment. Jim walked her to the front door.

Linda said, "Jim I can't ask you in. Hilda my roommate is there and our landlord does not want us to have men friends in our apartment after 10 p.m."

Jim, "That's okay Linda, I understand. May I kiss you good night?"

Linda, "Yes you may."

Jim took Linda in his arms and drew her close with an embrace. They kissed. Jim felt light-headed and very warm. Jim released his embrace and they kissed again. This was a shorter kiss.

Jim, "Thank you Linda. I had forgotten how good it feels to kiss a girl. I think you are great and I am glad I met you. Good night."

Linda, "Thank you Jim, I had a good time. Good night."

Jim caught a bus back to the hotel. He was on cloud nine. He realized that he and Linda had spent most of the time talking. He liked having a conversation with an attractive, intelligent woman. He resolved to call Linda the very next workday.

Jim and Linda dated several times during the ten days Jim had left on his R and R. They went to the movies, ate at the officer's club, and took a sight seeing tour of Honolulu and Oahu. Each date ended with kisses. Jim and Linda were drawing closer.

After the R and R was over the officers reported back to the *Spearfish*. They were anxious to find out about what their next patrol would be. The next day the skipper called for a meeting with the officers for a briefing. This would be in the officer's wardroom of the *Spearfish*.

Larry to the officers, "I see we are all here. I hope you enjoyed your R and R. Our next patrol will be near the Gilbert Islands. Our main targets are to be Japanese carriers and battleships. If there are no big boys we are next to go after troop ships, tankers, and freighters. You all know your jobs and I want everything checked out before we sail. We will shove off tomorrow at 0600. Are there any questions?

Jack spoke and said, "We are losing two crew members, but will get replacements. We are still short six enlisted men; maybe we will get four men this time. We are still short two officers, but will have to make do with what we have.

Larry, "As you may know it is not at all unusual to lose two or three crewmen or even officers after a patrol. Some men develop claustrophobia after three or four patrols. The navy understands that some people can develop a morbid fear of close quarters. As you all know the quarters are extremely close on a sub."

Jim was not aware of the claustrophobia problem, but could see why it could happen.

No one ask any questions. Larry, Jack, and Don left to start checking on things. Jim got maps and charts to start plotting routes. Al went to check on the supplies and ammunition. Mac left to check the fuel load and check with the engine mechanics.

Jim called Linda from a post telephone and told her they were leaving. He did not say when or where, but did tell her he would call her when they returned.

CHAPTER 4
THE GILBERT ISLANDS

THE GILBERT ISLANDS are a group of 16 islands in the central pacific. All the islands were small low coral reef islands. The Japanese occupied the islands. They had an important navy base and airfield on Tarawa the largest island in the group. The Japanese had a marine and army base on the island of Makin. They had radio and radar stations on several of the smaller islands.

It was a beautiful early spring day when the *Spearfish* set sail that morning. The sunrise gave a colorful glow on the water. The air was fresh and all seemed quiet and peaceful.

Larry, Jack, and Jim were on the bridge as they left Pearl Harbor. Jim felt lucky to be on watch with Larry and Jack. Jack soon went below to take charge in the control room. Two enlisted lookouts were in the crow's nest.

The *Spearfish* set a direct route to the Gilberts. It would take about 10 days for the *Spearfish* to be on station. As they got nearer their destination they became more alert.

They daily practiced their diving technique and other drills.

They had been out nine days. On the ninth night Jim and Jack were on night watch on the bridge. They were constantly scanning the horizon with their binoculars. The two enlisted men were also scanning the sky and sea. It was dark, but there was a three-quarter moon and its light reflected on the water. Jim and Jack had been in a low voice conversation.

Jim to Jack, "Jack how long have you been the Executive Officer on the Spearfish?"

Jack in a low voice to Jim, "This is my third patrol as XO. I have been in the sub service since December 7, 1941"

Jim, "I would think you would become a skipper after this or the next patrol."

Jack, "No, it will not happen Jim unless the policy is changed. You see someone has a notion that a sub skipper has to be a Naval Academe grad before 1937."

Jim had seen Jack's Annapolis ring so he knew he was a Grad. He said, "What year did you graduation?

Jack, "I graduated from Annapolis in 1938."

Jim, "That must be disappointing to you. But maybe they will change that rule and you will make skipper before long."

Jack, "No, I am not disappointed. I feel lucky. You see we lived on a farm just outside Meade, Kansas. My father owned 240 acres and rented about 200 acres more.

I had five brothers and two sisters. The depression hit hard in the early thirties. I dropped out of high school in 1932 and joined the navy."

Jim, "You came from a big family. How come the navy?"

Jack, "I joined the navy because I knew the local recruiter and they gave a $100 bonus. One hundred dollars looked might big in 1932."

Jim, "How did you get in Annapolis? Didn't they require a high school diploma?"

Jack, "Yes, they required a high school diploma. I took a navy GED test and got my degree. I attended a couple of navy schools. Every other year they would take a few Navy Academe plebes from the ranks. I took the test and was selected. I feel fortunate to be where I am today. That is why I am not disappointed. I am thankful."

Jim thought Jack has a good attitude and asked, "Jack are you married?"

Jack replied, "Oh yes. Ruby and I have two children. They live in Meade. Now Jim, tell me about you. I have been doing all the talking."

Jim told Jack about himself. He told only the high points, not all the details.

About that time control room contacted the bridge that sonar was picking up some ships off the port bow about 10,000 yards away.

Within five minutes one of the enlisted look outs said, "I see something off the port bow. It appears to be several miles away."

Jim and Jack immediately turned to the object. Through their binoculars they could tell that it was some kind of a ship.

Jack called on his intercom to the control room and asked sonar and radar operators to help them determine what they were looking at.

The sonar operator replied, "I've been watching the movement and it appears to be a convoy of four or five ships and it was heading our way."

Jack on intercom, "Control room notify the skipper. Sonar and radar keep the bridge informed. Those are probably Jap ships. We have no information about our ships being in this area."

Jim to Jack, "Seaman Pete Wojoski has the sonar duty. He is pretty good."

Jack, "Yes, Jim get on TBT and see if you can pick up any details on that convoy. Bridge to control room. Alert all personnel and stand by for action."

Within two minutes the crew was at their battle stations. The skipper was in the control room. Don had been in charge of the control room up to that time.

The skipper over the intercom, "Attention crew we have a Japanese convoy sighted and we will position ourselves to attack. It will probably be one hour before we are set to attack. Load all bow torpedo tubes. Load all stern torpedo tubes. We may make a surface attack, but no gun crews on deck. We want to be able to dive in a hurry. Feed all data through to give us a bearing, range and course of the enemy ships."

Jim had been able to determine the range on the Target Bearing Transmitter (TBT). Sonar could give a closer account of the convoy.

The skipper to control room and bridge, "Since we have about two hours of dark left we will initially make a surface attack. After the initial attack we will submerge to periscope depth and continue from there. It appears we have three tankers and one transport, and two escorts. The escorts are probably destroyers. There is one small vessel, probably a tender or junk."

Jack to Jim, "Jim you call the shots on the first one from the TBT."

Jim, "Yes sir, do you think I am ready for this responsibility."

Jack, "Yes you are Jim. Just remember each torpedo cost several thousand dollars. But also remember that a good spread will pay off. One on one is a long shot."

Jim, "I am sighting in on a destroyer. It is the first ship in the convoy. The second ship is one of the tankers. I think we will try for the first two at the same time."

Jim fed the data to the control room. The information set the torpedo-gyros.

Jim decided to shoot six torpedoes. He fired four by TBT at the lead destroyer. He fired three by radar at 900 yards at the first tanker. Two hit the destroyer and there was a loud explosion. One of the missed torpedoes hit the small ship, which turned out to be a minesweeper. The three torpedoes fired by radar hit the tanker. There was an explosion and a fire.

The other escort destroyer started shooting in the *Spearfish's* direction. At this point Jack gave the order to dive and level off at periscope depth. The lookouts and the officers on the bridge went below.

The skipper was in the conning tower looking through the periscope as the sub was submerging. The skipper congratulated Jack and Jim on hitting the enemy ships.

Larry said, "Good shooting Jim. You may have made history. This is the first time that I know about of hitting three ships with one shooting. The destroyer is breaking up and so is the tanker. At least two sinking, but the minesweeper was only damaged. The tanker is one of those big jobs that have watertight compartments. They are not easy to sink. We must have sunk 10,000 tons. Jack take a look."

Jack took the periscope and said, "Wow! I see two ships on fire and breaking up. Jim take a look."

Jim took the periscope and said, "What a sight. Good job men."

The enemy destroyer did not come after the *Spearfish*. She was like an old mother hen looking after her chicks. She stayed with the remaining convoy. A rainsquall came up and the Spearfish lost visual contact. They decided to track the convoy by radar and sonar and surface again to keep up with the Japanese convoy.

At daybreak Larry decided they would get back on their original patrol course. They resumed their original course traveling submerged since it was daytime.

The next day they were nearing Tarawa. Larry thought they might find some targets near the Jap Navy base. They received a coded message from headquarters congratulating them on sinking the two Jap ships. The *Spearfish* did not know it at the time, but their report of the Japanese convoy was of vital information to HQ intelligence. The convoy the *Spearfish* saw was going to rendezvous with a larger convoy to form a task force to reinforce the defense of Wake Island.

The *Spearfish* continued to watch outside the Jap Navel Base. There was some activity, but only smaller vessels were seen coming and going. Larry finally decided that they would move out into some of the known Jap sea-lanes. They sailed several miles west.

Larry on intercom to crew, "Attention men, we are moving to a sea lane between Tarawa and Truk. Both have navel bases so there should be some activity going on. When on the surface lookouts keep a sharp eye for Jap planes. There is a major Jap air base in the area."

Jim and Mac were on duty in the control room. Jim was at the navigation table and Mac was keeping an eye on the sonar operator. He had a new man that he was training.

Jim to Mac, "There is a lot of waiting and boring time between actions. We hurry up and wait. It seems we are bored for hours for a few minutes of excitement and near heart failure."

Jim continues, "You know Mac sometimes things settle into an easy routine, when no enemy ships are about. But being beneath the ocean is never dull. The crew does not seem to get bored, even though life sometimes becomes routine for a few days when there is no real action. But, when Jap ships are sighted the activity is hot and fast."

Mac to Jim, "Yeah it's like being on a date with a girl. You invest a lot of time and money for hours of boredom just to get a good night kiss."

Jim, "Mac you sound like a philosopher."

Mac, "Yeah, or a jilted lover."

Mac laughed and he and Jim returned to their duties.

The Sonar Operator blared out, "Sir, I have something and it's big. I think there is a convoy and one vessels is really big."

Mac, "Let me take a look. You are right it looks like we have three ships—a big ship and two smaller ones. Mr. Jackson should we alert the skipper?"

Jack to Mac, "Yes we had better alert the skipper and alert the men to go to their battle stations."

The *Spearfish* personnel knew the routine by now and were at their battle stations in record time. The skipper came into the control room and then joined Jack in the conning tower. The *Spearfish* had come up to periscope depth.

Larry to Jack, "Jack you keep command and direct our action."

Jack to Larry, "Aye, Aye, sir."

Larry taking the intercom, "This is the skipper, Mr. Jackson will be in command. You all know your jobs. Let's sink another Jap."

Jim and Mac had joined Jack and Larry in the conning tower. Jim thought that he learned something about command. Larry had delegated his authority and was giving Jack the freedom to act without being second-guessed.

Jack appearing through the periscope said, "I have visual contact. We have a heavy cruiser or a battleship and two escort ships. The heavy cruiser or battleship seems to be damaged. She is moving pretty slow. Jim standby to use periscope number two in case of trouble."

Larry said nothing. He was observing his officers and men. He was up and down splitting his time in the control room and the conning tower.

Jack on intercom to crew, "Men we have a heavy cruiser or battleship that is damaged and is being escorting to a dry dock somewhere. Load all torpedo tubes—bow and stern. At about 1,000 yards we will shoot. Don give me a TDC reading. Al give me a TBT reading. Make sure all data is ready to input on torpedoes."

After about five minutes Jack said, "Jim keep the time on the torpedo runs. Standby to shoot. Fire one . . . fire two . . . fire three . . . fire four . . . fire five . . . fire six."

Jim kept time and would read off how long it was before the expected hit.

It was about four minutes before the first torpedo hit. Out of five shots three were hits and one was exploded prematurely and one hit but did not explode. Jack then maneuvered the sub and shot four more torpedoes from the bow or aft tubes.

Jack looking through the periscope, "Good shooting men the cruiser is on fire and beginning to break up. Two of our stern shots hit. One bow torpedo was a dud and the other one missed. The two escorts have seen our periscope wake and or headed this way. Take her down. Crash dive. Prepare for depth charging. Skipper take a look."

Jack said, "Those damn Mark XIV torpedoes are not much improvement over the 12. When will they get us some really good torpedoes?"

Larry looked through the periscope and said, "Looking good. Another Jap takes the deep six."

Within 2 minutes the *Spearfish* was 150 feet deep. Jack gave the order "to take her down to 200 feet."

Within another five minutes the destroyers started depth charges. At first they were at least 200 yards away, but kept getting closer. Jack kept the *Spearfish* moving and order the helmsman to come to a heading that would take them out of the destroyer's path. One of the destroyers broke off the action. Jack surmised that she had gone to pick up survivors of the cruiser.

The depth charging continued for an hour. There were some leaks in the forward torpedo room and the glass facing on some of the instrument panels in the control room were cracked. During the depth charging the officers and men kept quiet. They were all sweating although the temperature in the sub was not abnormally hot.

Jim to Mac, "It is during this kind of time I wish I was back home."

Mac to Jim, "I know what you mean."

Finally the Japanese destroyer left the area. Jack gave command back to Larry. Larry decided that they would set sail for home base. They only had four torpedoes left, they had minor damage in the forward torpedo room, and they had a successful patrol. So far on this patrol they had sunk three ships with tonnage at about 14,000 tons and damaged a minesweeper. This had been a very successful patrol.

Ten days later they sailed into the sub base at Pearl Harbor.

CHAPTER 5
WORK AND PLAY

THE SKIPPER CALLED a meeting with the crew. They would meet in a conference room in a nearby warehouse. The conference room was really just part of the warehouse petitioned off. The crew assembled. Larry and Jack sat on a small platform facing the crew. A speaker's stand was in the center-front on a 12-inch high platform. The crewmembers were sitting in folding chairs. The officers of the *Spearfish* sat to one side.

Larry rose and went to the speaker's stand.

Larry said, "Men of the *Spearfish* I want to commend you on a successful patrol. We have received a letter of commendation from Admiral Lockwood. A copy of this letter will go in the personnel file of each officer and man on the *Spearfish*. At this time I cannot tell you how long we will be in port. The port crew will start to work on the *Spearfish* and assess the damage. I understand we will get up-dated sonar and radar equipment."

Larry continued, "We were given some orders when we docked. I'll ask Jack to tell you about those orders. Jack."

Jack took the stand and said, "From our orders it appears we may be in port at least two weeks or maybe three. Attention to orders: All officers and men will spend at least three days on the rifle range. Ensign Rush will be in charge of that detail. That is set for the next three days. After that the deck gun crew and alternates will spend two days on the 5" gun range. Ensign MacDonald will be in charge of that detail."

Jack paused to give what he had said time to be digested. There was some muttering among some crewmembers. The officers had been taking notes because they would have to see that the assignments were carried out.

Jack continued, "Our Engineering Officer Lieutenant (j.g.) Don M. Phillips, Ensign Al Valcheck, Seaman Pete Wojoski, Seaman Robert Nixon, Seaman Albert Schmitt, and chief petty office Mark Scott will attend a radar and sonar training four days next week. Lt. Phillips will be in charge of this group."

Again Jack hesitated to give time for the information to sink in.

Jim in a low voice to Mac, "Looks like we will be busy for the next couple of weeks. I hope I have some time to spend with Linda."

Mac to Jim, "Oh you will have time for Linda. Work her in between midnight and 0600."

Jim and Mac laughed. Mac and Jim turned their attention back to Jack and the stage.

Jack continued, "There will be small groups taking special up-dated training on diesel engines, enemy identification, navigation, navy strategy, and command. Lt. Commander Saxton and I will be in charge of these details. We will contact the individuals and give you specifics. Now I turn the meeting back to Commander Saxton."

Larry going to the stand, "Men it appears that the next two weeks will be very busy. You may have leave each night from 1700 to 2200 and on weekends. Now we want you to take your personal gear off the Spearfish and go to quarters assigned to you. Officers will stay in the BOQ number 3 and enlisted men will be billeted in the barracks buildings number 11 and 12. Check the bulletin boards at the respected buildings for room or bunk assignments. We will meet again when we have more news. Be sure to pick your mail up from the quartermaster. That is all for now."

The officers and men of the *Spearfish* would find a packet of letters waiting for them. At least they hoped so.

Jim, Mac, Don, and Al were all assigned to the same room. They took their luggage and picked up their mail and went to their room. It was a large room, at least it was large compared to what that had been use to on the *Spearfish*. Each officer selected a bunk and sat down to read his mail.

Before Jim read his mail he went to the orderly room to use the telephone. He called Linda.

Linda answering the telephone, "Special Orders Section, Miss Gower speaking, may I help you?"

Jim, "Yes, you may help me. I'm back in port and I have missed you. How are you doing good-looking?"

Linda, "Jim, it's you! I am fine. Are you okay? We have so much to talk about when can we get together?"

Jim, "We will be very busy this week, but I will be free Saturday and Sunday. Can I see you Saturday?"

Linda, "Yes that will be swell. I have to work until noon Saturday. How about 4 o'clock. Can you meet me at my apartment?"

Jim, "Yes, that will be swell. Hate to run, but I must. See you Saturday. Good by."

Linda, "Okay, good by Jim."

Jim returned to his room. Mac, Al, and Don were all engrossed in reading their mail. Jim was soon engrossed in reading his own mail. He had two letters from his folks, a letter from one of his old high school buddies, a letter from one of his aunts, and a letter from a cousin.

Jim's spirits were lifted as he read his mail. It was like a visit from home. His mother brought him up to date of the events in the community and family. He found out that cousin Molly had gotten married. That cousin Dan had joined the marines two months ago, and the next-door neighbor to the north; the Goodson's have a new grand baby.

Jim's letter also had some sad news that his cousin Ralph had been killed. His B-17 was shot down over Germany. Ralph had been a co-pilot. All of the crew was lost. Ralph had joined the Army Air Corp shortly after Pearl Harbor was bombed on December 7, 1941. Ralph had never married and was about three years older than Jim.

His aunt told him that she had read in the newspaper that his "old girl friend" Janet Hilton had made the dean's honor roll at O.U. His aunt brought him up to date on the aunts and uncles in the family. She also mentioned about Ralph being killed.

The men discussed the news from home.

Jim said, "My mom said that they had rationed meat, fats, and cheese. They issued them food stamps. My Dad runs a few head of cattle on my grandfather's farm so they will have plenty of meat. I had a cousin killed, his bomber was hit over Germany."

Al said, "Guess what, Edna, my sister who is 18 is engaged. Her fiancée' was drafted. Mom and dad are doing okay."

Mac piped in with, "FDR put a freeze on prices, wages, and salaries. My Dad was due a pay raise, but he won't get it now. This was to head off inflation. The freeze is supposed to stay on for the duration. I just learned that my best high school buddy, Charley Wilson was seriously wounded in action in North Africa."

Don said, "Not much news from my folks. All is well with Mildred and she is still working at Boeing. She is taking out a savings bond every other payday. I think it is the first time she ever saved any money."

Jim was very busy the next three days. He and a Marine Drill Instructor transported the crew of the *Spearfish* to and from the rifle range. Each man was expected to fire the M-1 rifle and the carbine at targets of 50, 100, and 150 yards. The officers and chiefs also had to fire the 45-caliber pistol.

The officers and men were tired at the end of the week. Most just wanted to lie in their bunks and rest. Jim, Mac, Al, and Don were resting in their quarters Friday night.

Jim to the others, "You know this week has been more like boot camp. But we needed the training."

Mac, "Yeah, and the Marine Drill Instructors seemed to get a kick out of our misery."

Don, "The skipper canceled our leave for tomorrow morning. He has called for a crew assembly tomorrow at 0800."

Al, "I wonder what that's all about?"

Jim, "He may have some news for us. He said he would keep us informed as he got information."

The crew of the *Spearfish* assembled in the conference room of the warehouse for the meeting. The Skipper, Lt. Commander Jackson the XO, and a third officer unknown to the men of the *Spearfish* were seated on the speaker's stand. The skipper, Larry Saxton, rose and walked to the speaker's stand.

Larry said, "Officers and men of the Spearfish our next patrol will leave on June 7. I cannot tell you where at this time. This means that you will have about one week free time, unless something comes up. We will give you more specifics later regarding the patrol. I am pleased to announce a new officer for our crew. As you know we have been short for sometime. The new officer is Lieutenant Mike Moreland. He will assume the duties as third officer. Now Lieutenant Jackson will give you further information."

Jack walked to the stand. He looked the crew over. He had a smile.

Jack said, "I have some good news for several of you. The promotion list came through. It is my pleasure to announce that Chief Andy Clark is promoted to Chief Petty Officer First Class."

A spontaneous applause broke out. Andy was well liked and he was a hard worker and always looked out and trained the men under him.

Jack continued, "Congratulations Andy. Please hold you applause until I have given all of the remaining promotions. Seaman Henry Thomas is promoted to Seaman third class, Seaman Robert Beach is promoted to Seaman third class, and Seaman Eugene Gray is promoted to Seaman second class."

Jack continued, "We have four new seaman reporting for duty. We have been short six enlisted men in our crew. Make them welcome. As you know we had two men who left the sub service."

Jack sat down and Larry came to the speaker's podium.

Larry said, "Baring any change in plans we will meet here again on June 6 for a patrol briefing. We want each officer and man to report in each morning you are not in training or otherwise on an assignment at 0800 here in this room. There may be some special assignments. That is all for now, you are dismissed."

After the meeting broke up the officers were anxious to find out about Lt. Mike Moreland. They gathered around Jack and asked him about Mike.

Jack said, "Lt. Moreland should be a asset to our boat. He is experienced and you officers know you have been pulling some double duty. Mike should be some relief for most of you. Mike is a 1937 graduate of the Navel Academy. He has been in the sub service for two years. He transferred from the *Sea Dog*. He is from Grand Rapids, Michigan. He is married and they have two children. He served in the sub service in the Atlantic before coming to Pearl about one year ago."

On Saturday at 4 p.m. Jim called on Linda at her apartment. He rang the doorbell. Linda opened the door. They locked into an embrace. Jim held Linda close and she clung to him. Jim and Linda then kissed for a long time.

Jim to Linda, "Linda, I really missed you. It's so good to hold you in my arms."

Linda to Jim, "I missed you Jim. I thought of you often while you were away. I told my co-workers about you. They have kidded me about having a 'steady boy friend.' They want to meet you. How did your patrol go?"

Jim brought Linda up to date on their patrol. She told Jim about her work activities.

Jim and Linda went to one of the movie theatres on base. They saw *Gone With the Wind*. Both had seen the movie before, but thought it was worth seeing again. After the movie they went to the officer's club for dinner. They had steak with all the usual vegetables.

Jim got Linda back to her apartment about midnight. They made a date for the next afternoon. They said their good nights with a kiss.

The next afternoon Jim and Linda met and sat in her apartment and "smooched." Jim reminded Linda of her landlord's rule of no male visitors.

Linda, laughed and said, "What he doesn't know won't hurt. Actually he and his wife are pretty good landlords. They are understanding people. My roommate is in and out and that will keep us legal."

Jim to Linda, "Where is your roommate?"

Linda replied, "Hilda had weekend duty at her office. She works for some Colonel and they have to keep a CQ on duty all the time. She will get here about five.

That evening Jim and Linda toured down town Honolulu. Jim had her back to her apartment by ten. He met Hilda. She seemed like a nice person.

Jim got back to his quarters and went to bed. He fell asleep immediately.

The next morning the officers reported to the conference room. Their assignment was to check the work being done on the *Spearfish*. Specifically they were to check their areas of responsibility.

The week turned out to be routine. The officers sat in on a briefing from the admiral's office. The overall strategy was discussed. They did receive some good news about the torpedoes. The problem of misfiring had been found and solved. The briefing included General MacArthur and Admiral Nimitz's strategies in their areas of the Pacific.

Later Jim, Mac, Don, and Al were talking in their quarters.

Mac to the others "Isn't it just like the navy. They make up things for us to do. It is another one of those hurry up and wait deals. They could just let us rest, but no they keep us busy with minor things."

Jim to others, "It is best we stay busy Mac. Time goes faster and besides things that may sound minor may be important."

Al to all, "Get Jim, he sounds like real navy. Jim do you plan to make a career in the navy after the war?"

Jim, "No Al, I plan to return to college. I am not sure what I want to do after the war."

Don, "Well I think I may stay in after the war. Where else can you receive pay on time, get you room and board, get you medical care, and retire after 20 or 30 years? I would just have to transfer from the reserve to the regular navy."

Jim, "What Don says makes a lot of sense. We all have come out of the great depression. Job security is important."

Mac, "I am not sure what I want do after the war. I guess I will get a job, get married, and have some kids. Say Jim, it looks like you will get to see that gal at least one more time before we shove off."

Jim said, "It looks like we will get together next Saturday. The skipper has called a meeting for Sunday afternoon. I may not get to see her Sunday night, we'll have to wait and see."

Jim and Linda had a date for Saturday night. They went to another movie and ate out afterwards. They went to Linda's apartment. Hilda was not there. Jim and Linda sat on the sofa embracing and kissing.

Jim could feel a hot wave go over his body. Linda sensed his passion.

Linda, "Jim I think we had better stop. Would you care for something to drink . . . a coke?"

Jim, "Linda, you are right we had better stop. Yes, I would like a coke."

Linda, "Thank you Jim. I am glad you feel like I do. I was afraid that you might be mad at me. You're a swell guy Jim and I really like you."

Jim, "You are a great gal. We are lucky to have found one another."

As Jim was getting ready to leave Hilda, Linda's roommate, came in. The three of them carried on a short conversation. Before Jim left he made a date to see Linda the next morning.

The next morning Jim and Linda attended chapel services together. Linda had a good singing voice. After chapel services they went to the officer's club for lunch. Jim did not think they had time to go into Honolulu since his crew had a meeting at 1500 hours (3 p.m.).

Jim told Linda that they would leave on patrol tomorrow. They would be busy with preparation to get under way this evening. He told her he would call when they made it back to port. They kissed. Jim returned to his quarters.

At 1500 hours the crew of the *Spearfish* met. Larry was standing at the podium as the officers and men came into the conference room.

Larry to the crew, "Men we will shove off tomorrow at 0600. I cannot tell you our destination. That will be revealed to you about one hour after we leave port. When I dismiss you I want you to check out of your quarters. Bring you personal gear aboard the *Spearfish*. Go over all checklist. I will met with all the officers in the wardroom at 1900 hours. You are dismissed."

CHAPTER 6
THE SEA OF JAPAN

AT 1900 HOURS the officers met with the skipper in the *Spearfish's* officer's wardroom. The skipper outlined in general terms their patrol.

Larry said, "I am not at liberty to give you all the details at this time. But you need to know generally where we are going. I want you to familiarize yourself with the area and especially study landmarks. Gentlemen, we are going to the Sea of Japan. No American submarines have been sent there before. H Q has decided to send subs there this summer. We will be one of the first. Jim as navigation officer what can you tell us about the Sea of Japan?"

Jim to the officers, "I don't know much about the Sea of Japan. I know it is a 'land locked sea.' The sea is located between Japan and China, Japan and Korea, and Japan and Manchuria, and Japan and Russia. There are three entrance points. I don't recall the names of the straits leading to the sea, but one is on the south and one in the middle and one on the north. The most northern strait is between a Japanese Island and Hokkaido, Japan. This strait is probably 50 miles wide at the narrowest point. This strait is not open in the wintertime. It freezes up. The middle route is a strait that is about 20 miles wide at its narrowest point. I assume the southern route is the least desirable route because it is closer to Japan."

Larry, "Very good Jim. Jim is correct on his geography. You will note the narrow straits. The Japs can mine and patrol these straits. They believe their shipping is safe within these waters. We should find good hunting."

Jack ask, "Larry which strait will we use or can you tell us now?"

Larry, "We will use the most northern strait. It is the widest and the narrowest point is in Japanese waters. The forays into the Sea of Japan are vertically landlocked. The southern strait is the Tsushema Strait, the middle strait is the Tsugam Strait, and the northern strait is the LaPetrouse. The Japs feel safe in 'their sea' so that should help us. Our biggest problem could be getting in and out of the sea."

Mac to Larry, "Sir, you said we should become familiar with the landmarks and other features. Why is that, sir?"

Larry, "Good question Mac. I want all the officers to become familiar with the land features because you will be on watch on the surface. We will not be far from some land mass most of the time. If we are submerged you may be looking through the periscope and need to be able to give us a location. You will know what details to look for I will brief you and the crew on that about one hour after we sail tomorrow morning. I don't want any of you looking at a map or studying anything until after we depart and I give the details to you and the men."

Larry adjourned the meeting and the officers went about their duties of preparing for sailing in the morning.

The *Spearfish* left promptly at 0600 on her patrol.

At 0800 the skipper got on the intercom and gave the entire crew the information he had given to the officers the day before. He promised to give further details of the mission once that had reached the LaPetrouse strait.

It was a 12-day journey from Pearl to the mouth of the LaPetrouse Strait. Upon arriving just out side the mouth of the northern strait the skipper waited until dark to enter the strait. The skipper called a meeting of the officers. They met in the officer's wardroom.

Larry address the officers, "Men this is top secret. You are not to divulge this information. We are going to enter the strait. From this strait it is about 500 miles south, southwest to a Russian Port called Vidivostak. We will observe this port. We will be looking for Japanese tankers loading up with Russian oil to take to Japan."

Map of Sea of Japan

Jack, "Men this part of our orders was given to us verbally by the Admiral. Intelligence suspects that Russia is selling oil to the Japs."

Jim said, "Wow! The United States ships oil to Russia for them to fight the Germans and Russia sells oil to Japan to fight us. What a crazy mixed up world."

Mac piped up, "How can the president let this happen?"

Don added, "He may not know anything about it. Intelligence may not be basing their knowledge on hard facts."

Mike their new third officer said, "It looks like we had better study up on Russian tankers and their siliques. And we had better know Jap shipping."

Al asked, "Skipper when will we be at this Russian port?"

The skipper said, "We are not close to the port now. We must get through this pass. We will wait until dark and go on the surface. Lookouts will have to be on their toes for Jap patrol boats and the officers on the bridge will have to keep a sharp eye on the harbor."

Jim asked, "Skipper what should we look for?"

Skipper responded, "Look for tankers and try to determine if they are coming or going from the port. See if they are riding low in the water, if so they are full of oil or fuel of some kind."

Mac asked, "Sir, what if there is no activity. How long do we wait?"

Skipper responded, "We will wait around long enough to tell if the loading is occurring at this port. That may take days."

Jim asked, "If they are not loading here do we go on to the next Russian port?"

Skipper, "You got it Jim. We came to sink Jap tankers and that is what I intend to do even if we have to follow them 500 miles."

Jack posted the duty roaster. Jim and Don had the 0200 to 0600 watch. All officers were assigned watch duty including the skipper. Two enlisted men were assigned to all surface watch times. At daybreak they would submerge and watch through the periscope.

If ships are sighted leaving the harbor the skipper is to be notified no matter when it occurs.

The entry into the strait was started at 1800 (6 p.m.). They were submerged. They did spot Jap patrol boats, but they had no underwater detection gear. Two hours of cat and mouse the *Spearfish* passed the most-narrow neck of the Strait. There were minefields and they had to maneuver around them or through them. This was a nerve-racking experience.

They were through the pass and soon at the Russian Port of Nikolaevsk. They sailed for the Russian Port of Vidivostak. This port was larger and the one that intelligence suspected of shipping oil.

At 02100 they surfaced. The cold long nigh watches began. Larry and Al had the first watch. Jim and Don would be next, followed by Jack and Mac. Mike would triple up with the first watch.

The routine was followed. Jim and Don were awakening at 0130. They would eat breakfast and then report to the control room. They would be briefed and then start their watch. The officers coming off the watch would become the officers working in the control room.

Jim, Don, and two enlisted men in the crow's nest were in their places by 0200. All of the watch personnel had binoculars and Don and Jim also had the TBT. As they watched Jim and Don would at times carry on a conversation in low voice. It helped pass the time.

Jim to Don, "Don you have been with the skipper for a while. Can you tell me about him."

Don in a low voice, "Lt. Commander Lawrence "Larry" Saxton is a 1935 Navel Academy graduate. He was ranked high in his class. He is from Clarksville, Tennessee and he is married. They have two children, ages five and two. He has been in the sub service for about five years. He is one of the younger sub commanders. The younger the commanders the more aggressive they are."

Jim to Don, "How many patrols has Larry been on?"

Don, "Let me see . . . I believe this is the skipper's sixth patrol as the captain of a submarine. I think he had one war patrol before he was promoted, but I am not sure. Most skippers are given a rest after six or seven patrols."

All the lookouts and the officers on the bridge were watching the port and keeping a lookout for other boats on the sea. The *Spearfish* was about three miles off shore.

One of the lookouts said, "I see some lights on the dock area in the harbor."

Don said, "I see it. Jim what do you make of that."

Jim looking through the TBT said, "Those are lights on a warehouse building, but I do see a ship starting up. It appears to be a tanker."

Don talking on the intercom to the control room, "Control room we have some ship movement in the harbor. It appears to be a tanker. It is too dark for us to make out much more."

Larry in the control room, "Keep a sharp eye. Do you see any other tankers? I would think they would make up a convoy of several ships."

Don to Larry, "We can't make out any others at this time, but we'll keep a sharp eye out."

Within an hour the picture became clearer. There were six tankers in the harbor apparently being filled. Don, Jim and the lookouts kept watch for any ship identity and movement. It appeared like the tankers were being filled. At 0600 Don, Jim, and the lookouts were relieved. Within one hour the skipper order the sub to submerge to periscope depth.

The *Spearfish* waited all the next day as the tankers were being filled. About sunset the tankers started coming out of the harbor. Larry wanted to wait until they could make positive identification and for them to clear the harbor by several miles. He instructed the helmsman's on a course to intercept the convoy about 20 miles down the coastline.

Jack was manning the periscope when he got a good look at the first tanker.

Jack reported, "The first tanker is defiantly Japanese. Skipper take a look and verify."

Larry taking the periscope, "You are right Jack the first tanker is Japanese. I can see the second one coming out now and it is Japanese. No doubt about it."

The *Spearfish's* course paralleled the convoy. There was one escort ship. It was a destroyer. About midnight Larry decided they would make a surface attack. Jim, and Don had the watch duty. Larry decided to join them on the bridge. Jack would be in charge of the control room.

All six tankers were in a line. The destroyer was moving in and out of the convoy. Larry took the TBT to direct the first firing. He had order that all torpedo tubes be loaded and that the settings on the torpedoes be made.

Larry, "Stand by to fire. Fire one . . . fire two . . . fire three. Give me a count on time Al. Helmsman bring her about two degrees to starboard. We will fire at number two before the fish hit number one. Stand by . . . fire four . . . fire five . . . fire six. Give me a count on the second shooting."

Hits began to be made. Two of the first three torpedoes hit the tanker below the stack and the forward end of the superstructure. Within two minutes the second tanker was hit. It appeared that all three torpedoes hit the tanker, but only two exploded. Both tankers were on fire and were beginning to break up.

They were firing at 800 yards. This was considered close. Within minutes other hits were made.

Larry gave orders for the sub to turn and he lined up a target for the bow tubes. He fired four torpedoes from the bow tubes. Another tanker was hit and was on fire. The destroyer had been firing its guns in all directions and finally started in the direction of the *Spearfish*. Larry gave the order to clear the bridge and to dive.

Larry had the *Spearfish* to submerge to 150 feet. The sonar was keeping track of the destroyer. The destroyer approached their location and started dropping depth charges. Larry gave orders for the helmsman to set a course to parallel the convoy and glide out from under the destroyer's path.

Two or three of the 30 depth charges dropped hit close enough to cause some minor damage to the *Spearfish*.

The crew did not seem to worry much about how things were going to turn out during a depth charge attack. At least the outward appearance would indicate little or no worry. They trusted Larry to get them out of any dangerous situation. But inside their guts were tight and their thoughts on prayer.

The *Spearfish* glided out from under the path of the destroyer and Larry ordered the sub to periscope depth. They had kept pace with the ships remaining in the convoy. Larry looked and confirmed that the three tankers were on fire and sinking.

Larry decided to "shoot the works" at the remaining three tankers. He ordered all tubes loaded. Lining up the middle tanker of the three he shot a spread of six torpedoes. One tanker was hit by at least two of the torpedoes. Another tanker was hit, but just damaged.

Larry said, "We hit one of the tankers with two of our fish. It is on fire. A second tanker was hit, but they must have got their watertight compartments close because she just appears damaged. I think two of our torpedoes missed everything.

It looks like it is beginning to get daylight and here comes that destroyer. Take her down to 200 feet. Helmsman set course to LaPetrouse Strait. I think we have stirred up a hornet's nest so let's get out of here.

Jim and Mac were still in the control room sweating it out.

Jim to Mac in a low voice, "Mac the skipper really showed skill in sinking those three tankers. He usually lets one of the other officer's do what he did today, but he did not delegate today. Do you suppose he is trying to tell us something?"

Mac to Jim, "Yeah, he could be doing a swan song. I have heard that submarine captains are given a rest break after five consecutive war patrols. The skipper may sense that this will be his last patrol."

Jim to Mac, "I think you are right. I wonder who would take his place?"

Mac replied, "I would hope it would be Jack, but you never know what headquarters will do. I guess it could be Mike. That may have been the reason for his being transferred to the *Spearfish*."

Larry decided to stay down deep to avoid enemy underwater search gear. That evening just after dark Larry decided to surface and "take a look around." It would probably be another day before they reached the narrowest point of the strait. This is the part of the patrol that really worried Larry and his crew.

As they surfaced Larry ordered that Lookouts to the bridge. Jim and Don were the two officers on lookout on the bridge. The two enlisted men took their positions in the crow's nest. Larry joined the two officers on the bridge. As soon as it was pronounced clear Larry left.

Larry as he was leaving the bridge, "I going to get some sleep, but if anything big happens wake he up."

Don, "Aye, aye, sir. Have a good sleep Larry we will keep a sharp lookout."

After Larry left, Jim said to Don, "Don how far are we from the narrowest point of the strait?"

Don, "I guess about 125 miles, but we have dodged around so I've lost my bearings. Hey, you're the navigator. I should be asking you where we are located in this sea."

Jim, "Yeah, I know, but I will have to get our bearings by the stars because I can't see any land mass to get a reading."

It was partly cloudy, but Jim finally found enough of the right starts to feed to the control room for them to figure out just where they were. The lookout crew saw no enemy ships. They were relieved at midnight, by Mike and Al. At last Jim and Don could get some sleep.

Before Jim and Don left the bridge they briefed Mike and Al on their approximate location.

Don to Mike and Al, "Keep a close lookout for Jap ships and when it starts to get light look for Jap planes."

Mike to Don, "Yes, thanks. You know you are right about Jap planes. I bet they are out looking for us at the crack of dawn. I think we will want to submerge then. Our batteries should be fully charged by then."

Don and Jim went to their quarters and immediately fell asleep. The last thing Jim thought about was how every one on a sub trusted everyone else. They trusted the watch crew and the control room crew to keep them safe.

Jim and Don were awakening at 0900. They had control room duty at 01000. They went to get breakfast. They ordered their meal and went to the wardroom.

Jim to Don, "We had a good eight or nine hours of sleep. I was really tired. I am hungry enough to eat a bear."

Don to Jim, "I am hungry too. I guess that's why I ordered three eggs, ham, biscuits and gravy"

Mike and Al joined Jim and Don in the wardroom. They had just come off watch and control room duty. They briefed Jim and Don.

Mike said, "We submerged about 0530 because it was beginning to get light in the east. We saw one Jap patrol boat about five miles away just before we submerged. I don't think he spotted us. We saw no Jap planes. A squall did come up about one hour after you guys left the bridge. It rained pretty hard. Visibility was about 200 yards or less".

Al, "Yeah and thank goodness for radar. It kept scanning the horizon and things stayed clear."

Don to Mike, "How deep are we Mike?"

Mike, "We are 225 feet deep. The skipper wants to stay deep for a while. He said something about going up to periscope depth just about dusk."

Jim, "You know I really trust the skipper. He has a feel for things that not many people have. He is a good skipper."

Mike to Jim, "Jim you are right about that. The admiral thinks a lot of Larry. Larry is rated high among the submarine commanders."

Jim and Don's meals were brought in and they started eating their breakfast. Within five minutes Mike and Al had their breakfast. All sat silently eating their food and drinking their coffee.

Al broke the silence, "You know what I really miss? A cigarette after my meal. But I understand the 'no smoking rule.' If 50 or so guys light up, the smoke would choke us to death because our ventilation system couldn't handle it. I agree with smoke breaks in the engine room or on deck in day time only."

Jim and Don left the wardroom to report for control room duty. They reported to the control room. Larry was in charge of the control room. Mac was also there looking over the shoulder of the sonar operator.

Larry briefed Jim and Don, "We are running at 200 feet deep. We are going about 12 knots an hour. We could go a little faster, but I did not want to put a strain on our engines. Sonar occasionally picks up a ship, but so far nothing close. About dusk we will go to periscope depth for a look. We can put our radar antenna up and check for enemy activity. We only have five torpedoes left so we will keep those for defense only."

Jim going over to the navigator's table asked, "Sir, I'll plot a course for us unless that has already been done."

Larry to Jim, "Go ahead Jim, plot our course. I suppose we can follow the same course out as we came in with. I think we finally got straightened out to resume our normal course."

About 1900 Larry gave the order to "take her up to periscope depth."

Larry immediately scanned the sea and sky with a 360-degree circle with the periscope. He then did a slow scan of just the sea area. He did a third one of just the sky.

Larry to conning tower crew, "All clear, pass the word to control and put up the radar antenna and give me their find."

Five minutes later the radar operator reported an "all clear."

Larry to crew on intercom, "This is the captain speaking. We will surface and try to go through the strait narrow tonight on the surface. All lookout crews and control room personnel stay alert. We don't want some Jap slipping up on us. Watch crew stand by, deck gun crew stand by . . . surface! Surface!"

Mike and Al had the first bridge watch. Jim and Don were scheduled to relieve them at Midnight. Jack and Mac were scheduled for the 0500 watch. The skipper kept all the crew on alert. This meant that they stayed at their battle stations.

Larry on intercom, "Attention, attention, this is the captain speaking. Men we will man our battle stations. I want us to be ready to fight, dive, or whatever we may have to do. I consider going through this strait to be a critical part of this patrol. I want to congratulate this crew on your work on this patrol. So far we have sunk three tankers with a tonnage of about 11,000 tons and damaged at least one other vessel of 2,500 tons. I realize many of you have been short-changed on your sleep. After we clear this strait we will all catch up on our sleep. That is all for now."

The lookout watch crew spotted a small vessel just as it was getting dark. They finally concluded that it must have been a Russian Fishing Trawler. After it turned dark they would rely more on radar or sonar to be the eyes and ears of the *Spearfish*.

At midnight Jim and Don came on watch. As near as Jim could figure they should pass through the narrowest neck of the LaPetrous Strait in about one hour. Jim notified the rest of the watch crew.

About 30 minutes later the sonar operator picked up a contact. It was about 5,000 yards off the port bow. All the lookouts turned their attention in that direction. Jim picked up the vessel at 3,500 yards on the TBT. It was difficult the make out the shape of the vessel. Jim finally blinked his eyes a few times and concluded that it was a Japanese patrol boat. The boat was about the size of the American PT boats.

The TBT read the course and speed of the patrol boat. If the patrol boat stayed on its present course he would be in range of the deck gun soon. However, the deck gun sighting was not that accurate, especially of a night. Don and Jim took it on themselves to fire a torpedo at the boat when it got to within 1,000 yards.

Jim notified the control room of their intent. Jack who was in charge of the control room gave them the go-ahead.

Don, "Ok Jim, you take the shot."

Jim, "Don you have more experience at this maybe you should take the shot."

Don, "No, go ahead. You will do alright."

Jim on intercom, "Control room load torpedo tubes one and two and stand by."

Jim sighting through the TBT said, "I can see the boat clearer now. It is a Jap patrol boat. He is coming directly at us. I don't think he has seen us yet. He is at 1,500 yards. When he is at 1,000 yards we will fire."

Don, "Jim you have fed all the data from the TBT to control, haven't you?"

Jim, "Yes Don, but thanks for the reminder. You know you have to think of a dozen things and at the same time concentrate on the target. He is at 1,000 yards. Don can you do the timing? Control room . . . Fire one . . . . Fire two."

Don, "The first torpedo should hit in 90 seconds. The second one in 120 seconds. I thought you was just going to use one torpedo."

Jim, "That was my intent, but I remembered that a spread is better than a one shot deal."

Don, "I'll start a count down at the ten second mark . . . . ten, nine, eight, seven, six, five, four, three, two, one."

An explosion occurred and it sounded like a clap of thunder to Jim. He knew they had hit the patrol boat with the first torpedo. The second torpedo also hit the boat. The little boat broke into a hundred pieces. Jim doubt if anyone could have lived through that.

Don and the two enlisted men gave a little cheer. Don reported their results to the control room. Jack had informed the skipper of the patrol boat and by the time the torpedoes hit Larry was in the control room.

Don, "Good shooting Jim."

Jim "Thanks Don, but we know it takes the whole crew to accomplish a sinking. The crew and the instruments we have. I doubt anyone person can take credit for a job that takes all the crew. We have the best on the *Spearfish*."

Unknown to Jim he had been on the intercom and the crew of the *Spearfish* heard him. A spontaneous applause broke out on the boat.

Larry came on the intercom, "Good job Jim. Good job crew. Now we must complete our journey through this pass. Let's concentrate on that job."

The lookout crew consisting of Jim, Don, and two enlisted men had 15 minutes to go on their watch. In the distant far east there was a glimmer of a rising sun.

The radar operator interrupted, "We have a blimp on the screen. It appears to be an aircraft at about 90 degrees of stern approximately 10 miles away."

Don, "Look outs below, gun crew below, prepare to dive. Dive . . . dive."

Within two minutes the *Spearfish* was still diving at 100 feet. At this point the skipper took over.

Larry said, "Level off at 150 feet. That should be deep enough that there will be no shadow to be seen from the air. Sonar keep alert to ships. That plane may have radioed for help if he had seen the wreckage of that patrol boat."

Larry to control room crew, "We will stay down and continue on our course through the strait. We dare not go to periscope depth because if that plane is around it could see our periscope wake. Things like that show very clear when observed from the sky. The plane is probably flying a set pattern of back and forth covering a hundred square miles."

Jim was near Mac and he said to Mac, "The skipper has just given us another lesson. This one on air surveillance."

Mac to Jim, "I believe you are right. How many more miles do we need to travel to clear this strait?"

Jim' reply, "This strait is about six hundred miles long. The narrowest part of the strait is just about 50 miles long. After this narrow part we will have about 150 miles more of the strait to navigate. We will soon be through the narrow part."

Jim and Mac fell silent and watched the sonar screen. For the next several hours the *Spearfish* travel submerged. At 0 twenty-one hundred hours (9 p.m.) Larry decided it was dark enough to take the sub up to periscope depth.

Larry to control room, "Take her up to periscope depth. Sonar do you read anything?"

Sonar's reply, "No, sir. I get no bleeps."

Larry, "I am going to the conning tower. Conning tower crew follow me."

Larry, Al, and two enlisted men climbed up into the conning tower. At 65 feet the periscope was raised and Larry took hold of it and started his observations.

Larry speaking over intercom to control room. "There is a rain squall on surface so visibility is limited. Raise the radar and radio antannas. Radar give me a report as soon as possible. Radio monitory for any radio activity of any kind. I can't see any ships, but my visibility is limited to about 500 yards or less."

Two minutes later the radar operator reported, "Skipper I have no activity on radar. The rainsquall cuts into my distance."

The radio operator reports, "Skipper I do not pick up any radio messages. All is quiet."

Larry to control room, "Take her up, surface . . . surface. Lookouts to the bridge. Stand by to surface. All crews to your battle stations."

Two minutes later the *Spearfish* surfaced.

Don and Jim had the bridge duty. They were part of the lookout crew. Two enlisted men joined them in the crow's nest.

The lookout crew scanned the sea and sky and reported all clear. The skipper gave the order to charge batteries. Larry also reminded the radar, sonar, and radiomen to be alert. He wanted to know of any activity.

On the bridge Don to Jim, "You know Jim this squall is a blessing. No enemy ships could see us. If they got close enough for their sonar or what ever they have to detect us our sonar and radar would pick them up first."

Jim to Don, "Don I think we are about through the strait. Of course that doesn't guarantee us safety, but it does give us more room to maneuver."

For the next six hours the *Spearfish* stayed with the squall. The men were getting tired. Many of them had not slept for 36 hours. Some were beginning to doze off at their duty stations. Larry observing the crew's weariness made a decision.

Larry on intercom, "Attention, attention, officers and men of the *Spearfish*. We need to rest. I am ordering a skeleton crew to remain in the control room to run the boat and order everyone else to get some sleep. We will submerge and run at a depth of 150 feet. Clear the bridge and clear the deck. Prepare to dive. Take her down at a 10 degree angle on the bow."

For the next ten hours all of the crew got some rest. Many of them got eight hours of sleep. They had cleared the strait so they ran on the surface that night. With eight hours on the surface they fully charged their batteries and it gave them a chance to pump in fresh air and expel stall air. They were on their way back to Pearl Harbor.

CHAPTER 7
THE TRANSITION

FIFTEEN DAYS LATER the *Spearfish* docked at Pearl Harbor. The patrol to the Sea of Japan had lasted 45 days. They sank three tankers, and one patrol boat. They damaged another tanker. The *Spearfish* had a successful patrol. Not many submarines had success in the Sea of Japan. Headquarters soon backed off sending patrols into the Sea of Japan.

When the *Spearfish* left on its patrol to the Sea of Japan it had been in the middle of summer. When they returned to Pearl it was early fall.

The men of the *Spearfish* were interested in catching up on the news. They learned that Leslie Howard the British actor had been killed when the airplane he was in was shot down. They learned that General MacArthur's forces had started a new offensive. They learned that the U.S. Navel and Japanese Navel forces had a battle near Bouganville. The men caught up on the major league baseball scores.

The day after the crew had disembarked off the *Spearfish* their mail was delivered. This was the best news of all.

Once again Jim, Mac, Don, and Al shared a room. They all sat around reading their mail then discussing it and then writing letters. Some had written letters while at sea. Those were mailed immediately. The discussion among the men was always informative and each man could keep up with the families of the others.

Jim went to the orderly room and telephone Linda. He called the operator and gave her the number and she dialed Linda's office.

Linda answering the telephone, "Special orders section, Miss. Gower speaking, may I help you."

Jim, "This is Jim, how are you doing Linda?"

Linda, "Jim, I am fine, how are you?"

Jim, "I'm okay. We just got in. Can I see you Saturday?"

Jim always got to the point as soon as possible when on a phone. The telephone was for important information and not small talk. He was courteous on the phone, but to the point and discuss the business at hand. His family's phone back home was on a six party line and you didn't tie up the telephone on trivial matters. He remembered that early training.

Linda, "Yes I am free Saturday after lunch. I have to work one-half a day Saturday. Why don't you come to my apartment about two or three o'clock?"

Jim, "Sounds good, I'll see you about three o'clock. Gosh it good to hear your voice. Good by."

Linda, "Good by Jim."

Jim returned to his room and told his roommates he had a date.

Mac commented, "Why is that you always seem so cheerful and upbeat when you know you have a date with Linda. You're old buddies just have to sit and suffered while you're happy."

Al piped up, "Maybe Jim is in love. I have to suffer just thinking about my fiancée and wondering when I will see her next."

Don, "Well fellows you are looking at a happy married man. But I wish Jim well."

Jim, "Al you have it wrong. I don't think I am in love, I just enjoy good female companionship."

Don changing the subject said, "I wonder what news the skipper will have tomorrow. Since he called a meeting at 0800 tomorrow he must have some news."

The next morning the crew assembled at 0800. All where present except Larry and Jack. The officers and crew passed the time carrying on conversation among small groups. This went on for about one hour. The crew was wondering what had happened to Larry and Jack. They were never late. About then Larry and Jack entered into the conference room. Jack sat down in a chair on the stage. Larry went to the speaker's stand.

Larry after a few seconds of hesitation, "Officers and men of the *Spearfish* I apologize for being late. It was unavoidable. The admiral kept us a little longer today. We have our sailing date. It is on the 21st. That gives us about 10 days. The shore crew should be through with their work by the 17th. I want the crew to assemble for a briefing on the 18th at 0800. Meet in this room at that time. Now Jack has some announcements."

Mac whispers to Jim, "The skipper always lets the Exec give the good news. So Jack will probably have the good stuff."

Jack rose from his chair and went to the stand. He had a clipboard in his hand.

Jack said, "Thanks, skipper. The skipper gives me the privilege of announcing the promotions. It is a privilege because we have an excellent crew. I am pleased to announce that Ensign Jim Rush is promoted to Lieutenant (j g.) This was effective on the second."

Jim was surprised. He couldn't believe it. He had only been an ensign a little over 16 months. Jim felt fortunate. Jim whispered to Mac.

Jim to Mac, "You should have gotten (j g) before me. You had time-in-grade on me by a month or so."

Mac to Jim, "No, I wasn't as qualified as you, congratulations. They knew what they were doing and you deserve it."

Jack continued with his promotion announcement, "I am pleased to announce that Chief Petty Officer Mark Scott is promoted to Master Chief Petty Officer; Seaman second class Pete Wojoski is promoted to third class seaman; Seaman Bill Schmitt is promoted to Seaman third class and Seaman Robert Nixon to promoted to Seaman third class. All of these promotions were effective on the second. Congratulations to all of you."

Jack added, "We may have some more good news on the 18th. Report each weekday back here at 0800. You may assume you have a pass when not on duty. That is all, you are dismissed."

The officers and several enlisted crewmembers lined up to congratulate Jim. Each one in his own way said Jim deserved it and they were glad. Jim felt humbled because he felt he got the promotion because of the work of the whole crew. He told many of the officers and enlisted men they helped him get the promotion.

Mac to Jim, "Jim I guess you know this calls for a celebration of some kind. How about tonight at the officer's club. You could invite Linda. She could bring some friends. Friends of the female type."

Jim, "I don't know if Linda can make it during the week. This will be rather short notice. How about tomorrow night?"

Mac, "Yeah Saturday night that will be even better. You are right it may take a little time for her to line up some girls."

Jim called Linda and since they already had a date planned that was no problem. He asked if she could get a couple friends for Mac and Al. The other officers were married.

Linda said she could probably get four or five girls. Jim said that would be fine.

Mac and Al took charge of organizing Jim's party. They decided to rent the small ballroom at the Royal Hawaiian Hotel. Since the navy had this hotel rented for a rest place they had no problem getting the ballroom. They also set the time, selected the food to be served, arranged for some entertainment, requested a cash liquor bar, and notified Linda of the time and place.

Mac and Al were very busy working very late that night. They sent invitations to Larry, Jack, and Mike. They expected all officers to attend. They even sent a general invitation to the enlisted crewmen of the *Spearfish*. Since time was so short the invitations were sent by courier. They had requested a count of the number expected.

By noon Saturday Mac and Al had a head count of the number expected. All officers said they would attend and 25 enlisted men said they would attend.

Since most of the enlisted men would be single Mac contacted the USO about some girls to attend for food and dance. Mac and Al wanted this to be an affair they would all remember.

Mac found a way around the rule about officers fraternizing with enlisted men. Their tables would be set up on the opposite side of the ballroom. The USO hostess would stay on the enlisted men's side of the room. He had asked Larry's advice on how to have enlisted personnel at a officer's party. Larry helped make arrangements so Mac knew that had to be okay. Larry and Jack had even invited an officer or two from headquarters.

They started gathering about 5 o'clock for the party. Mac and Al were the first ones there to see that things ran smoothly. Jim and Linda got there about 30 minutes later. Linda had brought two girls with her. Hilda her roommate and Rosa one of the girls from her office. Hilda and Rosa were Mac and Al's dates.

By 6 o'clock all were present and the waiters started serving the food. The food was delicious. As one of the *Spearfish* cook's, Bill Schmitt said it tasted great because they did not have to cook it.

The entertainment opened with one of the enlisted men playing the piano. He was very good. He played the *Saber Dance* and got a standing ovation. He played a number of popular tunes such as *Night and Day, Always, Donkey Serenade,* and several Glenn Miller numbers. This part of the entertainment lasted about 30 minutes.

Jim to Linda, "You know I did not know we had such talented men on our boat. That fellow's name is Sam Brooks and he was very good."

Linda to Jim, "I agree . . . I'm really enjoying this evening Jim. Again congratulations on the promotion. The men of the *Spearfish* are very likable and they seem to really care about one another."

Mac and Hilda were sitting near Jim and Linda and joined them in conversation.

Mac to the others, "Linda thank you for bring Hilda and Rosa. I hope they are having a good time."

Hilda, "Oh I am really enjoying myself. Thanks for inviting us."

Mac and Al took turns being the masters-of-ceremonies. Mainly they just introduced those at the head table and would tell what was on the program agenda.

After a 15-minute break, Mac announced that a band would play some dance music and everyone was invited to dance. The enlisted men really enjoyed this because they could dance with one of the USO girls. The dance phase of the program lasted about 45 minutes. Most men and women just enjoyed sitting and talking. Of course the men wanted to talk about home.

At one side of the ballroom a "cash bar" had been set up. Those who wanted a mixed drink went to the bar at some point during the evening. A few got intoxicated, but for most it was just social drinking in moderation.

Al announced that the next 30 minutes was set aside for just talking. At the end of that period of time he would call on the skipper for a few words.

Mac introduced the skipper, "Ladies and gentlemen I want to introduce the captain of the *Spearfish*. He is Lieutenant Commander Lawrence Saxton. Commander Saxton is a 1935 graduate from the U. S. Navel Academy at Annapolis. He is married and he and his wife have two children. He has been the skipper of the *Spearfish* since January 1942 and has been on seven war patrols. Commander Saxton."

Larry rises from his chair and goes to the podium. Larry takes a few seconds and looks over the audience with a smile on his face.

Larry says, "I hope all of you have enjoyed this evening. I know I have. We thank you for coming. I understand Ensigns MacDonald and Valcheck organized this party. You did a good job, gentlemen. I am glad you enlisted men came. You are really the backbone of the navy and we appreciate you. The *Spearfish* has crewmembers from 35 different states and one territory. They represent the best of the United States."

Larry continued after a slight pause, "You heard one of our crew member's play the piano. Did you know he was a farm boy from Iowa and he is an excellent sonar operator? Ladies we thank you for coming. You bring a fresh spring air to our party. Lieutenant Rush, we congratulate you and wish you well. You know Lieutenant Rush is just a small town boy from Oklahoma. Well enough from me I will turn the microphone over to Ensign MacDonald or Ensign Valcheck."

Mac stepped up and said, "Thanks skipper. He's the best. I will echo what the skipper said and thank you all for coming. Good night and God bless you."

As the party was breaking up the band played *Good Night Ladies* and the final number was *Auld Lang Sine*. Several stayed around talking as if they did not want the evening to end.

Jim and Linda were talking to Mac, Al, Hilda, and Rosa.

Jim said, "Mac, Al, thanks again. You guys did a swell job. Let me help you with some of the expenses. I know this must have cost you a couple of hundred dollars."

Mac to Jim, "No Jim you don't need to chip in. All of the officers chipped in. The hotel did not charge us for the ballroom since the navy had rented the hotel. The food service charge was very reasonable. Forget it . . . the tab is on us."

Jim, "Well thanks. I don't know how to really thank you guys."

Al changed the subject, "Say is that skipper something? He remembers names and places. He gave a nice little talk and did not have one note."

Mac said, "Yeah I have noticed on a number of occasions how Larry can remember things. He is still here let's ask him."

Mac, Al, and their dates along with Jim and Linda went over to where Larry and Jack were standing.

Mac to Larry, "Sir, may we ask you a question?"

Larry to Mac, "Certainly, Mac."

Mac continues, "We have noticed how good a memory you have for names and places. I bet you know the name of every man on the *Spearfish* and his home state. Did you have a memory course at Annapolis?"

Larry with a laugh, "I had a course or two in command school. We learned to think on our feet and give a speech without detailed notes. Part of the course consisted of learning how to remember,"

Jim was really interested and asks, "What is the method you use sir?"

Larry responded, "I use the method of association. You associate a name or place with something you will recall. Usually it is associated with something comical or ridiculous. For example, take your name, Jim Rush. I remember Jim by thinking about basketball. That is where do you play basketball? In a gym. I remember your last name by thinking of Mount Rushmore. So when I see Jim I think of Abe Lincoln dribbling a basketball. Mount Rushmore has the faces of Washington, Lincoln, Jefferson, and Teddy Roosevelt."

Al commented, "That seems like a lot of memory work just to remember. Wouldn't it be easier just to memorize?"

Larry to Al, "It would for some people Al. Each person really needs to find his or her own method of how to remember. The old fashion rote method is okay. It is used for such things as learning the multiplication tables. Just sit down and go over it repeatedly until you learn."

The small groups finally left the ballroom. The men called a cab to take the girls to their apartment. It was about midnight when they got the girls home.

Jim and Linda decided to get together the next afternoon.

The next morning Jim went to early chapel service. That afternoon he was at Linda's apartment by one o'clock. They went to a movie on base. They opted to go on post because they wanted to see *For Whom the Bell Tolls*. The military got movies before they were released to the public. The movie was just out and probably would not be shown in civilian theatres for two months.

After the movie they rode the post bus into town and ate at a nightclub called *Honolulu Harry's*. They discussed the movie. Both liked Gary Cooper and Ingrid Bergman.

Jim and Linda did not want the evening to end, but after several embraces and kisses Jim left to go back to the base. Before Jim left he and Linda had made a date for next Tuesday and Saturday night. Jim and Linda had decided that they would also start seeing each other during the week. Waiting on Saturday seemed like a long wait.

Jim felt very happy about the events of the weekend. He fell asleep within five minutes after he went to bed.

CHAPTER 8
THE CHANGE

THE NEXT MEETING of the *Spearfish* crew was on Saturday morning. They assembled in the conference room of the warehouse. All where present and they waited on Larry and Jack to appear. While they were waiting small groups engaged in small talk or talk about home.

Jim to Mac, "Mac who do you think will win the American and National League races?"

Mac, "I know the *Senators* won't win the American League. I like Boston, but it looks like it will be the *Yankees* again."

Jim, "I like the *Cardinals* in the national league. Yeah, I think the *Yanks* will take the American League. You know they both have good players in the service. But all the teams have players in the service. I read somewhere were the top 30 or 40 players in the majors are in the service."

The small talk continued until Larry and Jack entered the room. The men quieten down. Jack took a chair facing the group. Larry stepped to the speaker's stand. He looked to his right and saw all his officers seated to one side as usual. He looked back to the men of the crew.

Larry to crew, "Officers and men of the *Spearfish,* good morning."

The crew in unison, "Good morning, sir."

Larry to the crew, "I will bring you up to date on our orders. First you will be briefed on our patrol at 0800 on Saturday as we previously planned. I am pleased to announce that Lieutenant Jack Jackson our Exec has been promoted to Lieutenant Commander."

Larry hesitated to give the crew an opportunity to applaud. The crew whopped and hollered and clapped. The crew liked Jack and their enthusiasm at his promotion was genuine.

Jim to Mac with the noise in the background, "I am glad, Jack deserves the promotion. He is an excellent officer in my opinion."

Mac to Jim, "I agree 100%. I suppose this means a sub of his own."

Jim to Mac, "It might, but they will need to change the rule they have about being a 1936 Annapolis grad or earlier."

Mac said, "That's right. I think they should think about quality and merit not age and old school ties."

Jim chuckled and said, "I agree."

Unknown to Jim and Mac there had been a change in the policy regarding the selection of sub skippers. Larry was about to tell them. The crowd finished a short celebration. Jack had a smile on his face and it almost appeared like he had a tear come out of one eye. Jack had been moved by the crew's celebration.

Larry, holding up his right hand for quiet spoke, "Congratulations Jack. You see what the crew of the *Spearfish* thinks of you. I want to also announce that Lt. Commander Jackson will become a sub skipper."

The crew again whopped and hollered their approval. Now Larry was to drop a bomb on the crew.

Larry, "Jack will become the skipper of the *Spearfish*."

A stunned hush fell over the audience. The officers and men were stunned, because this would mean that Larry would no longer be their skipper. Larry waited two or three minutes before continuing.

Larry, "I will be leaving the *Spearfish*, but I will not be leaving you. I am being assigned to the Admiral's staff. I will be part of the Planning and Information Office in headquarters. Men, I hate to leave this crew, but the navy wants a sub commander to take a rest after five consecutive war patrols. They usually get a 30-day leave for rest and relaxation back in the states and home before being reassigned. I asked to stay on with this command so I was assigned to a job the admiral wanted me to do anyway."

RUSH TO VICTORY

The crew sat stunned. All was very quiet. Larry sat down. Jack rose from his chair and came to the speaker's rostrum.

Jack to crew, "Officers and men I know you are surprised as I was. We have had a great skipper in Larry. We wish him well in his new job. I know he will do a good job at what every assignment he is given. Men the good news is that Lieutenant Commander Lawrence Saxton has been promoted to full Commander."

With that news the silence of the crew was broken. Again whooping, hollering, whistling, and applause broke out among the officers and enlisted men. All rose to their feet and gave an applause that last two minutes. Larry was moved by the show of affection and respect.

Jack called for quiet, "Congratulations Larry. A well deserved promotion. We all wish you well and will not be surprised when you make admiral someday."

Jack was not through, but waited for the audience to settled down again. It seems that they had had a double dose of unexpected news. Again Jack called for quiet. The crew settled down.

Jack to crew, "Men you have had a lot of news today, but I have one more bit of information to pass on to you. Lieutenant Mike Moreland has been named as Executive Officer of the *Spearfish*."

There was a buzz among the crew. Then an applause broke out for Mike. Mike seemed surprised, not about his promotion to XO, but about the applause from the crew.

Jim in a low voice to Mac, "Headquarters had decided to make this change two patrols ago when Mike was transferred to the *Spearfish*."

Mac in a whisper to Jim, "You know, I think you may be right. I had not thought about this before. We have had a lot of news to adsorb today. What a day!"

Jack to all, "Remember we assemble here Saturday at 0800. All standing orders, policy, and procedures remain an effect. You are dismissed."

Officers and men gathered around Larry, Jack, and Mike to congratulate them on their promotions and to express their shock at losing Larry as a sub captain.

Jim to Larry, "Sir, we will miss you, but I want to wish you the very best. I admire you as a leader. You looked after us, taught us, and gave us leave way to carry out our duties. Thanks again. I hope we will be seeing you around."

Larry to Jim, "Thanks Jim for those kind words. Your appraisal tells you what I think of you as an officer. You are a good officer. Keep up the good work. In my new job you will probably see me around a lot."

Jim turned to Jack, "Jack congratulations. You deserve the promotion. We are behind you 100 percent. Good luck."

Jack to Jim, "Thanks Jim. I appreciate you and the crew."

Jack to Mike, "Mike, congratulations on being promoted to Executive Officer. We support you and if I can help in any way let me know."

Mike, who seemed a little surprised, "Why thanks Jim. I appreciate your support. I'll try to do a good job."

The meeting finally broke up about one hour later. The crew said farewell to Larry and that took some time. Several crewmembers started taking up funds for a gift for Larry. Don took up money from the officers and gave their contribution to the enlisted men. It was decided that the chief petty officers would take charge of purchasing an appropriate gift.

Jim, Mac, Al, and Don got back to their quarters about noon. They went to chow in the mess hall and back to lie in their bunks for a rest. They seemed tired even though they had done very little physical activity.

The men were still trying to digest all the news that had received that morning.

Don said, "Today we have seen a lot of changes. It all came about by one change of duty."

Jim said, "Yes, one action set off a chain of events. It was the domino effect. Orders involving one man caused at least three other changes. We never know what events will change the course of our lives."

Mac commented, "You are right Jim. I hate to lose Larry as the captain of the *Spearfish,* but by the same token I am glad for Jack."

Al added his comment, "I am glad we got Jack. He has worked under Larry and I think this will be a smooth transition in command for the crew I am personally glad that we did not get an 'outsider.' Mike may have been alright, but I am glad that Jack got the job."

Jim to group, "Well I hate to break up this high level meeting, but I have to get ready for a date."

Mac to group, "Jim would rather be with a pretty girl than be with this high level conversational group."

Mac laughed and the others joined him.

Jim showered and shaved to get ready for his date with Linda.

Jim and Linda decided to go into Honolulu for a movie and dinner. During dinner Jim brought Linda up to date on all the news of that day.

Linda to Jim, "It sounds like you guys had a lot of change to absorb. Jim will your duties change?"

Jim to Linda, "I think there could be some change with the promotion. I will still be doing the same job and have added duties with more responsibility"

Jim and Linda lingered in her apartment. They clung to one another as if this was the final farewell. The kissed and hugged. They drank cokes and talked. They listed to records. They sat silently listening to the music.

Linda to Jim, "Jim, you know that I am glad that we met and I really like you a lot. With the war and all I don't want to get real serious. It just doesn't seem like the right time and place."

Jim to Linda, "I feel the same way Linda. You are a great gal. I like you a lot. Forgive me if I don't say I love you. I really don't know if I do or not."

Linda to Jim, "You read my mind Jim. I don't know if I love you are not. I like you a lot, but that is not love . . . at least not my definition of love. We just need more time. We need to know one another longer. We may need to be in a different setting."

Jim, "Maybe we are not sure of our feelings because we are a long way from home. Time seems to have compacted. The war has changed how we feel and our outlook on life. I'm not explaining it very well."

Linda, "I think I know what you mean. These are unusual times and how would we act if things were normal?"

Jim, "Linda we both agree. We really like one another a great deal. But we are not ready for love and marriage. I am certainly content with our relationship as it is now we need more time."

Linda, "Yes we agree Jim. That may be another sign that we are compatible.

Jim kissed Linda long and hard before he left her that night. He finally left and returned to his quarters.

Jim slept late the next morning. He did get up in time to eat breakfast. After breakfast Jim, Mac, and Al were talking about the latest letters from home. Don had gone "shopping" at the PX. He and Mildred would soon be celebrating their fourth anniversary and he wanted to send her a gift.

The talk of Jim, Mac, and Al was suddenly interrupted. A message over the barracks squawk box blared forth, "Lieutenant Rush report to the orderly room. You have an emergency telephone call."

Several thoughts went through Jim's mind as he left his room and hurried to the orderly room. It couldn't be a call from home because no civilian calls could be made from the mainland. Unless it was the Red Cross! Jim rushed into the orderly room.

Jim, "Ensign, I am Lt. Rush, you have a telephone call for me?"

Ensign, "Yes sir, you may take it in the Chief's office for privacy."

Jim hurried into the other office and picked up the phone. He was gasping for breath because he had hurried and was very worried. Sweat was dropping from his brow. His mouth was dry and his tough felt thick.

Jim on phone, "Hello this is Lieutenant Rush."

Voice on phone, "Hello Jim, this is Linda."

Linda's voice sounded far away and somehow different. She sounded like she was down in a well.

Jim, "Linda, it's you. Is there some problem about our date tonight?"

Linda, "Yes Jim there is a problem. I have bad news. About four hours ago I got word from the Red Cross that my father died. I am leaving to go home and will not be back."

Jim could hardly believe his ears. It took a minute for Linda's news to sink in.

Jim, "Oh Linda, I am sorry to hear about you father passing away. What happened? How old was he?"

Linda, "Dad was 52 years old. He had a heart attack and passed away yesterday. I just found out this morning."

Jim, "When do you leave? Will I get to see you off?"

Linda, "I'm afraid there is not enough time to see me off Jim, sorry. My flight leaves in one hour. I am flying AATC and leave Hickam Field at 4 p.m."

Jim, "How come you will not be returning to Pearl?"

Linda, "My boss arranged for me to transfer to a civil service job closer to my home. That way I will be close to my mother and help her. My, older brother, David is stationed in North Africa in the army and will not be much help. This way I will not have to take leave without pay. I only had six days annual leave earned."

Jim, "Linda I offer my condolence on your loss. Is there anything you need me to do?"

Linda, "No I do not know of anything you need to do Jim. Jim I must hurry now. I will write you and let you know how things went."

Jim, "Linda I hate to say good by like this, but it has been a pleasure knowing you. I wish you well. You are a swell girl. Good luck."

Linda, "Thank you Jim. It has been good knowing you. You are a swell guy. Good by."

With that Linda hung up the phone. Jim sat stunned for a full minute. He finally rose from the chair and left the orderly room.

As Jim was leaving the orderly room the ensign on CQ duty spoke to him.

The ensign said, "Sir, I hope the news was not too bad."

Jim muttered, "Thanks, it was my girl friend. Her dad had passed away and she is going home."

The ensign had a puzzled look on his face as Jim left the Orderly Room. The ensign couldn't figure out why Jim's girl friend would he in Hawaii.

Don had joined Mac and Al by the time Jim returned to their quarters. They had been talking. When Jim entered the room the talking stopped.

Mac to Jim, "Jim I hope the news was not too bad?"

Jim, "It was Linda she called to tell me her dad died and she is going home."

Jim filled the others in on the details. Jim talked for 10 minutes explaining what he and Linda had talked about.

Don said, "Jim is there anything we can do to help. This may sound harsh, Jim but I believe, and have been taught, that everything happens for the best. It is hard to something believe that at the time of the event. It sometimes takes years for that to be realized."

Mac, "Jim I don't know what to say. We are with you buddy."

Al, "That's right Jim. We just don't know what to do or say, but we will be thinking of you and Linda."

Jim to the others, "Thanks fellows. I appreciate your support and just knowing you care gives me courage."

Mac to Jim, "I guess it is kind of hard to end your relationship with Linda this way."

Jim to the others, "Yes Mac it is hard to end our relationship. I liked Linda a lot and will miss her. This may sound strange, but by the same token I am glad our relationship has ended. I did not know how it would end. I dreaded ending it. Like I said this sounds crazy, but I feel sadness because our relationship ended, but at the same time I feel relief. Sounds crazy doesn't it?"

Mac to Jim, "No what you said does not sound crazy to me. You remember when I got the letter from Mary Jo breaking our engagement? Well at first I felt hurt to think she would 'throw me over' for some other guy. But later I left relief. I felt free and was glad it was over. I guess that sounds crazy? You probably noticed I did not dwell on the subject after I got the letter. I tried to get it off my mind by staying busy and thanking my lucky stars I found out about Mary Jo before we got married."

Don to Jim, "Jim what you say about feeling relief is good. This will free you from feeling a responsibility for Linda. We each feel responsibility and when we are no longer responsible in one area we can turn our attention to another. In your case you can concentrate on our next patrol and your work."

Jim to Don, "Don thanks for the wise thoughts. You know you should be a philosophy teacher."

Al to the others, "Fellows if you will follow me to the PX I will treat you all to a round of beer or what ever you want to drank."

All the men walked over to the PX, which was about two blocks away. On the way they talked about the weather and wondered what their next patrol would be. They would not have to wait long. Jack had called for a meeting tomorrow at 0800.

The next morning the officers and the men of the *Spearfish* assembled. Jack told them that he could not give all the details of their patrol until they sailed, but they were going to the Marians and Marshall Islands area. They may also return to the Gilbert Island group. Their first priority on this patrol would be lifeguard duty. Their secondary priority would be sink Japanese shipping. They had never heard the term lifeguard used before to describe a war patrol. They would soon learn more about the subject.

CHAPTER 9
LIFEGUARD PATROL

THE CREW OF the *Spearfish* learned that they would "shove off at 0600 in three days. They checked the sub out and doubled checked all the equipment. The cooks checked their grocery stores. The torpedo men check their torpedo firing mechanisms. The engineering personnel and mechanics checked the engines, the batteries, the fresh water storage, and the oxygen supplies. The gun crew checked the guns and ammunition. And so it went that every nook and cranny of the *Spearfish* was checked out.

As navigator Jim plotted a course using Tarawa Atoll in the Gilberts, Guam in the Mariana's and Kwajalein in the Marshall Islands as references. This patrol would involve more miles than any other patrol the *Spearfish* had been on. It would involve about 3500 miles to their farthest point.

Jim was working at the navigator's table and Mac was checking on the sonar scope. They sailed that morning. Jack would release details later.

Jim to Mac, "You know Mac, the Pacific Ocean is very big. There are many islands and it looks like we are following a chain to Japan proper. I wonder where we will invade next?"

Mac, "I think we will invade Tarawa next. I have a friend in the Second Marine Division and he told me that the 'scuttle butt' in his outfit was they would head for the Gilberts."

Jack came into the control room.

Rush to Victory

Jack picked up the mike and spoke, "Attention crew, this is the captain speaking. I promised you further information and I will give that to you now. We will first work near Guam in the Mariana Islands. The Japs are reinforcing their navy base on Guam. We will sink enemy ships caring supplies and troops."

There was a brief pause.

Jack said, "From Guam we will move about 1400 miles south, southeast to Kwajalein. We will be looking for Jap convoys near Kwajalein. Then we will travel southeast about 500 miles to work around Tarawa and Makin in the Gilbert Islands. We will be on lifeguard duty. We and seven other subs will set up a lifeline to pick up downed U.S. pilots. The fleet will report on down airmen and we will pick up them up. We will work as a 'wolf pack' with the other subs. As far as I know this is the first time we have worked in a pack and done lifeguard duty."

Jack continued, "As you can see we will be covering a large area. I know we can count on your best efforts to carry out our mission. We should be on our first station in about ten days. We will travel on the surface as much as possible. Lookouts be alert. We will follow our standard duty roaster for war zone areas. This may be a long patrol. Good luck and good hunting. That is all."

Jim, Mac, and Jack had control room duty during the day. Mike, Don, and Al had lookout duty on the bridge during daylight. The two shifts of officers would exchange duties each night and each morning. Each three-man crew would work in 12-hour shifts. One man out of the three could sleep when not in combat. The positions were rotated so that every man could get some rest. The enlisted men had their duty rosters.

The radioman monitored the airways for news when they were on the surface. They could extend the radio antenna. If atmospheric conditions were just right the radioman cold pick up broadcast from the west coast or Honolulu. He could pick up Japanese radio stations. Most of these were from Japanese bases or submarines. They were in code. ULTRA had broken some of the Jap navel code. Japanese submarines were very talkative. The U.S. code breakers could keep track of some Japanese convoys from the information picked up.

The skipper had given the radioman permission to pass on some news to the crew. This was a carry over authorization from Larry's command.

The radioman usually passed on major league baseball scores and college football scores. The latest war news was passed on to the crew. The crew appreciated knowing what was going on in the world.

The days went by fast. On the eighth day of the patrol they were definitely in Japanese waters. Jack decided to submerge during the day and run only on the surface at night. This meant that the day lookouts could help in the control room during the day and let some of the day control room crew get some sleep.

On the tenth night Jim and Mac were on the bridge. They had lookout duty. To help pass the time they would from time to time have a quiet conversation.

Jim said to Mac, "I guess you noticed that this patrol has three stations. We go the furthers east as we are going and start working our way back. I guess headquarters worked out this patrol for us to accomplish different objectives."

Mac to Jim, "Yeah, I noticed that. Looks like this patrol may last a lot longer than any we have been on before."

Jim, "I think you are right. I hope our supplies last."

Mac, "Yeah, especially the chow."

Just then Jim and Mac received a message from the control room on their headsets.

Control room, "Be alert, radar has picked up a number of ships about 10 miles out at 180 degrees directly toward our stern. We are adjusting our course to encounter."

Jim notified the two enlisted men in the crow's nest. All were looking for the first sign of a convoy but by the same token keeping a sharp lookout in all directions.

Control room to Jim and Mac, "We have information that a Jap convoy of three freighters and two escorts are in that convoy. We will stay on the surface and shoot from the bridge, but be ready to dive."

The Spearfish got into position to attack. The three fat freighters had their decks piled high with cargo. Jim could now see them on the TBT. He started feeding the information to the control room. They were in the right position and ready to shoot their torpedoes. Jim would have preferred to close the range some, but Larry suggested going ahead now.

Four torpedoes were fired from 2,500 yards. Two of the freighters were hit. Two more torpedoes were fired at 2,300 yards, but they missed or fail to explode. The bridge personnel could see large fires on two the freighters. They were breaking up. The escort vessels were firing. The *Spearfish* decided to dive and within three minutes they were down 100 feet.

The two Jap destroyers were pinging for the *Spearfish*, but so far they had not located her. Jack decided that they would get out of the area in a hurry. The destroyers dropped 20 to 30 depth changes within the next hour. None hit close to the *Spearfish*.

It was two hours before the *Spearfish* came up to periscope depth. Jack took the periscope and turned it 360 degrees to see if there was any active. Jack reported to the crew.

Jack on the intercom, "Men we have just sunk two big fat freighters. There is debris all over the area. It is raining on the surface and there is a squall. I do not see the rest of the convoy. Sonar, can you pick up anything?"

Sonar operator, "I can't pick up anything but the squall. The Japs must have ducked in behind the squall."

Larry to crew, "Good job men. Those supplies and equipment were on their way to Guam. The way those ships burned they must have had gasoline stored on deck. We will take her down to 100 feet. We will hang around this area another day or two."

After two days the *Spearfish* received no other information about Japanese shipping so they departed the area for Kwajalein.

It took four days and four nights to reach Kwajalein. The Japanese had a navy base and an airfield at Kwajalein. They had radar and radio stations on some of the smaller nearby islands. Kwajalein was on a Japanese water route.

The *Spearfish* was to rendezvous with two other submarines: the *Seawolf* and the *Perch*. The captain of the *Seawolf* would coordinate the activities. Jack contacted the other submarines by radio. Their messages were code. The other subs were already on station and reported no enemy convoy activity.

The submarines would stay submerged during the day and surface each night to charge their batteries and give crewmembers a short break on deck. They were stationed about 20 miles apart along a line that ran parallel to the Kwajalein Atoll. The *Seawolf* was stationed the farthest east, then the *Spearfish*, and then the *Perch* was the furthest west. They would coordinate any attack. This was a new concept to the crews.

Two days later the *Seawolf* sent a message to the other subs in the pack. They had sunk a Jap submarine and had spotted a convoy. The convoy consisted of several freighters and several destroyers. The course and speed was transmitted.

The *Spearfish* figured when and where they should intercept the Jap convoy. They would be ready and set to attack.

It was daylight so Jack took the *Spearfish* up to periscope depth. Jack, Al and three enlisted men were in the conning tower. Jim, Mac, Mike, Don, and seven enlisted men were in the control room.

Jack was looking through the periscope and would direct the action.

Jack over the intercom, "Attention crew I have seven Jap transports, one tanker, and four destroyers. The destroyers are providing a screen for the transports. We will shoot under the screen and try for one or two transports."

Information was fed into the system to set the torpedoes. Jack decided that they would shoot eight torpedoes under the destroyer screen to hit the transports. They would adjust the torpedo depth and try for a destroyer with two more torpedoes. If all went according to plan they would have ten torpedoes in the water at once. Eight torpedoes would be shot from the stern tubes and two from the bow tubes.

Jack, "Fire one . . . fire two . . . fire three . . . fire four . . . fire five . . . fire six . . . fire seven . . . fire eight, now bring her around and give me a bow shot. Don set the bow torpedoes. When they are set fire nine . . . fire ten."

Jack was concerned that the destroyer screen would see the wake of their torpedoes. And then spot their periscope wake. He wanted to wait until the last minute to dive.

Jack on intercom, "Bring her back to stern . . . 360 and reload all torpedo tubes."

Jack continued to look through the periscope.

He said, "The Jap destroyers have not spotted us yet. Mike how long before number one hits?"

Mike, "One more minute. We fired at 2300 yards."

Jack, "Let's move in closer. If we sink a destroyer we will need to be closer . . . down scope. We will move into about 1,000 yards and then raise the scope again."

Jim was watching the clock in the control room. A muffle explosion occurred. Again it reminded Jim of a clap of thunder.

Jim to Mac, "We must have hit one of the transports. The second should hit about now."

Mac, "Yeah, unless it's a dud.

The sonar man, "The Jap destroyers are pinging with their underwater gear. They are searching for us."

Jack on intercom, "Let's take a quick look see. Up scope."

The periscope was raised. About that time the crew heard two explosions.

Jack looking through the scope, "What a sight. We have hit two of the transports and torpedoes are still exploding. It looks like two of our fish exploded prematurely. The two for the destroyers missed. No wait! One of them hit a destroyer. It hit the destroyer in the fantail. It's only damaged. The other destroyers are like a bunch of angry wasp around a nest two of them are heading our way. Radioman, send a message to the other two subs. Tell them that we have sunk two transports and one destroyer is damaged. Tell the *Perch* that the convoy is heading their way. Dive quick as the messages are sent. Dive and prepare for depth charge attack."

The radioman sent the messages and Don, the diving officer, gave the order to dive. The Spearfish dove at a steep angle. It had been the steep's angle the crew had ever dove. Within two minutes the *Spearfish* was 150 feet deep.

The two destroyers dropped depth charges for the next two hours. The *Spearfish* played cat and mouse and tried to evade the destroyers. There were some close hits, but luckily no serious damage to the *Spearfish*. Several leaks sprung up and the crew stayed busy repair damage.

Finally the destroyers left. The sonar operator gave the all clear. Jack had decided to stay submerged because the Japs had an airfield nearby. They could have some planes in the air.

Mac to Jim, "You know Jim I was really scared during the depth charging. I was praying."

Jim to Mac, "I know Mac, I was scared and likewise I was praying. I almost forgot, Mac, you and I reported for duty on the Spearfish just a little over one year ago. Happy anniversary."

Mac, "Has it been that long? In one way it doesn't seem like it has been long. In another way it seems like a lifetime. Especially during depth changing I age about three times faster."

About this time the radioman came on the intercom.

Radioman, "Attention Spearfish crew. Here is the latest news I picked up yesterday and today. The World Series was between the Cardinals and the Yankees. The Yankees took the series in five games. See the sub newsletter for details. In college football Navy beat Army 13-0. On the book best seller list is *Guadalcanal Diary*. One of the latest movies from Hollywood is *Laura*. The captain wanted me to announce that you all did a great job. That is all the news for now."

The officers and men appreciated getting the news. They also enjoyed the bi-weekly sub newsletter. Three enlisted men under the supervision of an officer put out the newsletter. The one or two page letter was typewritten with five or six carbon copies. It was circulated among the crew.

Jack came on the intercom, "Attention, attention, this is the captain. We will leave this area and head to the Gilbert Islands. We have to be on station there by the 15th for 'Lifeguarding'. We will be standing off enemy islands during our carrier air strikes and our job will be to pick up U.S. airmen who are forced down in the sea. Radioman notify the other two submarines of our departcher. They knew we had another mission, but did not know when we would depart. Congratulations on a very successful patrol. That is all."

Jim checked his maps for the route directions and gave those to the helmsman. Jim had estimated that it would take two days and one night.

Jim, Mac, and Don were told to get some sleep. They would have the bridge and control room duty that night. Al would stand by for back-up duties.

Jim, Mac, and Don went to the officer's quarters to rest. They talked for a short time, but went to sleep within minutes. They knew that sleep time was at a premium and they wanted to make the most of it.

The CQ woke the three officers at nineteen hundred hours. They had to shower, shave, dress, and eat before reporting to the control room at twenty hundred hours.

Jim and Mac stood watch on the bridge that night. Don took charge of the control room. They encountered no trouble that night. They had to rely more on radar and sonar as their visibility was handicapped by fog and then a rainsquall came up.

Two days later the *Spearfish* joined seven other submarines for lifeguard duty. The pack was stationed just south of Tarawa and Makin Islands There was about ten miles between each sub. The *Spearfish* would coordinate the operation. This would keep the crew busier than normal.

The U. S. fleet consisting of four carriers, several battleships, cruisers, destroyers, tankers, transports, and other support vessels appeared about fifty miles away the next day. This was obviously and invasion fleet. The airplanes from the carriers started bombing and strafing targets on Tarawa and Makin. The U.S. planes also attacked Japanese shipping around the area.

As H-hour approached the air activity increased. The submarines surfaced and kept on the lookout. The Tarawa Atoll invasion began on Betio and was very bloody. The Second Marine Division was the invading force.

On the first day of the invasion the *Spearfish* received their first downed plane report. The fleet gave the approximately location and the *Spearfish* notified the nearest sub. The next day the report of a down aviator was in the *Spearfish's* sector.

Jim and Don where on the bridge. They and the two men in the crow's nest were on the alert. The *Spearfish* changed its course and headed toward the down airman. One of the men in the crow's nest was the first to see the down airman.

Lookout, "I see him. He is about 500 yards on our starboard"

Jim, "Yes, I see him now, helmsman come to 275 degree and slow sub to 12 knots for a stop. Rescue crew on deck"

Within 30 minutes the deck rescue crew pulled the downed aviator from his raft and helped him below.

Don, "Well that's our rescue and it feels good to save someone."

Jim, "Yes it does feel good to save someone. You know what other country would go to the trouble and expense to save a life? We have a great country."

Don, "Very few countries could afford to spend the resources that we are spending just to save a few lives. The Japs certainly do not."

Jim, "We in the United States value the worth of just one life. A lot of countries do not put the same value as we do on the life of a human being."

Within two hours Jim and Don were relieved. They and Mac were off duty and went to their quarters to rest. As they entered their quarters they saw the down aviator. He had a blanket around himself and was still shivering from being wet even two hours after being out of the water.

Downed aviator, "They put me in here I hope that is all right. I am sorry if I messed up you room."

Don to aviator, "You are okay. We knew they put you in our quarters. I am Don Phillips, this is Jim Rush and this is Mac MacDonald."

Jim, "Hi, welcome aboard."

Mac, "You are welcome ensign. I guess you had a pretty rough time."

Downed aviator, "Thanks for saving my life. I was really glad to see you guys. I am Joe Carter."

Jim, "Where is your home Joe?"

Joe, "I am from Sherman, Texas."

Don, "Joe, what were you flying? I assume a fighter?"

Joe, "Yes I am a fighter pilot. I was flying a Wildcat. I was scraffing and I guess I got too low and was hit by ground fire. I lost oil pressure and my engine started smoking so I had to set her down in the sea. What an experience. I thank the good Lord that I am alive."

The men chatted for another hour. Finally they all feel asleep, as they were very tired.

They were awaken when the CQ came in and told Joe that a rescue barge was sent to get him and take him to his carrier. They wished Joe good luck and he thanked them again for saving him. Jim, Don, and Mac fell back to sleep.

The lifeguard operation continued for the next several days. Seventeen airmen from seven down aircraft were picked up.

Finally the islands were secured. The "wolf pack" broke up and went their separate ways on their assignments.

Bill Schmitt, the chief cooks mate, went to Larry to report.

Bill to Larry, "Captain, I wish to report that we are very low on food supplies. We are having at least one meal a day of 'cold cuts'. That is we are having Spam sandwiches. We are out of fresh meat and vegetables. We have a few cans of potatoes and beans left. We have a couple of cases of C-rations. Sir, I think we probably have only enough food for four or five days. The men are beginning to grumble."

Larry to Bill, "Yes I have notice a decline in the quality and quantity of food. Even if we sail toward home today it will take ten days or so. I'll see what we can do. We may have to go to two meals a day. Bill, you will have do the best you can."

Bill to Larry, "I am sorry I had to bring you bad news Sir, but I put it off as long as possible."

Larry to Bill, "You did your duty. It's not your fault. Tell your crew that we appreciate what they are doing. It will not kill us to go a little hunger. Some fasting might do us some good."

As Bill left the Captain's cabin and the engineering officer, Al Valcheck, reported to Larry.

Al to Larry, "Sir I wish to report that we are running low on diesel fuel. I don't think we will have enough to make it back to Pearl."

Larry to Al, "If we run at the most efficient speed will that get us home?"

Al to Larry, "I don't think it will sir. As best I can figure it we will be about 300 miles short."

Larry to Al, "Okay Al, thanks for the report. Tell the helmsman to run at the speed that will give us maximum use of our fuel. I'll see what we can do to get a tanker."

Larry gave the radioman a message to send. He requested a tanker and some food supplies. He had Jim to give a map reference for a rendezvous point to the radioman to include in the message. The nearest supply depot was at Midway and it was almost as far as Pearl Harbor.

The Spearfish was low on fuel and supplies. They had been out 45 days on patrol. The men were tired. They headed toward Pearl Harbor and home.

Their speed had been decreased to conserve diesel. The cook had gone to two meals a day. Strangely enough the crew understood and there was very little complaining.

Jim, Mac, and Al were on duty. Jim and Mac had the lookout duty on the bridge. Al had control room duty.

Mac to Jim, "You know this crew is not complaining about the lack or food. I thought they might really be raising cane."

Jim to Mac, "This is an exceptional crew. I think they understand why we are low on supplies. I think they are thankful they are alive. That is why they are not 'belly-aching.' I doubt any of us will starve. We should be thankful for what we do have."

Mac to Jim, "You're right as usually Jim. How far are we from that rendezvous point?

Jim to Mac, "When I checked before we came on watch we had about 50 miles to go. We did change our course slightly to make the meeting point."

The radioman came on the intercom. He announced that the tanker was very near and that the captain said to keep a close "lookout." About that time the sonar operator came on the intercom and announced that he had a ship on his scope at about 10,000 yards directly ahead. There was one big ship with two smaller vessels.

Jim to Mac, "We better keep a sharp eye. It is probably our tanker, but it could be a Jap. We need to get positive I.D."

Mac looking through the TBT, "I see it! It's a tanker and it is one of ours."

The radioman confirmed that it was the tanker they expected. It took about two hours for the tanker to get hooked up to the *Spearfish* and put diesel into their tanks. The tanker had brought some food supplies and those crates were transferred to the sub.

Jack sent a thank you to the tanker. Flags using semaphore code sent Jack's message. This boosted the moral of the men. The captain of the tanker sent a message.

His message, "You are welcome for diesel and supplies. Among your food supplies you have turkey, dressing, potatoes, green beans, corn, and pumpkin pie with whipped cream. Merry Christmas."

"Tomorrow is Christmas! I had forgotten." Mac yelled.

Jim to Mac, "I think we all had forgotten or just didn't want to remind ourselves that it was Christmas."

Mac to Jim, "We will just have to celebrate Christmas at sea this year. We should be in port for New Year's. Eve"

They were soon on their way to Pearl.

CHAPTER 10
HOME AGAIN SAFE

AFTER ENJOYING A Christmas meal with all the trimmings the crew of the *Spearfish* was in good spirits when they docked three days later.

The day they docked Jim came down with a head cold. He had not been sick in three or four years. His head was "stopped up"; he had a headache, a sore throat, and felt miserable. He went to the *Spearfish*'s pharmacist mate. The pharmacist mate, Marvin VanRoyen gave him some pills, checked his pulse, his temperature and advised him to go to the dispensary if he was not feeling better in two or three days.

The start of this rest period followed the same pattern as the crew experienced after prior patrols. They followed the same routine. The skipper gave them an informational type talk, quarters were assigned, and they picked up their mail.

Jim, Mac, Al, and Don were roommates again. Jim was still not feeling well, but had improved. He lay on his bunk reading his mail. The other men were sitting on their bunks reading their mail. This was the quiet time. After about one hour the men began to stir.

Mac broke the silence, "Well everything is about the same at home. My uncle, Marion, you know the one in the Seabees; he is still on some South Seas island taking a rest. My mother said they heard they might stop rationing meat soon. My ex-fiancée, Mary Jo, called my mother and talked to her. Some nerve she has after breaking our engagement. My younger brother has finished jump school and earned his jump badge. He will be shipping out soon."

Don said, "Not much new to report from my neck of the woods. My wife is still working and my folk are doing okay. Mom told me that one of my best friends was reported missing in action. His B-24 was shot down over Germany."

Al spoke up, "I had told you guys that my sister's fiancée was drafted. He has finished his basic training. They gave him ten days furlough and shipped him to Camp Kilmer, New Jersey. That is the port of embarkation for the African/Europe theatre of operations. Dad is still working at the publishers."

Jim said, "I guess it's my time for a report. Things are about the same in my hometown. My high school boy's basketball team won the county tournament. My mother sent me a clipping out of the newspaper with my photo. The PIO took this when I got promoted and sent this to the newspaper. My mother said she was very proud of me."

Mac, "Let's see the clipping, pass it around,"

Mac looking at the clipping, "Good picture Jim. It makes you look better looking than you really are."

Mac laughed and passed the clipping around.

Don said, "I wonder where our next patrol will be. The skipper has called a meeting tomorrow, but I doubt that we would have an assignment that soon. Jim is your cold any better? You may want to go on sick call tomorrow."

Jim, "My cold is better. I don't think I will go on sick call. I'll see how it goes tonight.

Al to Jim, "Jim why not rub some Vicks on your throat and head. You need to gargle with some salt water. My mom use to rub us kids down with Vicks when we got a head cold."

Mac, "The best thing for a head cold and sore throat is some honey mixed with a little whiskey with a pinch of sugar added. If you would like I will buy the honey and whiskey. That always cleared up our head colds when I was a kid."

Don, "Well now there you have it Jim. Doc Mac and Al have just given you the remedy on how to get well"

Mac, "Don't make fun of my remedy it works. To prove it I will get the honey and a pint of whiskey. If Jim will take it I can prove my point. Jim if I get the stuff will you take it?"

Jim, "Well okay Mac, you get the honey and whiskey and as a favor to you I will take it."

After chow that evening Mac brought the honey, whiskey and sugar. As any professional he very carefully put the exact amounts together and mixed them up for Jim. Jim took Mac's medicine. After a few minutes his throat did feel better.

Mac, "Okay Jim, now in about two hours you can take another dose. We have to be scientific about this."

The others laughed at Mac. In the morning Jim felt much better. Mac gave him a third dose before breakfast and a fourth one after breakfast. Jim felt much better and they all left their quarters to go to the meeting Jack at called for 0900.

The crew of the *Spearfish* assembled in the conference room that they had become to know so well. It was 0900 and Jack and Mike were already seated on the platform.

Don reported, "Sir, all present and accounted for."

Jack went to the speaker's stand,

He said, "Good morning officers and men of the *Spearfish*. We do not have out next patrol assignment yet. I expect to receive that within the next ten days. The crew will stand by. Report here each morning at 0800 for possible assignments. All will have liberty on the 31st and the first. That of course, is New Year's. You will have liberty on the weekend. Enjoy yourself, but stay out of trouble. Now Lieutenant Mike Moreland will make some announcements."

Mac to Jim quietly, "Just like Larry use to do. Let the XO get to give the good news."

Jim to Mac, "I think you are right."

Mike to the crew, "Men I have the promotional list. Two officers and five enlisted men have received promotions. Lieutenant Don M. Phillips is promoted from Lieutenant (.j g) to full lieutenant; Ensign George 'Mac' MacDonald is promoted from ensign to lieutenant (j g.)"

Mike continued to list the five enlisted men who received promotion. Mac was so stunned that he couldn't hear what Mike was saying. Mike finally dismissed the crew.

Jim to Mac, "Congratulations Mac. You deserve it."

Jim to Don, "Don congratulations it is well deserved. Now you really have some news to write Mildred about."

Don to Jim, "Thanks Jim, I am grateful for the promotion and the increase in pay"

Don turning to Mac, "Mac congratulations. You are doing well. Just think only after your fourth patrol and you get a promotion. That is great."

Don turning to Al, "Al you will probably get a promotion after about two more patrols. You know we keep getting all these promotions and they will break up this old gang. We will become 'top heavy.' I bet we get a new ensign assigned to our crew before long."

Jack and Mike personally congratulated each officer and man who received a promotion. Several enlisted men congratulated Don and Mac. Likewise the officers shook hands and congratulated each enlisted man who received a promotion.

Very few of the crew had left when Jack raised his hand and asked for quiet.

Jack to all, "We will be throwing a New Year's Eve party Friday night. We will also celebrate the promotion of our fellow crewmen. Everyone is invited. Tell those who have already left. Mike and I will be in charge and host the event. This will be in one of the ballrooms at the Royal Hawaiian Hotel at 0w twenty hundred hours. That is 8 p.m. for those of you that are still civilians at heart."

The officers and men of the *Spearfish* got a laugh out of Jack's last comment. They applauded because they could already imagine food and women at the party. They were already taking up donations to help pay for the party.

Jim, Mac, Don, and Al returned to their room. They had just "settled in" when the mail clerk knocked on their door. Al got up and went to the door.

Mail orderly, "Sir I have some more mail for the *Spearfish*. I do not know where the enlisted men are. Can you see that they get their mail? There are a few pieces of late mail for you officers."

Al to orderly, "Yes we will see that they get their mail. Thanks for bring this to us."

The orderly left. The four officers gathered around a table and began to sort the small bundle of letters. Jim had a letter from Linda. Don had a letter from Mildred. Mac had a letter from his brother, and Al had a letter from Hazel his fiancée. They alphabetized the enlisted men's mail and Al took it over to their barracks.

The officers began reading their mail. It was a blessing to have more mail. Jim carefully read Linda's letter. It was not long, but Jim was so pleased to hear from Linda.

Linda's letter read as follows.

Dearest Jim,

I hope you are in good health. I am fine. I like my job here at the base.

It is the same kind of work I did in Hawaii.

I think about you and the good times we had. I am dating a fellow here. He is okay.

After my dad's funeral I helped my mother with all the estate stuff. I didn't realize there was so much to do. My mother seems to be coping with dad's death okay. I am glad I got home to help out. I still can't believe my dad is gone.

After we parted I began to wonder if it had indeed been too final. Perhaps we will meet in the future. I wonder if it would be a planned meeting, a chance meeting, or a sandwich and coffee "for old times' sake?"

Uncertainty has put our relationship on the "back burner."

You and I had some good times. No matter what I will always have a warm spot in my heart for you.

I know you are busy, but drop me a line if you can.

Love,
Linda

Linda's letter brought a flood of warm memories to Jim's mind. Jim realized, too late, that he really cared for Linda. He would put Linda from his mind for now and go on.

The officers started discussing their news from home.

Mac said, "Not much new from my brother. He has earned his jump badge and is waiting to be sent to Africa, Italy, or England. He is not sure which. Hey when we were sorting mail I noticed that Jim had a letter from his 'sweetie.' Tell us Jim what did Linda have to say. I bet she wrote a hot love letter."

Jim to the others, "Linda wrote a short letter. She got home okay and helped put her father away. She is working at a nearby base. It was not a love letter Mac. It was just a short note."

Don to the others, "Not any changes at my home. Mildred and my folks are doing fine."

Al said, "Hazel quit her job in the five and ten cent story. She has taken a government job on an army post. She is a typist in an office. She likes her job and says she feels like she is helping the war effort. She types letters of condolence to families who have lost loved ones. She and about twenty other typist work for some captain."

Mac to Al, "Watch out Al. Hazel may meet some army officer and throw you over."

Mac and the other laughed including Al.

Al retorted, "No not Hazel. She is a great little gal and I can depend on her being loyal to me."

Friday, the day of the New Year's Eve party came. Jim felt better, but was still not fully recovered. All the officers were at the ballroom ready to party by 8 p.m. A big crowd was there. There were girls and booze. Some of the men were already tight and a few were already drunk. A band was playing and couples started dancing.

Jim, Mac, Don, and Al were all sitting at the same table. Al was drinking and seemed tight. Mac went over and asked a girl to dance and almost got into a fight. It seems the girl was somebody's wife. Mac found another girl and they started dancing. Al went over to the bar for another drink. Jim and Don were sitting at the table talking.

Don to Jim, "Jim you don't look like you are feeling well."

Jim to Don, "I'm not feeling super, but I do feel better than I did this morning. I am getting better, but I have had a tough time shaking this cold. At least my throat is no longer sore."

Don, "Jim, you might get to feeling better if you asked one of the girls to dance."

Jim, "Maybe I will, but later."

Jack joined Jim and Don. Pretty soon Al returned to the table and sat down. He was nursing a drink. Mac was still dancing.

Jack to the others, "I hope you guys are enjoying this. Jim I understand you have been under the weather. How are you feeling now?"

Jim to Jack, "Yes sir, I have a head cold. It is better, but I am not at 100% yet."

Jack rising from his chair, "I had better mix and mingle. I'll see you guys later."

The music, food, drinking, dancing, and conversations continued for the next three hours. Finally, Jim decided he would try to meet a girl. He excused himself and went over to where there were several female's sitting. He had spotted a blonde who seemed to be friendly. Jim had been watching her for a few minutes. She had a neat hair do, had a good figure, and was attractive. At least Jim seemed attracted to her.

Jim to blonde, "Would you care to dance?"

Blonde, "Yes."

Jim to blonde, "My name is Jim Rush."

Blonde, "My name is Ann Rapp."

Jim and Ann went out on the dance floor. Jim put his right hand on Ann's shoulder and his left hand on her waist and she put one hand on his shoulder and one hand on his arm. They talked while they dance. After the first dance Jim held Ann closer. They talked about their homes, their past, their jobs, and a number of things. They danced for almost an hour.

Jim to Ann, "Ann you have beautiful eyes. I like your hair do. I enjoy dancing with you and I am not a good dancer."

Ann to Jim, "You dance well enough. I appreciate dancing with you. Most of the dances I had before were with partners who were two sheets to the wind. I don't know why folks think they have to drank liquor to have a good time."

Jim to Ann, "I agree."

At that time a bell went off signaling the New Year was here.

Jim to Ann, "Happy New Year Ann."

Ann to Jim, "Happy 1944 to you Jim."

Jim knew that Ann expected to be kissed. He took her in his arms and kissed her. He knew she expected to be kissed so he had not even bothered to ask her if he could kiss her. At first he intended to make it a short kiss, but the lights were turned out and he kissed Ann long and hard. Ann kissed him back. They both felt alone in the middle of a dance floor although they were with 50 other couples. After one minute the lights were turned back on.

Jim to Ann, "Thanks for the kiss Ann. It meant a lot to me."

Ann to Jim, "Thank you, it meant a lot to me to. We should both have a good new year."

About one a.m. the party broke up. Jim and Ann said their good byes knowing they would probably not see one another again.

Jim felt tired, but his head cold seemed a lot better. Jim and Mac had to help Al back to their quarters. Al was drunk and he vomited before that got to their quarters. They put Al to bed, clothes and all. He did not know anything.

Jim took a shower. He normally showered or took his bath at night and shaved in the morning. This way he was clean-shaven for inspection. He enjoyed the showers in the barracks because he could stay in the shower as long as he liked. Showering on a sub was timed and you only had three minutes per shower.

Jim, Mac, and Don all set up and talked awhile and finally went to bed and all slept very well.

The next morning Al woke up with a headache. Jim woke up feeling better. All went to the mess hall and ate breakfast. Not many people were eating at the mess hall that morning. The New Year's Eve parties had taken its toll.

The officers returned to their quarters. They were wondering what they would do that day. It was Saturday and Jim did not have a date. Mac suggested they take in a post movie later that day. They generally agreed that would go to a movie.

There was a knock at their door. Mac got up and went to the door. He opened the door and a young ensign stood in the doorway.

The ensign said, "Excuse me sir, but I have been assigned to these quarters. I hope that is okay."

Mac said, "Sure come in. As you can see we do have two empty bunks. Pick one. My name is George MacDonald. Everyone calls me Mac. What is your name?"

Ensign, "I am Richard Sisler. I prefer not to be called Dick. Here are my orders I am to report to the captain of the *Spearfish*."

Don, "Welcome. We are all from the *Spearfish*. This is Jim Rush and this is Al Valcheck. The skipper and executive are just down the hall. Get settled and we will take you to meet the skipper."

Jim to Richard, "Where are you from Richard?"

Richard to all, "I am from Long Beach. That is Long Beach, California. I was raised in Visalia, California. We moved to Long Beach about four years ago."

Don to Richard; "Tell us about yourself, are you married? Engaged? How long have you been in the navy? What did you do in civilian life? We are not nosy Richard. We just want to get to know you. You see sub crew's are very close."

Richard to all, "I am glad you want to know about me. I feel like you have accepted me. I am not married, but have a steady girl friend. I am 22 years old and got two years of college education. I joined the navy about one year ago. I got my commission four months ago."

Mac speaks, "Richard you are about mine and Jim's age. I think Jim is about one year younger. I just made (j g.). I was commissioned about one and one/half year ago. What about your family . . . you know your mother and father?

Richard responds, "I still live at home with mom and dad. I have two younger sisters and one younger brother. My dad works for the Kiser Ship Yards. He works on the Liberty Ships. My mother works in the home, but does volunteer Red Cross work."

Don to Richard, "Now that you have 'settled in' come with me and I'll take you to the skipper. We have a great skipper. He really knows his business. Richard you were lucky to be assigned to our crew."

Don and Richard went down the hall and knocked on Jack's door. He answered the door and Don introduced him to Richard. Jack asked for a copy of Richard's orders and he gave him a copy.

Jack, "Welcome aboard Richard. I'm pleased to have you on our crew."

Jack turns toward Mike and gestures with his arm pointing to Mike.

Jack continues, "Richard this is our Executive Officer Lieutenant Mike Moreland."

Mike, "Richard I am pleased to meet you, sir. I'll get with you tomorrow and go over what your duties will be. You have a bunch of great fellow officers. They will be worth listening to."

Jack to Don, "Oh Don, tell the officers that we will meet on the 15$^{th.}$ I should have some information about our next patrol. It will give us the chance to introduce Richard. We are getting two new enlisted men and will introduce them. We will make an announcement on the meeting date to the entire crew Monday at 0800."

Don and Richard returned to their quarters. Al was feeling better. They were all relaxed.

The officers attended a movie on post that afternoon. After the movie they went to the officers club for a meal.

The five officers were seated at a round table. They had order their meal and was eating the appetizer. Their conversation continued covering a number of things.

Jim said, "Some way to spend Saturday night."

Mac commented, "Get a load of that men, Jim would rather spend a Saturday night with Linda that with his old buddies."

Don said, "I can't say that I blame Jim. No reflection on the present company, but I would rather be with Mildred right now."

Al responded, "You guys are making me home sick. I wish I could spend just one hour with Hazel."

It was at this time that the main course of food was served to the officers. Jim had order a medium-well done beefsteak. Meat was still rationed to civilians, but the army and navy had plenty of meat.

Richard spoke, "My steady girl friend's name is Dorene and I miss her. Here fellas let me show you her picture."

Richard took Dorene's photo out of his wallet and passed around for the others to see.

Jim said, "She is a very attractive girl Richard."

Richard said, "Now men let me see the pictures of your girl friends or in your case Don your wife."

All the officers pulled out their wallets to show photos. They passed them around. All the photos had the name on back of the person pictured.

Richard, "Jim you have two photos of two different girls. What's the story?"

Jim, "Well both girls used to be my steady girl friend, this one is Janet. She and I went steady before I enlisted. We mutually parted company. The other girl is Linda. We dated here in Hawaii. She was a civilian employee, but left because her father passed away. So you see I do not have a current girl friend. I continue to carry their pictures to remind me what I am fighting for."

Richard, "Oh I see."

Mac, "Before you ask, the photo you have is my ex-fiancée's picture. She broke our engagement. I am unattached. Don't ask me why I still carry her picture."

Don, "The picture you have is of my wife Mildred. We just celebrated our fourth anniversary last month."

Al said, "The photo you are looking at is the best looking gal in Chicago. Hazel happens to be my fiancée."

Richard said, "Gee thanks for sharing you pictures with me. You know all this does make one a little home sick. Jim is right the girls pictures remind us of one of the things we are fighting for."

Mac said, "Say Richard you said you had two younger sisters. How much younger? Do you have any pictures? Are you sisters old enough to date? Would you be willing to introduce them to me?"

Richard said, "My sisters are ages 19 and 16. My brother is 12. I don't have any of their photos on me. Mac I would have to get to know you better before I would answer your last question."

The other officers laughed at Richard's reply.

Jim said, "This guy is pretty sharp. Richard you're okay."

Don said, "Good answer Richard."

Mac with a come back, "Yeah sure, just ask my ex-fiancée; she could give me a good recommendation."

The men walked back to their quarters.

The officers and men of the *Spearfish* stayed busy the next few days. They supervised and helped the shore crew repair, clean and repaint the *Spearfish*. Each sub received a new coat of paint inside and out after four patrols. Sometimes they were repainted more often. The ocean salt water could take its toll on metal.

As promised, Jack had the crew assemble on the 15th for information about their next patrol.

Don reported to Jack, "Sir all the crew is present or accounted for."

Jack to crew, "Good morning men."

Crew responded, "Good morning sir."

Jack to crew, "I want to introduce again some new men to our crew. They have been introduced before, but in case you have not met them I'll introduce them again. Men please stand as I call your name, Ensign Richard Sisler, Seaman 2nd Class Joe Harris, and Seaman 1st Class Fred Edwards. These men are additions to our crew, not replacements. For the first time we are fully staffed."

Mac whispers to Jim, "They are bringing more and more men into the fight. I understand they are drafting as young as age 18. and as old as age 38."

Jim whispers to Mac, "I think you are right. I had a 36-year-old single cousin who was drafted in early '42. They will let them enlist as young as age 17 with the parents consent."

Jack continues, "Men our next patrol will be to the Marshall Islands. I'll give specific information after we are underway. We will shove off tomorrow morning at 0900. Get you laundry, pack your bags, and report aboard the *Spearfish* tomorrow morning. I have been told that some of you may have some mail. Check with the quartermaster. That is all. You are dismissed."

CHAPTER 11
MISSION CHANGED

MAC WENT TO the quartermaster's office to see if any of the officers of the *Spearfish* had any mail. Al went to the supply room to pick up laundry for the officers. Jim checked them out of their quarters with the orderly room. Don double-checked their quarters to make sure they had got all their belongings.

They reported aboard the *Spearfish* and were ready to sail by 0900 on January 16, 1944.

Jack had instructed Jim to plot a course for the Marshall Islands. They were to patrol an area about 200 square miles between Kwajalein and Eniwetok. It would take about five or six days to reach their patrol area.

The third day out Jack called a meeting of the officers in the wardroom.

Jack to the officer's, "Gentlemen, we have just received a message from fleet headquarters. There has been a change in our orders. They have ordered us to divert and go to Wake Island. We are to seek out and sink any enemy ships we see. We are to be alert to lifeguard duty. They didn't say so, but it sounds like we may be going to take Wake back. As you may know Wake Island is about five or six hundred miles north of the Marshall Islands. It is half way between Hawaii and Guam."

Mike commented, "I hope we are going to take Wake Island back. We fought so hard to hold Wake after Pearl Harbor was bombed and the navy sent help and then recalled the help before it got to Wake. The garrison there had to surrender. Those marines and other personnel have been in Jap POW camps ever since. I have heard that the Japs executed 40 or 50 civilian workman on that island."

Jack gave instructions, "Jim plot us a course for Wake Island. I don't know if the Japs will send reinforcements or not, but let's all be on the alert for Jap shipping in that area. I will make the announcement to the crew in a few minutes. We will go on battle stations when we get within 100 miles of Wake."

Four days later the *Spearfish* arrived at its destination. Jack followed the pattern of staying submerged to periscope depth during the day and running on the surface at night. The Japs had a small navel force at Wake, but they were staying in port. They had a runway and a few airplanes.

The *Spearfish* received a message from the invasion fleet. The message wanted the *Spearfish* to be alert for cruisers and destroyers that may arrive at Wake. They asked the *Spearfish* to report any enemy shipping or air activity. Two other subs would be joining them. The two other subs would be the *Bowfin* and the *Seawolf*. The *Spearfish* would coordinate the attack. The invasion fleet should be on station tomorrow.

That night Don and Jim had the bridge lookout duty. Al and Richard had duty in the control room. Mike was in overall command. Jack and Mac were off duty sleeping.

About midnight sonar reported picking up a group of ships to the east. That had to be the U.S. invasion fleet. Radioman soon confirmed that it was the U.S. Fleet. The carriers would launch their first air attacks the next morning.

At dawn the *Spearfish* submerged to periscope depth. Don and Jim manned the periscope in the conning tower. They took turns staying on lookout. About 0700 Don was appearing through the periscope.

Don looking through the periscope, "I see them now. Our planes are bombing and strafing. The Japs are opening up with anti-aircraft fire. The Japs are starting to send some ships out of the harbor. Alert the captain. Load all stern and bow torpedo tubes. It looks like they have three small destroyers and one heavy cruiser and a minesweeper or some kind of a support vessel. Let's target the first ship out."

Don said, "Jim line up the first ship on the RBT and feed the info to control."

Jim responded, "Okay Don, Information transmitted to control. We are on a target."

Within minutes Jack was in the control room and took charge. He had Don and Jim to "man" the periscope and call the shots.

As the Japanese ships came out of the small harbor the *Spearfish* and the other subs would line them up and fire their torpedoes.

It was at this time that the *Spearfish* notified the two other U.S. subs of the plan of attack. They had formed a wolf pack and would each take a target in the order of *Spearfish, Seawolf,* and *Bowfin*.

The *Spearfish* shot four torpedoes at 2000 yards. They hit and sunk one of the destroyers. The *Bowfin* and the *Seawolf* each sank a destroyer. All three subs ganged up and sunk the cruiser. In the meantime the Japanese had managed to get a few planes in the air. Our planes and the Jap planes were having a "dog fight."

The subs did not want to surface with Japanese planes in the air. All the Japanese planes appeared to be fighters . . . Zero's and would not have bombs but their strafing of a sub could do great damage.

Within an hour the air seemed to be clear of Jap planes. All three subs decided to surface. There were four downed American airmen that the subs needed to rescue. It was decided to let the *Bowfin* pick up the downed airmen. The *Seawolf* and the *Spearfish* would stand guard duty.

The plan was changed when it was discovered that one of the down airman was within 500 yards of the *Spearfish*. Jack notified the other subs that the *Spearfish* would pick up one of the down aviator's.

The *Spearfish* lookouts saw the down airman. He was floating in a small life raft. The rescue crew helped the downed airman aboard. He was given some dry clothes and some food and coffee. He was soon picked up by a small craft and returned to his carrier.

Since it seemed safe Jack had four of his officers and as many enlisted men as he could spare to go up on deck and watch the landing party go ashore. Jim, Mac, Al, and Richard were all on the bridge to see the marines go ashore. Wake is a small island, really it was more like a sand dune in the ocean, but it took most of the day to take it from the Japs. Wake Island was declared secured by 1600. The Japanese garrison on the island had about 300 men. Only 25 prisoners were taken.

By this time it was getting dark. The setting sun gave a colorful glow. The cloud cover and a rainsquall several miles off to the west made an even more colorful sun set.

Jack sent a report back to Pearl.

Jack on PA system, "Attention this is the captain speaking. We have completed our mission at Wake Island. Good job men. We are waiting on further orders from Pearl. You may stand down from your battle stations. Keep a normal operating crew on duty. The remainder may get chow and rest.

About midnight the radioman reported he had received a message from headquarters. Jack told him to decode it and bring it to him. Jack called for a meeting with all his officers in the wardroom. He did leave Mike on duty in charge of the control room.

Jack, Don, Jim, Mac, Al, and Richard were all assembled in the wardroom drinking coffee when the radioman handed Jack the decoded message from Pearl.

Jack read the message, "To the commanding officer of the *USS Spearfish*. Good job. You may proceed on your original mission. You are to proceed to the Marshall Islands and carry out the orders originally given to you. You need not coordinate with *Bowfin* and *Seawolf*. We are communicating directly with them. They will remain at Wake for three days just in case of a counter attack. Good luck and God speed."

Jim, "Sir I have already plotted our course to the Marshall Islands. I have specifically used Kwajalein as a reference point."

Jack, "Okay, that's good Jim. Don let's run on the surface at night. I'll make a decision about submerging about day break."

Don, "Aye, Aye sir. I assume you want to use the normal speeds?"

Jack, "Yes, well gentlemen that is all for now. You may resume your normal assigned duties. Lets see, who has the first watch on the bridge? Is that you Don and Jim?"

Don, "Yes sir."

Jack, "Let me make a change. Don take command in the control room and let Mike get a rest. Mac you take Don's place with Jim on the bridge."

Mac, "Aye, Aye, sir."

Jim and Mac took their lookout positions on the bridge. The two enlisted men where all ready in the crow's nest. Jim had a feeling it would be a long night. Their destination was about 800 miles due south.

Jim said, "Mac it may be a long night because we have to go about 800 miles and there are no known Jap shipping lanes. It may be a quiet night."

Mac responded, "I hope it is quiet. How long do you think it will take?"

Jim, "Aw, about 40 to 48 hours. Depends on our speed. We should make good time tonight, but if we submerge tomorrow it will be slower."

Mac looking out across the sea, "It looks real peaceful. The sea can be kind and beautiful one minute and in a roar with high wind and waves the next. The sea is just like a beautiful woman. Relaxed and perfect one moment and a wildcat full of fire and brine stone the next. Boy, I will be glad when this war is over and I get home."

Jim chuckling, "Mac, how can you compare a women with the sea? Oh, I think I know what you mean anything that makes you think of home also makes you think of women."

Mac, "Yeah I guess that's right."

Jim checked with the two enlisted men lookouts. They reported "all clear."

CHAPTER 12
THE MARSHALL ISLANDS

THE *SPEARFISH* WAS on her patrol station two days later. Their patrol area consisted of the area between Kwajalein and Eniwetok Islands. This covered an area of about 600 miles. The *Spearfish* would patrol back and forth in this area looking for Japanese convoys.

For three days and three nights the *Spearfish* moved along a line between Kwajalein and Eniwetok. On the fourth day they received a message telling them that Ultra had intercepted a Japanese radio message and that a convoy would be in their area later today or early the next day. They were given a route and the map reference where to intercept the convoy.

The helmsman changed their course and steered them toward the intercept point. When they reached that point Jack had the sub submerge and brought her back to periscope depth. The crew was put on alert and manned their battle stations.

Jack was in the conning tower manning the periscope. Al and Richard were with him. Jim, Don, Mac, and Mike were all in the control room. Mike was in charge in the control room. Of course Jack was in overall command.

The sonar operator was the first to sound the alert.

Sonar operator, "I am getting several pips. I count six, no seven ships. One pip is very big. That could be a battleship. Going by the size of the pips I would say we have three or four tankers or freighters and two or three destroyers."

Jack, "Radar, are you picking up anything?"

Radar, "No sir, except the same formation that sonar has."

Jack, "Radio man are you picking up anything?"

Radio, "Yes sir, I am getting some Japanese, but I have no idea what is being said,"

Jack, "The Japs are probably talking among themselves in the convoy. They probably feel secure or they wouldn't be so talkative. Load all torpedo tubes and standby for a set-up."

Jack, "Sonar give me a range."

Mac, "8,000 yards and closing."

Jim to Mac, "I expect we will wait until we have a much closer range, unless the wake from our periscope gives us away. I'll bet Jack has us to slow down since the convoy is headed toward us."

Mac, "Jim I think you are right. You know you are beginning to call the shots. One of these days you should command your own sub."

Jim, "Not me Mac. I can talk a good game, but I wouldn't want all that responsibility and headaches. Besides I am not an academy grad."

Jack on intercom, "Slow speed to 5 knots. I don't want our wake to give us away. We are at the point of attack. We will wait on the convoy to get closer. The big job is a cruiser. I think we'll try for her first and then a tanker or freighter. I'll feed the information into the SRF so the torpedoes can be set, Stand by"

To those in the control room it seemed like an hour went by. In reality it was only ten minutes before the convoy approach the range Jack wanted.

Jack on the intercom, "Give me the range."

Jim, "The range is 3,000 yards."

Jack, "When the range gets to 2,000 yards let me know. We will fire tubes one, two, three, and four, on my command."

At 2,300 yards, Jim began to counted down every 100 yards.

Jim, "Range 2,300 yards . . . 2,200 yards . . . 2,100 yards . . . 2,000 yards."

Jack, "Fire all stern tubes. Reload all tubes. Swing the bow around 360 and we will take a shot at a freighter."

At 1,800 yards the *Spearfish* fired two torpedoes from her bow tubes.

The *Spearfish* scored three hits out of the four torpedoes on the cruiser. One torpedo hit near the stern, one below the stack, and one under the bridge. The two bow torpedoes missed or exploded premature.

Jack maneuver the *Spearfish* into another set up and fired four more torpedoes. They hit a freighter. The cruiser and the freighter were on fire and breaking up when Jack gave the order to dive. Two of the destroyers had headed toward them.

They dove down to 250 feet. It was the deepest Jim remembered going. They tried to glide out from under the depth charging, but couldn't throw off the destroyers. The two destroyers dropped at least 40 depth changes, but thank goodness they must have had them set for 150 feet. The depth changing lasted about two hours. The *Spearfish* escaped with very little damage.

The *Spearfish* continued to track the convoy with sonar. The convoy had moved about thirty miles while the Spearfish was evading the depth charges.

The two Japanese destroyers apparently stayed around to pick up survivors from the sunken cruiser. They were now racing to catch up with their convoy.

Jack on the intercom, "We are going after that Jap convoy. We will have to run on the surface to have a chance to catch it. There is some risk in that so I want every officer and man to be alert. We will surface and I want three officers on the bridge instead of two. I want two enlisted men in the crow's nest Sonar, can you tell me where the two destroyers are?"

Sonar operator, "The two destroyers have left the area and heading east toward the convoy. They are about 3 miles away"

Jack on intercom, "Take her up to periscope depth. Stand by your battle stations.

Jack checked the surroundings through the periscope. Seeing nothing he ordered the Spearfish to surface. He ordered the lookouts to the crow's nest and the bridge.

He ordered Don, Mac, and Jim to the bridge. He wanted experience on look out and order two experienced enlisted men to the crow's nest.

Jack gave general orders on the PA, "This is the captain speaking. All other officers stay in the control room. All men at a duty station remain.

The remainder of the crew may stand down for now. Be ready to go to battle stations with a two-minute warning. We are going to try to catch that Jap convoy. Expect to go on battle alert about 0700. That is all for now."

The officers on the bridge heard Jack's announcement over their headset.

Don, "You know I think Jack really wants that Jap convoy. He is more aggressive than I thought, but I like it."

Jim, "You are right Don. Jack is a good skipper and my admiration for him grows with each action we undertake."

Mac, "Jim how long do you think it will take us to overtake that convoy?"

Jim, "I would estimate about two hours. Then allow another hour to get set and get a good fix on a target. So probably three hours in all."

Mac, "That means we can expect action about sunrise."

Don, "Mac, remember sunrise comes real early this time of the year in this part of the world. Jack will have to decide if we keep on the surface by about 0500."

The sun was just beginning to glow a little in the east. When the sonar man broke the quiet with a message.

Sonar man, "We have passed the Jap convoy. They are 5,000 yards to our rear and off the port about 4,000 yards."

Jim, "Jack let Pete Wojoski, the sonar man, make the announcement. Pete has been tracking the convoy all night and is probably tired. Jack rewarded him by letting him tell about the location of the convoy. Most skippers would have given the news, just to remind everyone who was in charge."

Don, "Jim you are right. What Jack did shows that he is good at delegating and does not need to feed his own ego."

Mac, "I agree that is a mark of a good leader."

About this time Jack came on the intercom system.

Jack, "Attention, lookouts below. Take her down to periscope depth. Dive, dive. Change course to get us in an attack positions. Jim and Don help the helmsman work out our course. Mike and Al join me in the conning tower for periscope duty. Mac and Richard help with sonar and radar duties. All hands go to your battle stations. Load all torpedo tubs and stand by for action."

The *Spearfish* worked her way into an attack position.

Jack appearing through the periscope, "Here they come. One destroyer is leading. The other two destroyers are one on either side of the three freighters and one tanker. There is one more Jap ship than we thought. We will shoot for a freighter and the tanker. Standby to fire."

Jack decided to shoot a spread of torpedoes. He would shoot eight torpedoes at three different targets. He had decided to try for one of the destroyers. He wanted in closer to increase the chances of hitting all the targets. He knew if their torpedoes were spotted that the destroyers would probably have time to maneuver out of the way.

Jack on intercom, "Quick as we shoot the torpedoes I want the tubes reloading as quickly as possible. The torpedo men you will have to work fast. I want to immediately shoot another spread."

Mac, "We can do it. Jim I am going to the forward torpedo room and help them. Mike gave Mac permission to leave the control room.

Jim, "Good luck Mac."

Mac went to the forward torpedo room. He would help, but it showed the enlisted men that officers were not afraid of manual work.

Jack on intercom, "Set range for 800 yards. From this point blank range we can't miss. The Japs haven't seen us yet. The sun is just rising. Fire all tubes with 15 seconds between shots.

The *Spearfish* shot four torpedoes within 60 seconds. The first three torpedoes hit the tanker. Two hit directly under the stack, and one at the forward end of the super structure. There was a loud explosion as the tanker started burning and exploding. Two torpedoes hit a freighter. They hit in the middle of the ship and there was a loud explosion.

Within two minutes the forward torpedo room reported that all tubs were reloaded. Jack order that all four of the torpedoes be shot. Two of the four hit one of the destroyers. It was hit enough that it was stopped in the water.

Jack looking through the periscope, "I see one tanker going down, one freighter is burning and sinking, one destroyer hit and stopped in the water. The other two destroyers are shooting in every direction. I don't think they have spotted us yet. Take her down. Dive, dive, take her down to 200 feet."

The action had been swift and mind bottling. It had been hard for the crew to keep up with all the action. They were all busy doing their own jobs and it was hard to see the complete picture until it was over.

For some reason the destroyers did not pursue the *Spearfish*. The crew felt lucky. So did Jack. He decided that he would rest the crew for a little while.

Jack on PA, "Attention, this is the captain. Good work men. You have sunk two Jap ships and damaged at least one other. We will stay down for the day. We need to get some rest. Keep a minimum on duty and the rest go eat and rest. Relieve those who remain on duty within four hours so they may eat and rest. We will not pursue this convoy any longer. There is a Jap airbase nearby and they will have air cover. Thanks for a job well done. That is all."

Jack and Richard stayed on duty in the control room. The other officers went to the officer's wardroom and ordered breakfast. They ate their meal and drank coffee.

Mac to the other officers, "I am all 'tuckered out' I think I'll go to our quarters and hit the sack."

Mike said, "I am exhausted I'm going to hit my cot and sleep."

Jim and Al followed Mac to their quarters. The men quickly fell asleep.

Jim woke up about five hours later. He thought that two of them should relieve Jack and Richard. Normally the executive office relieved the skipper. So he woke Mike up. Jim and Mike went to the control room. They relieved Jack and Richard.

The enlisted men were in the process of relieving enlisted men in the control room. Normally there would have been eight to ten enlisted men in the control room. But at this time there was a skeleton crew of five.

Within four hours Mike and Jim were relieved. So were the on-duty enlisted men. The crew was unselfish is spreading the eating and resting around. The crew rested the remainder of the day.

At 2200 Jack gave orders to get underway. He wanted to get back on their patrol route. Since it was nighttime, the *Spearfish* ran on the surface. They were sailing west toward Eniwetok Island. The Japs had a big air base there and a smaller navy base. They would have to keep the island supplied.

As soon as they surfaced Jack sent a report by radio to headquarters. He reported the number of torpedoes shot. He gave the number and type of ships that were hit. The number of ships sunk. Jack gave the number of ships damaged and the estimated tonnage sunk.

The total number of crew at work was what they normally had when on a battle patrol. This meant two officers and two enlisted men on lookout on the bridge and two officers and eight enlisted men on duty in the control room. This also meant that five torpedo men were on standby duty, at least one cook was on duty, at least four mechanics looking after the engines, a deck gun crew of five on standby, two 50 caliber machine gun crew of four were on standby, and at least one corpsman on call. The radioman, although in a separate room, was considered part of the control room crew.

Jim and Don were scheduled to relieve the lookouts on the bridge at 0600. This meant they could grab a few more hours of sleep.

At 0500 the *Spearfish* radioman woke the skipper to give him an important message from sub headquarters. The radioman knocked on Jack's doorway.

Jack waking up, "Yes, you may come in."

Radioman Nick Franklin said, "Sir we have an important message from headquarters."

Jack was still coming out of a deep sleep and felt groggy.

Jack to Nick, "Okay Nick, read the message."

Nick reading, "To *USS Spearfish*. This is a top priority message. Ultra has intercepted a Japanese message that says that a supply boat with food and 'many classified' documents is being sent to Kwajalein Island. The Japanese boat should be coming your way at about 0900. Intelligence thinks the classified documents could include new Japanese Naval codebooks. Intercept, and if possible capture boat and documents. Message to follow will give map co ordinance and time boat will arrive your area. Be on the alert for other enemy ships or aircraft."

Jack, "Nick notify all officers to meet me in the wardroom in ten minutes, with the exception of the officers in the control room."

Nick, "Aye, aye, sir."

Jack met with Don, Jim, Mac, and Al. Mike and Richard were on duty in the control room or on lookout duty.

Jack read the message to the officers.

Jack to the officers, "This will be a tough nut to crack. If that boat is carrying what headquarters thinks they will not surrender without a fight. I can't image the Japs sending a lone boat on such an important mission."

Don said, "Do you want us on the surface?"

Jack, "Don that is a good question. If this boat is alone and there is no air cover we will attack on the surface. A surface attack is really the only way I can see of us capturing those classified documents."

Jim, "Skipper, do we try to capture with the deck gun or use torpedoes?"

Jack, "If we are on the surface we will try to use the deck gun. Also I want the two 50s on the bridge to help."

Mac, "Sir, Don and Jack have the lookout duty. I request permission to be on the bridge with the 50-caliber gun crew. If not there I request permission to be with the 5" gun crew on deck."

Jack, "Let me think that over Mac. Right now I think I would prefer to have you in the control room, but maybe it would be a good idea to be with the deck gun crew. I'll let you know before 0900."

Jack continuing as though he was thinking out loud. "If we have to stay submerged then we will have no choice, but to use our fish and sink the boat. Then when we can we try to retrieve any documents. This would be a real long shot."

Jim, "Sir, if they do not have much escort maybe we could still risk it on the surface. Let's say if they have only one destroyer escort."

Jack, "We will have to size up the situation when the boat gets here. I have already given the helmsman our intercept point. We should be there within one hour."

Jack went to the control room and briefed the officers and men there. He announced the plan of action over the PA. All the crew was alerted and Jack told them he would call them to their battle stations at 0700.

The question was: when it gets daylight will the *Spearfish* stay on the surface or submerge.

At 0600 when Don and Jim took their place on the bridge it was starting to get light. Jim and Don scanned the horizon and the two men in the crow's nest looked in the sky and sea. All pronounced an "all clear." The lookouts stayed glued to their binoculars looking and searching the sea and sky.

After checking with sonar, radar, and radio Jack decided to stay on the surface for the time being. He sent the deck gun crew up to ready the 5" gun. The 50 caliber gun crews reported to the bridge and set up their guns. Jack had given Mac permission to be with the deck gun crew.

Jim to Don, "It is getting light enough now. Our visibility range on the TBT is about 10,000 yards. I don't see anything yet."

Don, "Jim keep looking to the west. It is a little early yet for us to spot the Jap boat."

Jim, "Don . . . I think I see some kind of a vessel at 12 o'clock. Check me on that."

Don, "I can't see anything with my binoculars. You have more range on the TBT. Let me look through that."

Jim moving to one side lets Don look through the TBT.

Don, "Jim you are right. I do see something, but it is too far away to make it out. We should be able to see it better within a couple of minutes."

Jim takes the TBT and squints as he looks into the instrument.

Don on intercom, "Control room, we have spotted something about 10,000 yards ahead. We can't make it out yet. Is sonar or radar picking up anything?"

Al in control room, "Bridge we are not picking up anything yet. We will search more diligently."

Jim said, "If we can see them, then they can see us."

Don, "Not necessarily Jim. We have a TBT. I doubt they have anything comparable to that. But we will soon find out because they're getting closer. I can now see them with my binoculars."

Jim, "I can see them much clearer now. It's not a Jap ship! It is a Chinese junk. What would a junk be doing in this area?"

Don, "Carrying Japanese classified documents. What better way to send something even without an escort that to disguise the messenger"

Don reported their findings to the control room. Jack agreed that probably the boat they were expecting. Jack asked Don how big was the junk and if it carried any armor.

Jim appearing through the TBT reported, "I don't see any armor, but there is a canvas covering over something on the deck. This is a big junk. It appears to be 250 feet long. The sail is a fake because they are moving at 18 knots an hour. The range is 5,000 yards."

Jack on intercom, "Use your judgment as to when to fire at the junk. Perhaps a warning would only alert them and give them time to radio for help or destroy the documents. Don you call the shots."

Don, "Jim what do you think. At what range should we fire?"

Jim, "I don't know. Let me check with Mac."

Jim motioned for Mac to meet him below the bridge on the deck.

Jim, "Mac at what range should we fire. How accurate are your guys?"

Mac, "They are fairly accurate up to 800 yards. Of course, the closer the better."

Jim returned to his post on the bridge and told Don what Mac had said.

Don, "I think we will wait until the range is 750 yards unless the junk starts to take evasive action."

The junk did not veer off course. This mystified Jim and Don.

Jim, "Don they are really a junk or there are playing the cat and mouse game to the bitter end."

Don, "Jim I think this is a trick. I think they have a gun on that crate."

Jim, "Don they are at 800 yards. They are now at 780 yards."

Don, "Gun crew on deck open fire."

The five-inch gun opened up on the junk. The first shot was about 20 yards short. The second shot hit the front of the junk. The third shot hit the mast of the junk. The junk veered and opened fire.

Jim, "Son of a gun they have a three inch gun."

The junk fired three shots two of them short, but the third one hit the conning tower. The *Spearfish's* gun finished off the junk. It started to sink. The damage to the conning tower seemed to be minor.

Jack had been following all the action and had a crew on deck to try to gather up all the debris they could. He still hoped to get some of the classified documents. The Spearfish got closer to the burning junk. Some of the *Spearfish's* crew jumped in the water and started swimming toward anything a float.

Part of the crew of the junk had taken to the water still wanting to fight. The Spearfish's two 50-caliber machine guns killed all the remaining junk's crew.

The *Spearfish* swimmers and men in three small rubber rafts were picking up anything that looked like a book, map, or paper.

Jack urged hast because that junk may have radioed for help. There were bound to be Jap planes show up any minute. The men hurried aboard bring their retrieved goods. Those would be sorted, dried, and evaluated later. Jack ordered all gun crews below. He order the lookouts below.

Don on the intercom, "Skipper we have two wound men on the bridge and need help to get them off the bridge."

Jack turning to men in the control room said, "Quick! You first five men help them down. Mike alert the Pharmacist Mate. Have him report to the control room."

Within five minutes the two wounded men where lying on the control room-floor. The dive order had been given and the sub submerged to 100 feet. There was a shell hole in the outer wall of the conning tower, but it had not penetrated the inner wall. The radar antenna had been bent.

Al yelled, "Don who was wounded."

Don in a calm voice, "Seaman Frank Stone and Lt. Jim Rush have been hit."

Jim and Frank were taken to sickbay. Chief Petty Officer Marvin VanRoyen, the pharmacist mate, began to attend to their wounds and try to determine how badly they had been hit.

Jack was back to check on the wounded men immediately. He had given orders to dive the sub. It was just in time because Japanese airplanes were already lining up to dive on the *Spearfish*.

Jack asked the pharmacist mate, "How badly are they wounded Marvin?"

Marvin, "I can't say yet sir, Seaman Stone was hit in the back and Mr. Rush was hit in the left side about the rib cage area. I have stopped most of the bleeding. I will know more in a few minutes."

Mac stuck his head in the sick bay room, "Jim are you conscious? Can you talk?"

Jim, "Yes I am conscious Mac. Why are you so wet?"

Mac ignoring Jim's question, "How badly are you hurting buddy?"

Jim, "It hurts some, and I think I am still in shock."

Marvin, "He is in shock sir. My assistant is warming some blankets for them. I don't think any of the wounds are death threatening."

Mac, "I guess that is what I wanted to hear. Chief take good care of them."

Marvin VanRoyen, "Oh I will sir."

About one hour later Jack checked back on the wounded men. He would have to make a report so he had to try to piece together what had happened and how sever the wounds. Jack gather information and wrote his report.

Jack found that it took him two hours to gather information and another hour to put it together.

Jack's report was concise and accurate. Here is what he found out.

The third enemy shell hit the conning tower. Shell fragments and metal from the conning tower had hit Jim and Frank. They had been on that side of the bridge just starting to leave. Jim threw up his left arm to protect his head and Frank tuned his back and hunkered down to protect the front of his body.

The pharmacist mate reported that Seaman Frank Stone had 10 to 15 pieces of small metal partials in his back. He found no other parts of Seaman Stone's body had been hit. Lt Jim Rush had eight or ten pieces of metal that started under the left armpit down to just below the rid cage. The Pharmacist Mate could get many of the smaller fragments out of both men. Many of the smaller fragments were just below the skin.

The Pharmacist Mate said that Lieutenant Rush and Seaman Stone needed to be ex-rayed. That would show where the fragments were located and the depth. He said Lieutenant Rush had a larger piece of metal that had gone pass the ribs and he thought it might be close to Mr. Rush's heart. He was afraid of infection and had given each man an antibiotic and a pain pill. He recommended that both men get hospital medical attention as soon as possible.

Jack radioed his report to headquarters. He reported on the two wounded men and asked for fast transportation to the hospital. His report included the action and the retrieval of some of the classified materials.

Within 30 minutes Jack received a reply to his message. He was instructed to proceed to Midway. A PBY would fly Jim and Frank to the hospital at Pearl. They requested that the captured classified papers or what was left of them be sent with the wounded men. Jack was instructed to see if he could repair his damages at Midway. If so he was to re-supply and refuel and proceed on another patrol.

The *Spearfish* set a course for Midway Island.

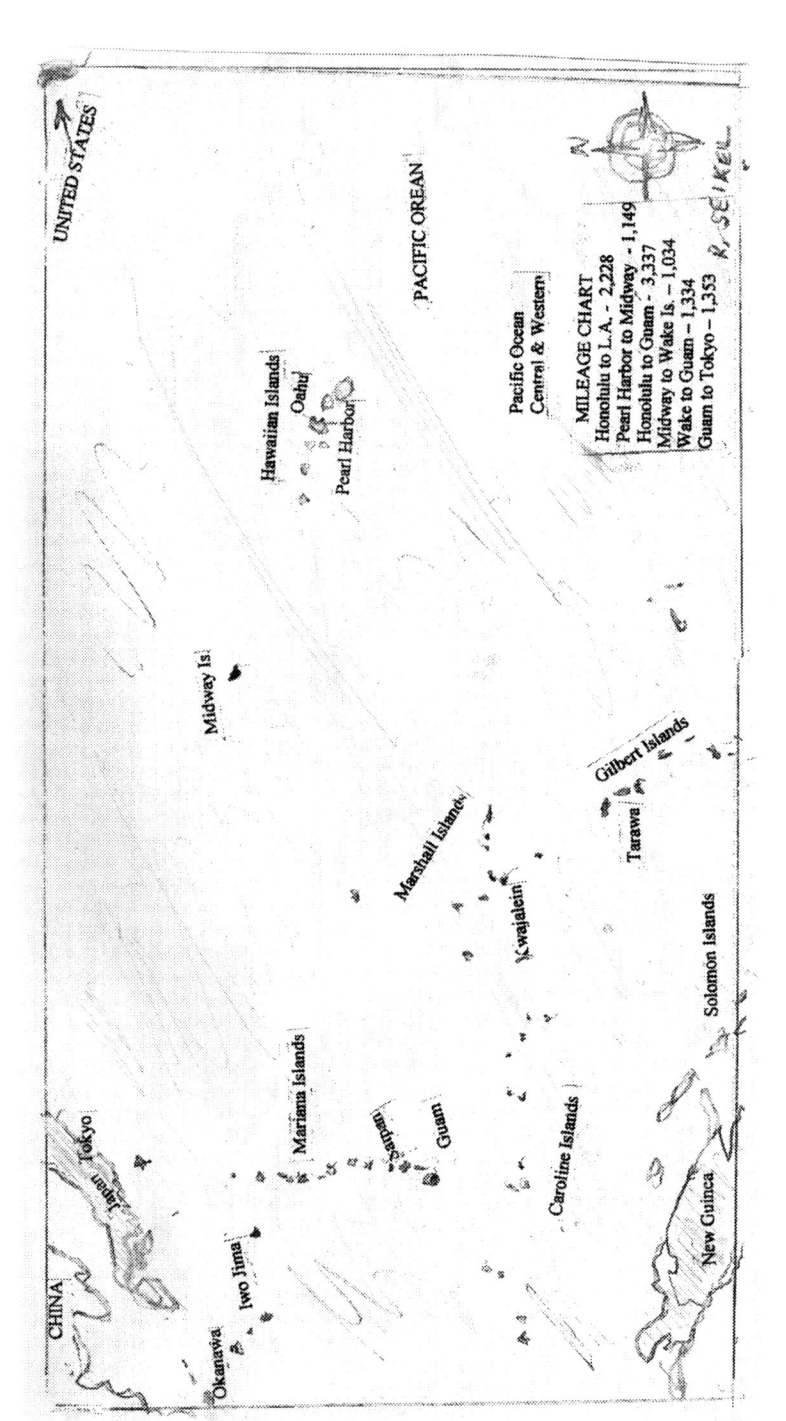

South and Central Pacific Ocean

CHAPTER 13
THE FLIGHT

IT TOOK THE *Spearfish* two days to reach Midway. During the trip Pharmacist Mate, Marvin VanRoyen, continued to give Jim and Frank antibiotics and pain pills. Marvin continued to pick pieces of metal out of their bodies.

Marvin picking out pieces of metal, "Mr. Rush I have picked out about 8 or 9 more pieces of srapneal out of you. I have seen this stuff work its way out. Sometime it will works its way deeper. That is why I don't want to try for any of the deeper stuff."

Jim, "Thanks Marvin you are a good doctor. What do you plan to do after the war?

Marvin, "I plan to go back to medical school and become a doctor. I hear the government may have a program to pay for some of my education. I already have three years of college, but it will take at least five or six more years before I can become an M.D."

Jim, "You have a worthy goal to shoot for Marvin. Stay with it and achieve your goal."

Jim and Frank were placed on stretchers. As they were being carried out of their quarters Mac, Don, and Al were there to meet them.

Jim in a low voice, "Mac would you see that my personal items get packed and sent with me."

Mac, "Sure thing Jim. Don't worry about it we will take care of it."

Don, "Jim good luck we will be thinking about you. Try to get word to us on how you get along."

Al, "Jim get well and stay away from all those pretty nurses. They will just keep you excited."

As they carried the two wounded men out on the deck and were starting down the gangplank Jack appeared at the bottom of the gangplank.

Jack, "Hold up a moment attendants. I want a word with my men. Jim, Frank, I want to wish you the best. Your plane will be here and ready to take you to Pearl in about two hours. Midway has a clinic and you will be held there until you plane is ready to leave. You personal gear will be with you. We are also sending what we salvaged of the classified Japanese documents. There are three sealed boxes about one by two feet in size. The admiral is expecting them. So long men."

Frank, "Thank you sir, we appreciate your seeing about us. We hope to join the crew again soon."

Jim, "Skipper, Frank is right we hope to join you guys soon. We think you are a swell skipper."

Jim and Frank were loaded in an ambulance and taken to the clinic. There were two wards in the clinic. They placed Jim and Frank in the officer's ward, as the enlisted ward was full.

There was one doctor on Midway. He made a curser check of Jim and Frank. He gave them a pain pill and had a corpsman change their bandages. They had a small ex-ray machine. He had ex-rays taken. He read the ex-rays and said these would be sent with them.

Both Jim and Frank were hungry, but did not feel much like eating. They were served some soup and crackers. They were also served some hot coffee.

Frank, "Mr. Rush I don't feel too swift. I am as weak as a pop corn fart."

Jim, "Frank, I am the same way. I am hungry, but don't feel like eating. I was thirsty, but that coffee tasted like it was a week old."

Frank, "Yeah I can't say much for the water either. It has a funny taste. Too much chlorine."

Jim, "That's because it's distill seawater. That plus the fact our taste buds are all out of kilter."

One of the medical attendants came to Jim and Frank's cots.

Medical attendant to Jim, "Sir, we are getting ready to transfer you and Seaman Stone to the pier to get on you airplane. The ambulance is here now and they will be here in a minute to get you."

Jim, "Do you know and are you at liberty to tell us what the ex-rays showed?"

Attendant, "Sir they showed all the buck shot that you guys are carrying around. Most of the shrapnel is small, but there is one larger chuck in you sir. It is about the size of a nickel. Some of the metal you guys are carrying came from the enemy shell and some of it was from the metal on your submarine."

The attendants loaded Jim and Frank in the ambulance and took them to the pier they were to be transferred to the four engine PBY transport seaplane. At the pier were two SPs guarding the three boxes of classified material, and Don and Mac.

Mac to Jim, "We come to see you off. We have a special escort as you can see. How are you feeling Jim?"

Jim, "A little better thanks. The doc gave us some pain pills. What are you guys doing here? I mean besides seeing us off. I mean can they repair the *Spearfish*?"

Don, "We are waiting on the sub base here to tell us if they can repair the damage to the *Spearfish*. We know they can supply us with food, torpedoes, and ammo, but their sheet metal shop may not have the gauge of metal to repair our conning tower."

Mac added, "Yeah and we need a new radar antenna. They can't straighten ours out."

Don, "Jack wanted us to see you guys off. He said to tell you God Speed."

Frank, "Mr. Phillips tell the captain we 'thank him' and tell the rest of the guys I said hello."

Don, "We sure will. We had better let them put you guys on board so you can get on your way to Pearl."

Jim and Frank are taken on the PBY plane. A plane with a compartment with built-in stacked bunks that had been placed for the job as transporting wounded and sick. There is even a pharmacist's mate in attendance to care for the wounded.

As the plane is warming up to take off the pharmacist mate looked over the medical charts of Jim and Frank. The airplane is soon airborne.

The pharmacist mate spoke, "I am seaman third class Dewey Whittington. I'll be your nurse during this flight. I will give you a big sleeping pill in about one hour. You should sleep most of the way. Is there anything I can get you?"

Jim to Dewey, "This is my ship-mate seaman third class Frank Stone. I am Lieutenant (j g.) Jim Rush. We were part of the crew on the submarine *Spearfish*. They're shipping us to the hospital at Pearl. Of course, you know that. Thanks for looking after us. How long will it take us to get to Pearl?"

Dewey to Jim, "Sir, it is about 2,000 miles from Midway to Pearl . . . give or take a hundred miles. We will be flying at about 275 miles per hour. So I guess it will take about seven hours. Would you care for a cup of coffee or anything to eat?"

Frank, "I am not hungry, but I would like a cup of water. Better yet do you have any orange juice?"

Dewey, "No sorry, no juice. I'll get you both some water before I give you the sleeping pill."

Jim and Frank drank their water. Dewey gave them their sleeping pill. Within a few minutes Jim was feeling very sleepy.

Jim muttered, "Frank I am about to go to sleep. My thought process is slow. You know I like the drone of the engines. They sort of hum me to sleep."

Jim and Frank did sleep most of the flying time to Pearl. Dewey woke them up about twenty minutes before they landed. After they landed they were placed on stretchers and placed in an ambulance.

Jim had been able to keep his sense of direction until he was placed in the ambulance. It seemed like the ambulance was going in circles to Jim. Anyway by this time Jim could not tell north from south. Jim and Frank were lying flat on their backs and at times Jim though the ambulance was spinning around.

Jim did not know how many miles they drove or how long it took to get them to the hospital because he fell asleep again. When Jim woke up he was in a ward with about 20 beds. Most of them were empty.

An orderly visited Jim. He told Jim that he was in the officer's ward for surgery patients. The orderly took his vital signs and put sulfur drug on his wounds.

Jim wondered what was next.

CHAPTER 14
THE HOSPITAL

JIM HAD JUST dozed off when a petite female RN came up to his bedside. She had a chart in her hand. She had a big smile on her face and her eyes sparkled.

The nurse said, "Hello Lieutenant. I am Lieutenant (j. g.) Ginny Jennings and I am your day nurse. You may call me Ginny and I will call you Jim. Is that all right?"

Jim, "Yes that is okay, by me. Good to meet you."

Ginny rechecked Jim's pulse, temperature, blood pressure, and examined his wound. She seem very capable to Jim. She took out a needle and drew some thick looking liquid out of a vile.

Ginny, "Jim this is penicillin and I am going to give you a shot. I will give this in the hip because you will be getting a shot every three hours. Please turn over and pull open your gown."

Jim did as Ginny instructed. She gave the shot. It did sting and burn for a few seconds. The medicine felt like it was cold.

Ginny, "Penicillin is a new drug that they have discovered that it is great for fighting infection. It is so powerful that we have to give it in three hours doses. A patient couldn't stand a large dose. Actually penicillin was discovered in about 1928, but they have just discovered how effective it is now. It took a war to really learn the value of the drug."

Jim, "That shot did hurt. How long will I have to take these shots?"

Ginny, "I really don't know Jim. It will depend on us getting the infection under control. I would guess about three days and three nights."

Jim, "Ginny, can I get out of bed to go to the head?"

Ginny, "No, we will have to bring the urinal and bedpan to you Jim. Sorry about that. The doctor wants you to be still so that shrapnel in you won't move around."

Jim, "When will I get to see the doctor?"

Ginny, "He should be around this afternoon or evening. Get some rest now Jim. I will see you in about three hours. If you need anything just punch this button."

Jim was served a tray of soft food. He ate most of the food. It could have been his imagination, but he thought he felt a little better already. As he looked up he saw Ginny coming down the isle. She had the needle ready to give him another shot.

Jim dreaded the shot because it hurt. He had made up his mind that he was not going to show any pain or fear and he was not going to complain.

As Ginny was giving the shot she said, "Jim has anyone every told you that you have a good looking butt."

Jim, "Aw Ginny, I bet you tell all the boys that."

Ginny laughed and said, "I'm glad you have a good sense of humor. Humor helps one heal and it's a sign you feel better."

Jim, "I guess so. When will the doctor see me?"

Ginny, "He is coming into the ward now. He should see one other patient and then you."

Within 15 minutes the doctor approach Jim. The doctor had Jim's chart in his hand. He had been reading it. The doctor was an older distinguished looking man. He stopped next to Jim's bed and Ginny stepped behind the doctor.

The doctor said, "Hello Lieutenant, I am Doctor Hubbard. I'll be doing your surgery.

Jim, "Doctor Hubbard I am please to meet you. What can you tell me about my wounds?"

Dr. Hubbard, "Oh yes, may I call you Jim?'

Jim, "Yes sir, please do."

Doctor Hubbard, "We will be doing surgery to remove the shrapnel that is in your side. There are several small pieces and one large piece. The large piece is deeper than the other pieces. We are going to ex-ray you again this evening."

Jim, "Thanks Doctor. You make me feel better already."

Doctor Hubbard smiled and Jim thought that the doctor must be at least 45 years old. He was a distinguished looking man and carried himself in a confident manner.

Jim, "Sir I noticed that you are a Lieutenant Commander. I hope you don't take this wrong, but you obviously were not drafted".

Doctor Hubbard laughed, "No Jim, I volunteered. You see I am 48 years old. I have a son in the navy and a son the army air corps. I wanted to do my share so I volunteered my services. I came in the navy at the rank of Lieutenant a little over one year ago. I had a very good practice in civilian life, but the U.S. of A. has been good to me and I wanted to give back something."

Jim feeling much better said, "Doctor Hubbard when do you operate?"

Doctor Hubbard, "You're scheduled for tomorrow morning. That is tentative. We will want to look at the ex-rays again and evaluate other factors. The other factors would include the infection . . . we want to have that under control before we do surgery. The penicillin shots will continue and probably go for a couple of days after the surgery."

Doctor Hubbard left to continue his rounds. Ginny was reading Jim's chart to see what orders the doctor had left. The doctor always told the nurse of any change in orders and he hadn't mentioned anything new, but she wanted to make sure.

Ginny to Jim, "You know I think the doctor likes you. He was talkative and I could tell he liked you. Your about the age of his sons."

Jim, "Since he is going to cut on me I hope he likes me. I am relieved to get an experienced doctor. I was afraid I might get a young doctor still in training."

Ginny, "It takes a surgeon in your case Jim and most of those are the older fellows."

Jim was taken to ex-ray that afternoon. He was fed a liquid meal at 1700 hours. The night nurse gave Jim a sleeping pill. She told him this was to help him relax. He finally went to sleep. The only time his sleep was interrupted is when the nurse came in to give him his shot.

The next morning Jim was told he would get no breakfast. He could have no liquid. The surgery was going as planned. Jim took that as good news.

Ginny wished Jim good luck when the attendants came to 'wheel him' to surgery.

Doctor Hubbard had his surgery gown on and was getting his groves on when they took Jim into the surgery room. There were four or five people around. Jim had no idea who they were, but they each seem to have a job.

Doctor Hubbard, "Jim we will give you an anesthesia that will knock you out. I have good news for you. The latest ex-ray showed that the piece of shrapnel that was near you heart has actually worked it way toward the surface. It moved just enough to make our surgery easier. I am glad it did not work its way deeper. I anticipate that the surgery will take about two hours. You will be in recovery about two hours and then back in the ward to sleep off the anesthesia. We will be using ether to put you to sleep."

A voice said, "Start counting from 100 backwards."

Jim, "100 . . . 99 . . . 98 . . . 97 . . . 96 . . . 95 . . ."

The last number Jim remembered was 95.

Later Jim came to in the recovery room. He was sleepy and everything seemed in a haze. He was glad the surgery was over. He said a silent prayer of thanks.

The nurse in the Recovery Room said, "You did fine in the surgery. It was a success and everything went as planned. I'll pull that tube out of your throat in a minute. Are you cold? Do you want another blanket?"

Jim was not even aware of a tube down his throat. He felt cold and was shivering.

He said, "I am cold and shaking. I need another blanket. Sorry, I can't keep from shaking."

The nurse, "Don't worry about the shaking. That is natural and that is the shock of the surgery. Here is another blanket. I'll pull the tube now. Try to rest some and we will soon take you back to your ward."

Jim fell back to sleep. After about two hours he was taken back to his ward and placed in his bed. He continued to sleep and was having some strange dreams.

Jim was in a deep sleep. He began to wake up just a little. He could still smell the either. Then he heard a soft female voice, it sounded far away. He couldn't recognize the voice, but in a way it sounded familiar.

The voice, "Jim you need to wake up."

Jim muttered, "Who is talking to me?"

The voice, "Jimmy . . . James Robert Rush, you had better wake up."

Jim was still bewildered and could just barley open his eyes, but everything was a blur. It was difficult to see and wake up.

Jim said, "Have I died and gone to heaven? No one has called me Jimmy since high school. Only my mother used my full legal name . . . James Robert. She only used it when she really needed to get my attention. Who are you?

The voice, "It is I, Janet Ann. Janet Ann Hilton an old friend from Shawnee. You know me."

Jim's eyes opened wide and he could see, but still had some blur.

Jim said, "Is that really you Janet? What are you doing here?"

Janet said, "I'll explain it all later after you are completely awake. The doctor wanted us to wake you up and check on you."

Jim still confused, "How come you are here Janet? Who sent you? My mother?"

Janet repeating, "I'll explain it all later. For now go back to sleep and I'll see you later."

Jim muttered, "I couldn't believe what had just happened. Was it real or did I dream it? What is going on?"

He felt cheerful and thought he would sleep a little longer and then sort things out later.

When Jim was next awakening it was dark outside. He was hunger. The night nurse ordered a tray of food. In about 30 minutes the tray was delivered. Jim didn't seem so hungry any more, he just picked at his food. The ether had killed his appetite.

He asked the nurse if he had a visitor by the name of Janet that afternoon. She did not know since that was before she came on duty. He asked if Ginny was still there. The answer was no.

Jim was not sure that what had happened was real or a dream. He reasoned that if it were real he would know tomorrow. He chatted with the patient next to him for a few minutes. He asked him if he had seen a female visitor during the day talking to Jim. The man in the next bed said he had not seen any females, except nurses.

Patient next to Jim, "That ether will make you have all kinds of weird dreams. I dreamed I was back home as a kid and my mother was calling me in for supper. It was so real. Crazy. You didn't dream that Betty Grable or Lana Turner was visiting you, did you? Send one of them over here, ha, ha."

Jim remembered that they probably had placed the temporary folding screens around his bed to provide some privacy. This would mean others in the ward couldn't know if he had visitors or not. If the patient next to him was still under the influence of ether he wouldn't have know what was going on.

Jim stayed awake for about two hours. The nurse took his temperature, his pulse, checked his surgery bandage, and gave him his penicillin shot. He then fell asleep.

CHAPTER 15
THE RECOVERY

THE NEXT MORNING after breakfast Jim saw this good-looking nurse come into the ward. She started down the isle. The figure and the walk looked familiar. Jim recognized her!

Jim in an excited voice, "Janet! Is that really you? You were here yesterday weren't you?"

By then Janet had reached Jim's bed and pulled up a folding screen for some privacy. She sat down next to Jim on the side of his bed.

Janet, "Yes, I was here yesterday. Your doctor asked me to wake you up."

Jim, "What are you doing here? The last I had heard you were in nursing school."

Janet, "I am an RN based in this hospital. I am a Lieutenant (j g) in the Navy Nurse Corps. I saw your name on a report. I was surprised and wanted to check and make sure it was the Jim Rush I had known."

Jim, "Gosh it's good to see you. How have you been?"

Janet, "I have been fine Jim. It's good to see you."

Jim, "We have a lot of catching up to do. How are you? How are your folks?"

Janet, "My folks are fine, thanks for asking."

Jim, "Janet . . . did . . . did you ever marry?"

Janet, "Ha, ha, no Jim I never married. I have been too busy for that."

Jim, "Tell me about your nursing career. You must have excelled in school to be an RN and a j.g.this soon."

Janet, "I think you have had enough company for one time. We have a lot of catching up to do, but we have plenty of time."

Jim, "Before you go, promise you will be back . . . and real soon."

Janet, "I promise I will be back. Now you had better get some rest. I'll be seeing you."

Janet left and Jim felt good. It was so good to see Janet. He really had not thought that much about her. He wondered had he missed out on something when they were courting before he enlisted?

Ginny took the screen down. She dressed his wound.

Ginny asked, "Jim can you bathe yourself? I noticed your visitor. I knew Janet since we reported to work at Pearl about the same time. She is okay. It was like old home week wasn't it?"

Jim, "I can bath myself. Tell the aide to just leave the pan of water and a washrag. Yes, Janet is an old friend, well we dated for awhile back home. That seems like it was along time ago. Ginny, could I get up and go to the head to shave?"

Ginny, "Let me check to see if it is okay for you to get out of bed. If you feel up to it you could sit on the edge of your bed and try to get your bearing."

Ginny left.

The Patient in the bed next to Jim said, "I saw that good looking gal. Your old girl friend huh. You are lucky . . . your dream came true. But if Lana or Betty show up send them over . . . ha, ha."

Jim to patient, "You are very funny . . . I'll tell you what if Marjorie Main shows up I'll send her over."

Patient next bed, "Ha, ha, you are a barrel of laughs."

Ginny returned to Jim's bedside in ten minutes.

Ginny said, "The doctor said you could get up, but we must have an orderly with you to help you. Jim keep your left arm down and do not raise it above the shoulder for five or six days. They don't want you to tear the stitches out."

Jim went to the head. He relieved himself and shaved. An orderly accompanied him to help, but Jim didn't need much help. He was a little rocky on his feet. He didn't realize how weak he had become.

When Jim returned to his bed there was a small stack of letters on his pillow. His mail had caught up to him. It was a miracle. Jim was busy the next two hours reading his letters over and over. He had three letters from his folks, a letter from his grandmother, and a letter from a cousin and one from one of his high school classmates.

Jim's morale soared. Seeing Janet and then getting this mail from home was a great boost. Jim forgot about his wounds. The letters from his folks, really his mom, as his dad was not much on writing, gave him all the information about the family and the whole town.

He learned that his cousin, Joe, in the air corps in England was a waist gunner on a B-17. His cousin was also on the company basketball team. Jim had played high school basketball and baseball with Joe. Joe was a very good athlete.

Jim's mother told him that she had talked to Wilma Dean, one of his high school classmates, and she had told her that of the 15 boys in his graduating high school class that 12 were in the service. Two were 4-F and one deferred as an essential worker.

After supper Jim set about writing letters. He wrote one to his folks and told them about his wound . . . he played that down, because he knew the navy had already notified them he had been wounded. He did not want to worry them, but reassure them that everything was okay. He told them of meeting up with Janet.

He wrote to his cousin and told him about the five patrols he had been on. He had to be careful what he wrote because the censurers would "clean it up." He wrote his dear old grandmother and told her again how much he missed her wise counseling and her fried apricot pies. He really did not know how to tell his grandmother how much he loved her.

About one hour before "lights out" Janet paid Jim another visit. She had got off duty at duty at 1700 hours. She had been to her quarters had her meal and changed into her dress uniform.

Jim, "Janet you look beautiful."

Janet, "Thanks Jim, it's the uniform"

Jim, "It's not the uniform. You would look good in anything. I am glad you came by. I know you must be tired being on you feet all day."

Janet, "I am a little tired. I can't stay long Jim. I just dropped by to see how you are doing."

Jim, "I doing better. They will even let me get up and walk to the head."

Janet, "Jim I see that Dr. Hubbard has just come into the ward. He will want to be seeing you. That is my cue to go. Good by, I'll see you tomorrow. Oh, tomorrow is Sunday and I have the day off and will be able to spend the day with you."

Jim, "Hey, that sounds great. So Long Janet, I look forward to seeing you tomorrow."

Dr Hubbard followed by the evening shift nurse came over to Jim's bed. Dr. Hubbard had been reading Jim's chart.

Dr. Hubbard to Jim, "Jim your surgery went well. How are you feeling? Your chart shows that your vital signs are good. Lab tests show that infection is about wiped out. You are making good progress."

Jim, "Sir, I feel pretty good. After I was able to get up I felt even better."

Dr. Hubbard, "Oh Jim, I have a present for you."

Doctor Hubbard pulled a small vile out of his smock pocket. He handed it to Jim.

Dr. Hubbard, "Here is a little souvenir for you. It's the shrapnel that we took out of you. There are eight small ones and a large one. The large one is about the size of a dime, and it was the one that was near your heart."

Jim took the container and looked at the pieces of metal. He thought, "I will save this as a reminder."

Jim spoke, "Thanks doctor. I will keep this and some day show it to my grandkids."

Dr. Hubbard, "Jim you may get out of bed and walk a couple of hours a day. We will stop the penicillin shots tomorrow morning. Remember keep you left arm down; do not raise the arm higher than the shoulder for about five more days. I'll see you Monday or Tuesday."

Sunday morning came and Jim would get his last penicillin shot. The nurse was not Ginny. Ginny had the day off.

The nurse said, "Your bottom looks like a pin cushion. I know we must be hitting some of the same places over and over. I am sorry, but I know you are glad this is the last one."

Jim to nurse, "I am glad it is the last one, but I'm not complaining. After all the shots helped save my life."

Nurse to Jim, "That is a good way to look at it. We can complain, but sometimes forget to be thankful for what we have."

Jim, "You're right."

Jim ate his breakfast. He cleaned his tray. It was the first time since he had been wounded that he really had been hungry and thought the food tasted good. He went to the head and showed and shaved. He put on a clean pair of pajamas and a housecoat. He had graduated from the hospital gown to the pajamas.

About 0900 the ambulatory patients in the ward were given the opportunity to go to the hospital chapel services. Jim went and was back by 0945.

About 1000 Janet came into the ward. It was like a breath of fresh air for Jim. She sat down next to Jim on his bed.

Janet, "Jim do you want to go outside and we can sit under a tree?"

Jim, "I would like that very much. It looks like it is a beautiful day and I have not been outside in two weeks."

Janet, "Great I'll clear it with your nurse."

Two minutes later.

Janet, "The nurse said is was okay. She wants you to take a wheel chair just in case you get tired."

Jim, "Well okay."

Jim and Janet go down the long hospital corridor and go outside. They find a bench with a view of the ocean and sit down.

Jim, "Boy this is great. What a beautiful day. Now, Janet fill me in on how you got to Pearl."

Janet, "Well after I finished high school I qualified for a scholarship at the University of Oklahoma. I decided to go to nursing school. I had debated between nursing and teaching. Anyway I had completed two of the three years of nursing school. The navy and the army had a special program for nurses. They had a shortage of nurses.

Jim, "Yeah the war changed many things"

Janet, "The navy had a program where you could enlist in the navy nurse corps if you had two years of nursing education. You entered the program as an ensign. After one year of training and working in a hospital the navy awarded the registered nurse degree and a lieutenant (j.g.)'s rank. The university recognized and approved of the program and they also gave the college degree. The war put a lot of things on the 'fast track.' Now Jim fill me in on how you got to Pearl."

Jim, "As you know I enlisted. They sent me to San Diego for boot camp. I applied for officer's candidate school and was accepted. After I completed NOCS I wanted to be a flyer—aviator—but I was too tall. So I went to sub school in New London, and from there I was sent to Pearl."

Janet, "Tell me about your job and how you got wounded?"

Jim told Janet about the five war patrols and how he got wounded. He told her about his buddies on the *Spearfish* and how it was like a bother hood or a fraternity.

They sat on the bench talking. Jim looked at Janet and thought Janet is better looking than I remembered. They continued to talk. Jim saw his shipmate Frank Stone. Frank was walking along the walk nearby.

Jim yelling, "Hey Seaman Stone. How are you? Come on over"

Frank broke out with a big grin and hurried over to where Jim and Janet were sitting.

Jim. "Frank I want you to meet Janet."

Frank, "Hi Janet, glad to meet you."

Janet, "Good to meet you. Jim said you were wounded at the same time he was. How are you doing?

Frank, "Aw, I am doing okay. They let me out of the ward yesterday for walking. I think they will let me out of the hospital in a day or two. Mister Rush I am worried. They said something about I would probably be sent to the replacement center for assignment."

Jim, "Frank I wouldn't worry about it. The skipper told me he had requested for you and me to be put on orders assigning us back to the *Spearfish.*"

Jim and Frank exchanged information about their surgeries and their hospital experiences. Jim explained his relationship with Janet. He described her as a very good friend. They talked about the last patrol and their buddies on the *Spearfish*. Frank left and was on his way to the hospital PX.

Janet, "Frank seemed like a very nice boy. I noticed you called him by his first name. Aren't officers and enlisted men supposed to remain a little more formal?"

Jim, "Yes Janet, we are more formal in public. But on the sub or in private conversation we are very informal. The relationship between officers and men on a sub is a very close working relationship. The informality is permitted on the sub or in private between men and their officers."

Janet, "Do you think there is a chance that you and Frank will not be reassigned to the *Spearfish*?"

Jim, "There is always a chance we both could be reassigned. Headquarters will decide where they want you. I know a lot of experienced submariners who have been reassigned. There is something about a submariner's work ethic that the navy likes."

Janet, "Jim it is close to lunch time. Shall we go eat?"

Jim, "Yes, we could go to the galley or mess hall. How about going to the snack bar at the PX and getting a hamburger?"

Janet, "A hamburger sounds good to me."

Jim, "I forgot I don't have my wallet. I have no money."

Janet, "That's okay, this will be my treat."

Jim and Janet went to the hospital PX. Jim pushed his wheel chair, but finally did get a little tired and he rode in the wheel chair part of the way. They enjoyed their hamburgers and cokes.

Janet, "Jim this is just like old times. Remember when we used to get a burger and coke?"

Jim, "Yeah, at the drive-in and sit in my 36' Ford and eat and talk. I miss those days Janet."

Janet, "Yes I miss those days also. They are gone forever, but the memories are still with us. Remember us sitting in you 36' Ford and hugging and kissing?"

Jim, "Yes I remember. We used to really have some good smooching. Those were happy times"

After their lunch Jim and Janet decided to walk outside, They soon found a bench and sat down. The cool spring breeze off the ocean felt good.

Jim, "Janet tell me about what you did after I went in the navy."

Janet, "After we were both noble and decided to go our separate ways. I finished high school and went to college."

Jim, "Yeah, I know that. What about boy friends and dates? Did you have any steady boy friends? Were you engaged? Did you have a boy friend after I left?"

Janet laughed and said, "Yes, I guess you could say that I had a boy friend. At any rate I dated two or three boys in high school. You might say I 'played the field.' I had a boy friend in college. He wanted to get serious, but I didn't. So we broke up when I went in the nurse corps."

Jim, "Then you are not engaged?"

Janet, "No."

Jim, "Janet tell me about your folks. How are they? What did they think of you joining the navy?"

Janet, "My parents are fine. Dad is still working of course. He is still with the same oil company. Mother is still active in church work and keeps house. She volunteers at church preparing meals for the service men who are coming and going."

Janet, "Being the only child, dad still takes on after me. Mother did not want me to go in the nurse corps. She thought I should go to work in one of the local doctor's office or hospital. Dad did not want me to leave home either, but I finally won dad over. Mother thought I should stay home, settle down and get married."

Jim, "What will they think about you running into me?"

Janet, "I think they will be pleased to know I have seen someone I know."

Jim, "Janet why didn't you and I write to one another? I am thinking we could have continued some kind of a relationship.

Janet, "Remember Jim we were very young, you was 18 and I was 16. Who knows what teenagers think. We both decided to call it quits. I guess we both wanted the freedom from a steady permanent relationship.

Jim, "Yeah, your right. Just two teenagers not knowing what they wanted. You would have been 17 in August and I would have been 19 the next February. We are only three years older but have experienced so much during that time. We have learned a lot. You know I continued to carry your picture and think about you often."

Janet, "Well we have those memories. I am glad we 'ran into one another.' It has been great."

Jim looked into Janet's eyes. She moved closer to him. He took her cheek in his hand and turned her face and kissed her. Janet kissed back. Jim felt the flicker of her tough and thought it has been a long time since I have kissed Janet.

After they kissed, Jim continued to hold Janet close. She snuggled closer to him. Finally with a sigh Janet released her hold on Jim's arm.

Jim spoke, "That brings back old memories. No one kisses like you Janet. I hope you don't think I was out of place."

Janet, "No not at all Jim. I am glad we kissed."

Jim, "I've wanted to do that every since I saw you come into the ward. You're a swell girl Janet."

Janet, "And I have wanted to kiss you from the first time I saw you after your surgery."

Jim and Janet continued to sit on the bench. Not saying anything. Just holding hands. Each one was lost in thought.

Finally Jim said, "Janet, do you suppose we could go back to the ward. I am getting a little tired?"

Janet, "Sure Jim. What we have done might put a strain on your heart. Just joking of course. I have to get back to my quarters I have some laundry to do."

Jim and Janet went back to the ward. They said their good byes. Jim got into bed and shortly fell asleep. Janet left to go to her quarters.

Janet visited Jim each day he was in the hospital. Some days she stayed a little longer, but usually had to get back to duty. Even thought the visits were short they lifted Jim's spirits.

Two days later, Jim had just finished his breakfast and had showered and shaved and had returned to his bed. Ginny came sailing down the isle with a grin on her face.

Ginny, "Jim you are going to have a visitor. A high-ranking officer. Do you know a Commander Saxton?"

Jim, "Yes I sure do. Is he coming to see me?"

Ginny, "Yes, I overheard him talking to the doctor about you."

At that time Commander Lawrence "Larry" Saxton came into the ward. He saw Jim and came back to his bed. He had a junior grade officer with him.

Larry, "Jim it's good to see you. You look fine and the doctor tells me they will probably dismiss you within a week. Jim, this is my aide, Ensign Phillip Johnson."

Jim, "Sir it is good to see you. Please to meet you Mister Johnson."

Larry, "My visit is two fold Jim. One just to say hello. The other part is to tell you the Awards Board has approved awarding you the Purple Heart. Congratulations."

Jim, "Thank you sir. I had not even thought about a Purple Heart. Sir, did they award Seaman Frank Stone a Purple Heart. After all he was wound at the same time I was."

Larry, "Yes Seaman Stone was award a Purple Heart also. Do you know who else was award a medal?"

Jim, "No sir. I don't know. Who was he?"

Larry, "You old buddy, George 'Mac' MacDonald, was awarded the Bronze Star."

Jim, "I'm glad to hear that. What did Mac do?"

Larry, "After you and Frank were wounded the Jap boat was sunk. Debris including the 'classified documents' was all floating around. Jack sent a crew upon deck to try to save as many documents as possible. He had six men with three small rafts trying to retrieve document."

Jim, "Yes, I remember a little of what was going on, but we were stretched out with the pharmacist mate working on us and everything was a bite hazy."

Larry, "Well, Mac was on deck with his gun crew. He could see that the documents and papers were scattered. The men in the rafts were only able to reach a few. Mac pulled his shirt and shoes off and order the gun crew to do they same. He asked if everyone could swim. Then they jumped in the water and started swimming."

Jim, "I would have liked to have seen that."

Larry, "Well Mac and his men picked up documents that was scattered over about a 200 square foot area. They would swim and give them to the men in the rafts. They gathered up ten times the amount that the retrieval crew did."

Jim, "I saw the boxes the material was put in. The boxes were on the same flight as Frank and I were on. I am surprised they did not reprimand Mac for leaving his post."

Larry, "Well would you believe some arm chair commando officer wanted to court marshal Mac for desertion of duty in time of combat."

Jim, "How did they get Mac out of that?"

Larry, "Well Jack raised hell and wrote a scorching report. He explained that there was an 'all clear' after the sinking of the Jap boat. He also included a letter from Commander Joe Rochefort from the Intelligent Branch and the Code Breakers about how useful the information contained in the captured documents was and would save many lives. The court marshal charges were dropped."

Jim, "I am glad. Thank goodness for officers like Commanders Jack Jackson, Joseph Rochefort, and you sir."

Larry, "Thanks Jim. I understand you will get a short leave to recuperate after they dismiss you. Enjoy it, and I see you again in a few days."

Jim, "Thank you sir for coming by. I know you must be very busy. Sir, one question, when will the *Spearfish* be docking?"

Larry, "That is classified and I can't tell you when the *Spearfish* will be docking, but if I wanted to see them come in I might be down on pier five in seven days at about 0900. I have to be going now. See you later."

Jim, "So long sir."

Before Larry and his aide, Phillip Johnson, departed the aide told Jim that a reporter from the Public Information Office (PIO) would be coming by for an interview. They would want to send a news release to his hometown newspaper.

Later that day a reporter came and visited Jim. He asked Jim several questions. The reporter told Jim they wanted to send a press release to his hometown newspaper publizing his being wounded and receiving the Purple Heart. When Jim told him his hometown did not have a newspaper the reported wanted the names of newspapers in the area. He wanted to get the name of newspapers that people in Jim's hometown read. Jim gave him three names and cities that published a newspaper that he knew his folks read.

The reporter told Jim that they would send a photographer when he was actually given the medal. It seems this would be a second article his "hometown newspaper" would get.

Within two days Ginny gave Jim the good news. They were going to dismiss him just as soon as Dr. Hubbard saw Jim and wrote the orders. Jim started packing his things. His duffle bag had caught up with him so he had his clothing and personal items.

Dr. Hubbard made his rounds and told Jim he was dismissing him. Janet, Ginny, and two aids where there to give Jim a farewell good bye. Ginny gave a short speech.

Ginny, "Jim, we wish you the best. You were a very good patient. We will miss you and I'm going to kiss you on the cheek."

Ginny kissed Jim on the cheek. She had a tear in her eyes.

Jim, "Ginny you have been a wonderful nurse. You really care for people. Thanks for looking after me. I will always consider you a friend."

Janet, "Ginny, thanks, I will always consider you a friend.

Jim was dismissed from the hospital. He was given a five-day recuperation leave. Before Jim left the hospital he made a date with Janet for Saturday.

CHAPTER 16
THE RECUPERATION

JIM CHECKED INTO the Royal Hawaiian Hotel again. This time it was for five days recuperation leave. He shared the room with one other officer. He rarely saw his roommate. After his five days here he would be billeted in the bachelor officers quarters on base.

Saturday afternoon Jim called at Janet's quarters. Janet had her dress uniform on and looked good to Jim.

Jim to Janet, "Hello Janet, you look great."

Janet to Jim, "Hi Jim it's good to see you. Come in,"

Jim, "Janet what would you like to do?"

Janet, "I don't have anything special in mind Jim."

Jim, "Janet I would like to go see the movie, *Thirty Seconds over Tokyo*. I've heard that it is a good film. It stars Spencer Tracy and Van Johnson."

Janet, "That sounds okay to me, where is it playing."

Jim, "It is playing at the main post theatre. It hasn't been released to the general public yet. That is how new it is."

Janet, "Okay. Let's go."

Jim, "I thought we could eat out after the movie."

After the movie Jim and Janet went to the Officer's Club. They ordered their meal. They enjoyed the meal and conversation was continued about the movie, about old times and home.

Jim, "Say do you want to see my plush quarters? The navy checked me into the Royal Hawaiian Hotel on Waikiki Beach."

Janet, "Sure why not."

Jim and Janet rode a base bus into town. They got off the bus and went into Jim's hotel. Jim showed her the dinning room, the ballroom, and other sights around the hotel. They took the elevator up to Jim's floor. Jim opened the door to his room. His roommate was just leaving. Jim introduced Janet to him.

Jim, "Come in and see my quarters. One extra large room with a small bedroom and bath."

Janet, "Isn't it against regulations to have women in your room?"

Jim, "You know, I don't know if the hotel follows the navy regulations are not. Anyway I doubt that the hotel cares about navy regulations. I'll take you to your quarters when every you say."

Janet, "I was kidding about the regulations Jim. What the navy doesn't know won't hurt them. I guess I had better be going it is getting late"

Jim, "Before we go I want to kiss you."

Janet, "Okay."

Jim took Janet in his arms. He felt her body press against his. They kissed and kissed again. Jim released his embrace and looked Janet in the eyes.

Jim, "Janet, I love you. I don't want to leave you."

Janet, "Jim, I love you too. And I want to be with you. It is getting late we had better go. I need to get back to my quarters."

Jim, "Okay we will go now, but promise me I can see you tomorrow afternoon."

Janet, "Okay call at my quarters about one o'clock or I guess 1300 hours."

They both laughed and Jim took Janet to her quarters. He kissed her good night at her door and returned to his hotel.

That morning Jim went to chapel services. That afternoon he called on Janet. They decided to go to a photo studio that Janet knew and get a picture of the two of them in their uniforms. Even though it was Sunday the studio was open and they got two or three poses made.

After that they rented a car and drove out of Honolulu along the coastline. The view was breathing taking. They stopped at a lookout point and just watched the waves coming in and going out.

Jim, "Janet this has been a great day. To be with you and now see the beauty of nature"

Janet, "It has been a good day. You know Jim we both said we loved each other last night. I think I love you, but we both could feel lonely. Here we are 4,000 miles from home in a war, not knowing what the future holds. Are we just wanting one another or is this love?"

Jim, "I haven't tried to analyze our relationship Janet. The war has sped up everything. 4,000 miles from home and we are lonely even though surrounded by people. Yes, we miss home and security. We can't recapture the past, but we can control what we do now. I do believe I want to spend the rest of my life with you."

Janet, "What is love? Maybe it's all the things we have said and more. I was not ready for any long-term commitments when you and I dated as teenagers. I didn't even think about love."

Jim, "When we dated as teens I didn't think about love. I may have loved you, but didn't have enough sense to realize it. We were dating and smooching, but love was not a part of it . . . I don't think . . . who knows may be it was."

Janet, "Some things only come up once in life. Life can be an adventure or we can just let it slip by. I think fate has brought us together"

Jim, "Let's not lose what we have by waiting. Let's not let events pass us by. Janet let's get married."

Janet hesitated as though she was really thinking over the proposal.

Janet, "Yes, Jim I will marry you."

Jim, "Great honey. When?"

Janet, "I don't know. I have to give that some thought. Jim I have always wanted a big church wedding with bride's maids, flower girls, and all the trimmings."

Jim, "But honey you are talking about waiting until we get back home. I don't want to wait that long. I need you now. We could get married in one of the chapels on base."

Janet, "Okay, but promise me we will have a second ceremony in the church with all the things that go with a big wedding."

Jim, "I will agree to that, of course we can Janet. After the war and we get back home we will have that big wedding."

Janet, "I have to check into the rules on getting married. I think I can still stay in the navy. I hope so."

Jim, "Yeah there will be a certain amount of red tape. With the war going on and the services needing men and women I can't image us getting married will cause either of us to lose our jobs."

Jim and Janet sealed their marriage proposal with several kisses. Jim and Janet drove back to Honolulu and returned the rental car. They rode the bus to the base and got off in front of Janet's quarters. Jim kissed Janet goodnight and caught the bus back to his hotel.

The next day Jim went to the Adjuent General's Office to get information and see what paper work was needed. Since they were both American citizens they only had to fill out one form each.

Jim next visited with a Chaplin he had gotten acquainted with. The Chaplin said he would help them arranged to use one of the chapels on base. The Chaplin had been a church of Christ preacher in civilian life. Both being members of the same church, as Jim and Janet would make the married ceremony even more memorable.

The next day Jim and Janet visited with the Chaplin in his office to finalize the arrangements.

Jim, "Chaplin this my fiancée Janet. Janet this is Lieutenant Jack Hill. Jack is from Searcy, Arkansas. He's practically a neighbor."

Janet, "Jack I am pleased to meet you. It is swell of you to help us."

Jack, "Glad to meet you Janet. You will make a beautiful bride. I'm glad to help you two."

Janet, "What will we need to do Jack? Can I have a bride's maid? Can Jim have a best man?"

Jack with a laugh, "Yes you can have all those things and about anything else you want. Now let's look at the calendar and set a date."

A date was set. Jim and Janet had to submit their application and Jack would do that for them. Jack would help Jim get a Territory of Hawaii license and a navy or government license. They would need a blood test. Janet and Jim would need to arrange for a maid of honor and a best man.

Jim and Janet discussed the wedding and Janet was going to ask Ginny to be her maid of honor. Jim was going to get Mac as his best man if he was in port. If Mac were not in port he would ask Larry.

Jim next arranged to rent a "honey moon suite" from one of the less expensive hotels. It was difficult to get rooms. Every hotel seemed to be booked up for months.

Jim's five days were up at the Royal Hawaiian and he was assigned a room with one other officer in one of the bachelor officer's quarters. He was in barracks five and he understood that the officers from the *Spearfish* would be next door in barracks four.

On the day the Spearfish was to dock Jim went to the pier at 0900. The *Spearfish* was one hour late. It was another hour before the crew started to disembark.

One of the officer's to come down the gangplank was George "Mac" McDonald.

Jim yelled, "Mac."

Mac yelled, "Jim,"

The two men greeted one another with a handshake and a pat on the back. They were happy for the reunion.

Jim said, "It's good to see you Mac. Congratulations on the medal. You deserve it. How did things go after I left you guys?"

Mac, "I'm glad to see you Jim. Obviously your surgery was a success. We had one bad experience Jim. We sunk another transport and we where depth charged for four hours. It really got scary for a while. The boat had some serious damage. A couple of men got hurt, but otherwise things were routine."

Jim, "Where did you go when you left Midway?"

Mac, "We went to Guam. We are invading the Mariana Islands. I'll fill you in on the details later."

Before Mac and Jim could finish their conversation, Jim saw Don, Al, and Richard coming down the gangplank.

Jim yelled, "Hello Don . . . hello Al . . . hello Richard."

Jim said hello to Jack, Mike, and several of the enlisted men. Several of the men asked about Seaman Frank Stone. Jim reported that Frank was doing fine and waiting to see them.

Don said, "Say we are billeted in the BOQ number four, let's meet in our room and have a confab. But first, somebody pick up our mail."

Mac said, "It sounds good to me lets meet in about one hour in our room. I'll pick up the mail."

All agreed to meet, except Jack, the skipper, and Mike, the XO, they would have to make a report to headquarters. Jim went with Mac and they talked as they walked along to the quartermaster and then to the BOQ.

Mac, Al, Don, and Richard read their mail. That was always the first order of business. After that they all sat with Jim and talked for two hours. They told Jim about their patrol. Jim told them about his hospital stay and his getting engaged to Janet.

Jim's friends were surprised to hear that he was about to get married. They all congratulated him.

Don, "Jim congratulations, we wish you the very best."

Al piped up, "Couldn't go any longer without getting a little."

Jim, "No it's nothing like that Al. I am really in love and want to spend the rest of my life with Janet."

Don, "Jim that sounds like a winning attitude for a long and happy marriage."

Mac, "Did you say you are going to get married on the 30th?"

Jim, "Yes that's right."

Mac, "Great we will still be in port. Jim if you are reassigned to the *Spearfish* that will mean a very short honeymoon. Jack said by the time they get the repair work done it will be the fourth or fifth before we ship out. We can all go to the wedding."

Jim, "That reminds me Mac I was going to ask you to be my best man."

Mac, "Yeah, you bet."

There was a knock on the door. It was Jack.

Jack, "I have orders for Mac, Jim, and Frank to be in dress uniform and be on the squadron parade field at 0900 Friday to get your medals. Here is a copy of the orders for all of you. Don will you see that Frank gets his copy?"

Don, "Aye, aye sir. Jack, we just heard the news that Jim is getting married on the 30th. Can you arrange for us all to be on leave at that time."

Jack, "Well congratulations Jim I assume the bride to be is Janet. Of course I'll arrange for you guys to be off. That happens to be a Sunday and you can have the day off."

All of the officers laughed. The officers sat around talking for another hour before they broke up and unpacked. Jim went to his quarters. They would all meet later for supper at the officer's club.

Later Jim, Mac, and Don went to eat at the officer's club. Al and Richard were going to eat in the mess hall and then go see a movie. They mention about going for a "few beers" after the movie.

During their meal at the officer's club Jim ask Mac about his bravery that won him a medal. Mac laughed some as he told the story to Jim.

Mac said, "Well Jim it was like this. It was a hot day and I thought a little dip would cool me off. The men wanted to join me. As we were swimming this bites of rubbish kept getting in our way. So we picked up the trash and gave it to these guys in the rafts."

Jim, "That's not the way I heard it Mac. Someone said you yelled 'I have not yet begun to fight' and jump into the water."

Mac, "No that's not so. Anyway after it was all over they flipped a coin to see if they would court marshal me or give me a medal."

Jim, "And that's not the way I heard that either."

Don, "Jim you probably got the straight of the story. Actually there were sharks in the water and it was dangerous. I understand the Intelligence and Code Breaker guys were able to pick up a lot of important information."

Jim, "Well anyway Mac we are all proud of you."

After the meal the three officers went back to their barracks. They called it a day.

Jim, Mac, and Frank were dressed in their dress uniforms and assembled on the parade field. There were several other men getting medals that day. It seems that once a month these ceremonies were held for the awarding of medals.

The three from the *Spearfish* got their medals. Admiral Charles Lockwood gave out the medals and congratulated the men. The PIO photographer was there to take the awardees photo just as the Admiral pin the medal on.

Jim was disappointed that Janet couldn't be there, but she was on duty and could not get away for the ceremony. He thought that his folks would be proud of him if the picture were run in the newspapers back home. Jim felt that there was too much fan fare, but he supposed that was just a part of navy life.

Larry, Jack, Don, Al, and Richard were there. Many of the men from the *Spearfish* were there. There was a large crowd sitting in the viewing stands. Finally everyone was dismissed.

A group gathered around Jim, Mac, and Frank. There were a lot of congratulations going on.

Jim said, "I feel like they are making a lot of fuss over us. I don't deserve all of this attention."

Larry said, "Yes, you guys do deserve a lot of fuss Jim. Did you know this is the first time that three men on the same submarine were award medals for the same patrol action? So you guys have something to be proud about. I am proud to know you men."

Jack said, "I am proud of you guys. You know Larry deserves some credit. After all he was the skipper for seven patrols and he trained us all."

Larry laughed and said, "Now Jack it does no good to 'butter me up' I am not on the promotion board."

All the men around laughed.

Larry said, Jack I would like to meet with you, Mike, and Jim in my office at 1500. Can you men make it?"

All said yes. Jim wondered why he was included. Usually just the skipper and his exec met with headquarters to get assignments. Jim decided he had better keep his dress uniform on.

The group broke up and the *Spearfish* officers went back to their barracks.

Jack, Mike, and Jim reported to Larry at 1500. Jim was especially curious as to why he was requested to be there. He would soon find out.

Larry, "Be seated men. It is good to see you all again."

Jack, "Thank you sir."

Larry, "The reason I wanted to meet with you officers is for two reasons. One the next patrol of the *Spearfish* and the second is the reassignment of Jim."

Jim did not say anything, but now he knew he would not be going out with the *Spearfish* on the next patrol.

Larry, "The *Spearfish* took some serious damage and will not be ready to go until the 6th or the 7th. I will have your patrol assignment and give you further information on that about the first. The *Spearfish* is considered old based on her combat experience. She will probably be sent to the east coast for a complete overall after this patrol. Jack that means you will probably get a new submarine. If so you and your officers will have to get some special training that will last about two weeks"

Jack, "A new sub huh. That sounds good to me, but I hate to lose Jim."

Larry, "We will be assigning a new officer to replace Jim's slot. He will be reporting to you early next week. Incidentally, you will be getting Seaman Frank Stone back."

Jack, "That is good news, thanks."

Larry handed Jack two sheets of paper.

Larry, "Jack here is a copy of Frank's and the new man's orders. The new man's name, rank etc is shown."

Jim had said nothing; he was waiting for Larry to get to him.

Larry, "Jim, you are being reassigned to the Intelligence and Planning branch in headquarters. I and P is a small office and they need someone with your experience. We lose a lot of good submariners to other branches. What do you think?"

Jim, "If that is where the navy thinks I need to be then I suppose I have no complaint. I would prefer to have stayed with the *Spearfish* though. I'll really miss the officers and men of the *Spearfish*."

Larry, "It is only natural to want to stay with your friends. Once you have been through the rigors of battle with a group you feel a kin-ship. I did not want to leave the *Spearfish* either Jim so I know how you feel."

Jack, "Jim we will miss you, but remember you can still see us after each patrol."

Jim to Larry, "Sir, when do I report for duty?"

Larry, "Well I got this authorization for one Lieutenant (j g) James R. Rush and one Lieutenant (j g) Janet A. Hilton to get married and have leave for five days. So it looks like you will report for duty on the eighth at 0700. Congratulations on the marriage."

Jim, "Thank you sir."

Mike had not said anything. He had a big smile on his face and he laughed.

Mike said, "Jim this way you get to set up housekeeping just like normal married folks. No more patrols. You won't be away from home at night."

Larry, "Well that's a good thing about your reassignment Jim. But the navy did not consider your marital status in selecting you for the new job. Gentlemen if there are no other questions, you are dismissed."

CHAPTER 17
THE WEDDING

THE NEXT AFTERNOON Jim called on Janet at her quarters. They planned to go into Honolulu and take a tour of the city. Janet was not quite ready and asked Jim to come in and be seated. Janet proceeded to put her makeup on while they talked.

Janet, "Jim I did make it to the awards ceremony yesterday. I was glad that I did. You looked handsome."

Jim, "Janet why didn't you come down after the awards where completed?"

Janet, "I had to get back to work. My supervisor was kind enough to let me off a few minutes for the awards so I didn't want to abuse the favor."

Jim, "I have some news for you. Guess what? I am being reassigned to the Intelligence and Planning Branch in headquarters."

Janet, "Oh Jim! That is good news. You and I will be together more. I won't worry about you so much."

Jim, "Janet, I have something for you. This is even better news."

Janet, "What's that?"

Jim pulled a small box out of his pocket and opening a ring box and took out an engagement ring. Janet came over to him.

Jim, "Give me you hand. I have a ring for you."

Jim slipped the ring on Janet's finger. She smiled and kissed Jim.

Jim, "I guess I should have let you pick it out, but there didn't seem to be time. However, the jeweler says I can bring you in for the wedding ring selection and if you want another engagement ring we can trade this one in."

Janet, "Oh Jim this engagement ring is beautiful. We will not trade this in. I am so happy Jim."

Janet and Jim went to the jewelry store where Jim had bought the engagement ring. The owner waited on Janet and Jim. Janet picked out the wedding ring. They spent three hours on a tour of Honolulu. They went to a first class restaurant and ate. They discussed renting an apartment. Jim suggested they see if there were any married quarters on base. Since they both worked on base they would be closer if they lived on base or at least nearby.

Jim talked to Janet about his new assignment. He would be on base and no longer on patrol in a submarine. Janet was very happy about Jim's new assignment.

Janet, "Oh Jim, things have really worked out for us. We have a lot to be thankful for"

Jim took Janet to her quarters. Her roommate was gone. They sat on the sofa talking. They were sitting very close.

Janet kissed Jim and Jim kissed her back. They embraced and continued to kiss. Jim could feel that he was getting "carried away" and he put his left hand on Janet's right breast. She did not object. He carefully massaged her breast. Jim was wondering what her breast would feel like under her blouse and bra.

Janet, "Oh Jim, wait a minute. Let me take my bra off."

Jim was surprised but thought I've wondered what Janet looked like without clothes.

At least I can see what her breast look like before our wedding night.

As he massaged her breast he said, "Janet you have beautiful breast. They are bigger than I thought. They feel good. I have never seen a woman's breast before."

Janet, "Ha, ha, how do you know they are beautiful?"

Jim, "I've seen pictures. You dress so modesty that you don't advertise how big of breast you do have."

Janet, "I have always dressed modestly. That was the way I was raised."

Janet and Jim continued to kiss. Janet let Jim continue to massage her breast. They both were breathing heavy and they felt like they may get "carried away." Jim moved his hand from Janet's breast and put it under Janet's skirt. He moved his hand up her leg. He got to just above the knee.

Janet, "No Jim, please don't go further. Sex is a big step and I just can't do it outside of marriage. Surely honey you can wait a week."

Jim, "Of course I can wait Janet. I'll think about you all next week. I am glad you stopped me Janet. We can both start married life as virgins."

Janet, "We both feel the same way about this, but passion was about to take us into doing wrong."

Janet put her bra back on and straightened her clothing. Jim went to use the bathroom and straightened his clothing.

Jim was just leaving Janet's quarters when her roommate came in. Jim made a date with Janet for the next morning. They would attend chapel services together.

Sunday morning Jim and Janet went to chapel services. They attended where Jack Hill was delivering the sermon.

After the chapel services Jim and Janet went to the officer's club for lunch. They saw Mac, Don, Al, and Richard there. The club was too crowded to get a table for all six. Jim and Janet sat at a table for two and the others at a four-person booth. After they ate they all went back to Jim quarters. They sat and talked.

Mac, Don, Al and Richard left after a few minutes. They were going to a movie. Jim and Janet were alone.

Janet, "Jim I thought Jack delivered a good sermon this morning. I am glad he is going to perform our marriage ceremony."

Jim, "I am too."

Janet, "Jim when do you report to your new job."

Jim, "I have to report on the 8th. How much leave did you get for our honeymoon?"

Janet, "I have to go back to work on the 6th. If they get some emergency cases in I could get called back sooner."

Jim, "Let's hope they don't get any emergency cases. I think I may drop into my new work place one day next week and get acquainted."

Janet, "Sounds like a good idea. You know Jim not many people would check out their new work place on their leave. You are very conscientious."

Jim, "Shall we go to a movie?"

Janet, "I guess so."

Janet and Jim went to a movie. They saw *Going My Way* with Bing Crosby. Afterwards they had supper. Jim took Janet to her quarters. They kissed and necked some and Jim finally left about midnight.

Janet was counting the days until the wedding. She showed her engagement ring to all the nurses she came in contact with. She wrote her parents about getting engaged and about going to be married within a week. Janet thought, "I'll be married by the time they get my letter"

Janet wondered what her mother would think about her getting married.

She told Jim, "My mother will probably be upset. I can hear her now. You run off and have a wartime romance and got carried away. I hope you know what you are doing."

Jim response to Janet, "When she finds out it is me you are marrying she will think that she and your dad will be lucky to have a son-in-law like me. Ha, ha, don't you think that is funny?"

Janet, "Yes, I think that is funny, but you know I really don't care what they think. I do care what they think, but they will get over it. Anyway Daddy will see it my way eventually and he will convert mother."

The week before the wedding Jim and Janet stayed busy. They saw each other each night. Janet had her job during the day. Jim was still on convalescing leave so he visited his friends from the *Spearfish*.

On Wednesday Jim visited the I and P offices. He introduced himself to the chief of the I and P. The chief was Lieutenant Glen Harper. He was about 25 years old and Jim thought he seemed a little young to be in charge of this office.

Jim and Glen sat in Glen's office and visited for about an hour. Jim liked Glen and he though Glen liked him. They talked about the kind of work they did in the I & P branch. They exchanged personal information such as hometowns, marital status, their homes and many other things.

Glen asked Jim about his combat experience. Jim told him about some of the patrols.

Glen to Jim, "Jim I am envious of you. I wanted combat but have been stuck at a desk every since I graduated form the academe."

Jim, "What year did you graduate from Annapolis?"

Glen, "1940."

Jim, "You must have been a good student to end up in intelligence and planning work."

Glen, "I made good grades, but I don't know if that made me a good student. I did test out with a high I Q and I think they thought I was smart."

Jim, "You said you were from New York. I think everyone thinks of New York City, but where is your home town?"

Glen, "I am from Syracuse. That is I am from a suburban area called Mattydale."

Jim, "As I mentioned earlier Janet and I are getting married Sunday at 1300 hours in chapel number one. You and you staff are invited."

Glen, "Thanks for the invitation. Speaking of staff let me introduce you around. I have given you the numbers and job titles. Come on out and I'll introduce you."

Jim met Glen's staff members. The I & P office had a staff of 15 people. Twelve were navy personnel. Each a specialist of some kind. There were three civilian personnel. One high-ranking GS civil service type and two clerk-typist.

The main purpose of the I & P was to keep informed about naval and submarine stratigy and to gather information and plan for patrols. Part of Jim's job would require him to sit in on headquarters discussion about the plans to defeat the Japanese. Carry out the plans by selecting targets and working out details. Jim found out that Larry was the coordinator between the admirals office and the I & P.

Glen explained to Jim that his job would require a "top secret" clearance. Jim would be exposed to a lot of high level planning that had to be kept secret.

The Navy Department had in fact started the top-secret investigation of Jim a month ago.

Jim left thinking he might like the work even though it took him away from action to behind a desk.

That afternoon he told Mac, Don, Al, and Richard about his new job. Later that evening he told Janet about his new job.

Jim and Janet spent most of Saturday before their wedding the next day together. They talked of their plans.

Janet, "Jim I just got a letter from my folks. Guess what my mother did not seem upset. She wanted to be here, but sent her best. Oh yes! She sent a newspaper clipping of your picture getting the Purple Heart. She thinks you are hero. I think dad won her over quicker than I thought."

Jim, "I am glad. But had your mother had time to get your letter and respond?"

Janet, "You know you are right. Mother must have been talking about our engagement, not the marriage. Maybe she was talking about the newspaper article."

Jim, "What do you want to do after the war?"

Janet, "Jim we really can't make too many plans until the war is over. What do you want to do after the war?"

Jim, "I really don't know what I want to do. I do know I want to go back and finish college. Finish nothing—I only had one semester; it will be like starting over. What do you think we should do?":

Janet, "I think you should finish college and that I should get a job nursing. I may want to consider an RN job in some hospital"

Jim, "Is it too early to consider children . . . a family?"

Janet, "I have thought about that. I can tell you I want at least two children. I was an only child and I always wanted a sister or brother. We have plenty of time to think about that . . . I guess."

Jim, "We will have plenty of time later to sort all this out. Let's just get through the next few days. We live in perilous times, but we must look forward."

Janet, "You are right. The main thing is that we love each other and want our marriage to be for a life time."

Jim. "We had one wedding rehearasl is that enough?"

Janet, "I think so. There really isn't all that much to do. Are you nervous?"

Jim, "No, I am not nervous I am calm, do you know why?"

Janet, "No what makes you so calm?"

Jim, "I keep thinking of our honeymoon and what will take place that night. Everything else is just a necessary step to bliss."

Janet, "Ha, ha. Jim you are very funny."

Jim and Janet parted that night. They were ready for the big day.

The day of the wedding arrived. At 1300 on the 30th Jim and Janet were married in Chapel number one on the navy base at Pearl Harbor. There were 30 or 40 people in attendance. Jim and Janet had not expected that many guests.

The officers and some of the enlisted men from the *Spearfish* were at the wedding. Other guest included several nurses and those who took part in the wedding. This included the officers with the crossed sabers that Jim and Janet marched under upon leaving the chapel.

Lieutenant (j g) Jack Hill, the chaplain, did a good job on performing the ceremony. It was just the right length and he said just the right words. Jim and Janet were pleased with the ceremony.

Ginny looked lovely as a bride's maid and Mac made a handsome "best man."

Jim had rented a car. As Janet and Jim came out of the chapel and passed under the honor guard swords Janet threw her bouquet of flowers for the girls to catch. Jim and Janet then got in the car and drove off.

They drove to the hotel. Jim and Janet enjoyed their honeymoon. They took a tour of Oahu Island and saw a lot of things they had not seen before. Janet later described their honeymoon as a blissful get acquainted time.

They attended a party given by the *Spearfish* crew, took in a movie or two, visited with friends, and went apartment hunting.

The navy had converted an old wooden barracks into small apartments for married officers who had their wife's at Pearl. There were not many. Most were like Jim and Janet; that is married after they got to Pearl.

Jim and Janet had a small three-room apartment. The living room was a good size room, the bedroom was smaller, and the kitchen was even smaller. They had one bathroom and one closet. It was furnished and best of all it was provided as their housing allowance. This meant it was rent-free.

Jim and Janet spent one day repainting the living room and cleaning up the apartment. It was on the second floor and only about three miles from the hospital where Janet worked and about four miles from Jim's new office. They could ride the base bus to and from work.

Janet could ride the bus to the commissary to buy groceries. Janet and Jim made a budget and decided to keep buying savings war bonds for their future. They were happy with the way things turned out. They did not know what the future held.

CHAPTER 18
A NEW ASSIGNMENT

JIM REPORTED FOR duty at the I & P Branch at headquarters at the date and time specified in his orders. The first two days were spent in orientation. Commander Larry Saxton, his former sub skipper, Lieutenant Glen Harper, and two other officers gave Jim briefings on the job he was to do and what the duties of the I & P were.

Larry to Jim, "We will cover Admiral Nimitz invasion plans for the central pacific tomorrow. Jim you will have access to the intelligent gathered by the HQ Staff and other top-secret information. For those reasons you will be sworn to secrecy."

Jim, "Aye, aye sir."

Larry, "Jim you will be required to sign a statement agreeing to the code of a top-secret clearance."

Jim, "Yes sir, I understood that I would be investigated. How long will that take?"

Larry, "Unknown to you Jim you have already been investigated and cleared before you had been assigned to IPO. It usually takes several weeks for the investigation to be completed, but since you lived in virtually one place all your civilian life it did not take as long."

Jim laughed and said, "No there on secrets in our little town. Everyone for miles around can tell you all about everybody."

Larry directed Jim to Glen who had Jim fill out some papers and sign the oath. He was directed to another officer from the Code Breakers

Group. After this orientation he was turned over to another officer who took him around and introduced him to various department heads and other people that he might deal with.

At the end of the day Jim's head was spinning. Mentally he was fatigued. When he got to the apartment Janet was already there and was cooking supper.

Jim told Janet about his first day. Of course he did not reveal any secrets. They ate scrambled eggs and bacon.

Jim, "Janet that was a good meal. You did a good job. You are a good cook."

Janet, "Thanks honey, but eggs, bacon, coffee, and toast are no test for a cooked meal. It was something I could fix quickly. Anyone can cook bacon and eggs. I am not all that good of a cook. But thanks for bragging on me."

The next day Jim reported for work. He was 30 minutes early. He wanted to read some material he had been given. He soon found out that the second day orientation was really getting his first assignment with a briefing.

Jim's second day at I & P was a busy one. Four men from the I & P office attended a briefing by Admiral Nimitz' Chief Of Staff. The four men were Jim, Glen, Ensign Tim Spencer and Ensign Paul Essary.

The briefing consisted of the Admiral's plans already made and area of future consideration. The I & P men learned that the Mariana Islands where the next to be invaded. The islands of Guam, Tinian, and Saipan where schedule for invasion. The invasions dates were in June and/or July. The dates were subject to change.

They were informed that task force routes had been selected. The task force make up had been decided. Submarine patrols had been planned and their mission would to take lifeguard action and of course, sink Jap ships. Since the Mariana's were much closer to Japan they expected the fighting to be harder.

The I & P was instructed to give sub patrol missions for the invasion of the target islands. On the longer range they were told to plan sub patrols areas. They were "running out of sea room and targets." Jim's office was to plan into the future for possible Japanese shipping lanes and areas where submarines might fine targets.

The four I & P Officers returned to their offices with a renewed enthusiasm. Jim's orientation continued. He went over the office layout, given the location of various files, and the job of each person in the office. Jim learned that a big part of his job was thinking, research, and discussion.

Jim found out that one of the woman in his office knew Janet. They had roomed in the same building at one time. Her name was Kathy Holt, from Houston, Texas and she was a civilian GS-4 clerk-typist. Jim made friends easily and got acquainted with most of the staff that day.

That evening when Jim got to the apartment he had a lot of news for Janet. They talked about their day. They were beginning to settle into a routine for married life.

Jim had gotten a letter from his folks. They congratulated Jim on his marriage and wanted him to send them some wedding pictures. They sent Jim a page out of the newspaper that had the article and picture of him receiving the Purple Heart.

Jim to Janet, "My folks said congratulations on our marriage. They welcome you to the family. They also requested some pictures of our wedding. When do you think we will be getting the pictures?"

Janet, "Jim the photo studio called me today. Our wedding pictures can be ready by next Friday. I need to let them know how many copies we want. What do you think?"

Jim, "Hum . . . let me see. One set for us, one for your folks and mine, and one set for friends and other relatives. I would say let's get five sets. How many pictures in a set?"

Janet, "There were 12 photos in each set. Five sets would cost us $25.00. Can we afford that?"

Jim, "Yeah, sure . . . let's get five sets. We will squeeze our budget for the cost. The memories captured in the photos are worth it."

Janet had made ham and cheese sandwiches for supper. She warmed a can of soup to go with the sandwiches. Once again Jim compliment Janet on her ability to put a good meal on the table after she had worked hard all day.

The next day the staff in Jim's office set about planning sub patrols in the Guam, Tinian, and Saipan areas. Jim had patrolled this area so his experienced help. He suggested they put a priority on the rescue of down fliers. He remembers the look of relief and appreciation on the faces of the down airmen.

The staff studied reports by sub skipper's who had been in the area. Jim noticed that Larry and Jack's reports were well written and very informative. Some sub skipper's were very good and others brief and not so informative. A few skippers only reported the number and tonnage sunk. Jim made a mental note to interview Jack on the area when the *Spearfish* next docks.

Jim now had access to the information on the coming and goings of submarines. He knew that the Spearfish was due at Pearl within a week. He made a mental note, "I'll get information from Jack, Mike, Don, Mac, Al, and Richard about the area."

Glen and other members of the staff commented that they were glad to have a former submariner on their staff. His experience was going to be helpful. Plans were drawn up for three wolf packs of at least four submarines in each pack to be used for the three islands. Their plan was sent up to headquarters.

They waited for word on their plan for two weeks. While they were sweating out that word they were busy gather information on their second assignment. This was a more difficult assignment, "pick areas for war patrols and look in places where there might be Jap shipping going on." They were aware that, "they were running out of sea and targets."

Jim and Janet were settling in to their married life routine. They were happy and couldn't believe that they could be so happy in the middle of a war with so much unhappiness going on.

Janet and Jim did their grocery shopping at the commissary. Since their apartment was furnished that did not have to invest much in household items. They did purchase a coffee pot and some silverware. There were plates, bowls, pots, pans, cups, and glasses furnished with the apartment.

When the *Spearfish* docked Jim was there to meet the officers and men. They had orders for all the officers to report to headquarters. This is the first time they could remember all officers being called for a debriefing.

They met in a small conference room in an annex to the headquarters building.

Jack, "Jim what's this all about? We are not in trouble are we?"

ROBERT E. SEIKEL

Jim, "No Jack it's nothing to worry about. You see we want to pick you guys brains."

Mac, "Jim is our inside man now. He is in good with the management. We are probably going to get a leave."

Jim laughing, "No Mac, No leave. You will find out in a minute."

About that time Commander Larry Saxton entered the room and sat at the head of the conference table. An officer who had accompanied Larry sat down on Larry's right.

Larry, "Good morning gentlemen. It is good to see you. Your friend, Lieutenant (j. g.) Jim Rush suggested that you men could be of a great help to us"

For the first time it dawn on Jim that he had a mentor in Larry. Larry was in a position to help Jim, but it had not occurred to him.

Larry, "You see we want information and your opinion on patrol duty in the Mariana's. We cannot tell you why, but it will help us in our job. But first we should go around the table and introduce ourselves. There are three or four officers here that do not know all of the officers."

Larry, "I am Commander Lawrence "Larry" Saxton. We will start on my left."

Jim, "I am Lieutenant (j g) Jim Rush of the I & P office."

Glen, "I am Lieutenant Glen Harper, head of the I & P office."

Tim, "I am Ensign Tim Spencer of the I & P office."

Jack, "I am Lieutenant. Commander Jack Jackson captain of the *Spearfish*.

Mike, "I am Lieutenant Mike Moreland Executive Officer of the *Spearfish*.

Don, "I am Lieutenant (j g) Don Phillips of the *Spearfish*."

Mac, "I am Lieutenant (j g) George "Mac" MacDonald of the *Spearfish*."

Al, "I am Ensign Albert "Al" Valcheck of the *Spearfish*."

Richard, "I am Ensign Richard Sisler of the *Spearfish*."

Larry's Aide, "I am Lieutenant Robert Dykes aide to Commander Saxton."

Larry, "Okay now that we know one another lets get down to brass tacks. We would like your recommendations on patrolling the waters about Guan, Tinian, and Saipan."

During the next hour the officers from the *Spearfish* freely gave their ideas and opinions. The officers of the I & P office made notes and ask questions. Larry soon dismissed the officers. He did ask Larry and Mike to make a patrol report before going to their quarters.

The remainder of the *Spearfish's* staff made a dash to pick up their mail and get to their quarters. They had invited Jim, but he still had work to do. He told them he would see them about 1900 hours. He wanted to go to the apartment and see Janet first. He would invite her to go with him.

That evening Jim filled Janet in on his work activities for that day. She was glad that he got to see his old "ship mates." Janet turned down Jim's offer to accompany him to visit with the officers of the *Spearfish*.

Janet, "Jim, thanks for the invitation, but I will just stay here and rest. I think it would be boring for me to sit in on your bull session."

Jim, "You are probably right. But at some point I do want to show you off to the boys again."

Janet, "I have an idea Jim. Why not invite them over to the apartment some night for supper?"

Jim, "I would, but wouldn't that put a lot of work on you? Will our budget afford it?"

Janet, "We could make it a Friday or Saturday night. I think we can stretch our budget to cover it. We may have beans and cornbread."

Jim, "Okay. I know you were joking about the beans and cornbread, but that would be a good meal for them. Add fried potatoes and onion and you have a meal fit for a king."

Janet, "Just let me know when so I can prepare."

Jim left to visit with his old buddies. They met in the BOQ and talked until nearly midnight. Jim remembered he had work the next day. He asked them over for supper and they told him they would let him know when.

Saturday at 6 p.m. Mac, Don, Al, and Richard came to Jim and Janet's apartment. Janet had invited Ginny over. Ginny remember the others from the wedding. They gathered in the small apartment. The men talking while Janet and Ginny finished preparing the meal and setting the table.

The seven of them crowded around the kitchen table. Janet had added a leaf in the table and that helped. Sure enough Janet was serving pinto beans, fried potatoes, cornbread, butter, onions, with ice tea, water, or coffee to drink. There was an added attraction. Janet had managed to get some beefsteaks because they had just stopped meat rationing in the states.

Everyone enjoyed the meal and fellowship. Al had never had pinto beans and cornbread before, but he bragged on Janet's cooking. All were complimentary and seem to truly enjoy themselves.

Mac, "Janet that was a good meal. Thank you. Ginny it's good to see the bride's maid again. I bet you helped with the cooking."

Ginny, "Mac I am glad you liked the meal. I didn't do much. Janet had it all going when I got here."

Don, "It is good to get a good home cooked meal. It reminds me of home, my wife, and the good things in life."

Al, "Janet I need to get your receipt for the cornbread. I had never tasted it before, but it was super."

Richard, "Janet, Ginny, and Jim thanks for having us over. Jim, I can see that you have a great wife and a good home."

Jim's friends left about 11 p.m. Janet and Jim where along.

Janet, "Jim I am glad we had the crew over. Did Mac take Ginny home?"

Jim, "You where wonderful honey. I love you. You made a hit with the boys. I think Mac may have escorted Ginny back to her room. Is Ginny married or engaged??

Janet, "Ginny was engaged, but her fiancée was killed at Guadalcanal. I don't think she wants to get close with anyone until the war is over. She told me once that she did not want to go through losing another."

Jim helped Janet clean up the kitchen and then they went to bed.

Monday morning Lieutenant Glen Harper raced out of his office into the general work area waving a paper.

He shouted, "Guess what? Headquarters has approved our plan. The Admiral signed off on this last week. Things are already set in motion."

Jim, "That's good news. Did they make any changes?"

Glen, "No changes. After work I'll buy the beer for the staff at the PX."

Tim, "Does that mean that the submarines have already sailed out on patrol?"

Glen, "Yes, I think two of the wolf packs sailed from Pearl and one wolf pack from Midway."

Paul Emery, "Jim, I guess that means that the *Spearfish* is not on this patrol. Will they be disappointed?"

Jim, "I guess so. I am sure they will."

The next two months events seemed to snow ball. James Forestall was named Secretary of Navy. Frank Knox had been the secretary, but he died in April. From June 6 through June 18th B-29s bombed the Japanese mainland. That was the first air raids on Japan since April 1942. The Doolittle raid on Tokyo and other Japanese cities had been the only other air raid up to this time. Submarines were to set up lifeguard lines.

During early June the battle of the Philippians Sea took place. The Japanese lost 400 planes in a four-day battle. U. S. forces attacked Saipan on June 15th. By July 9th Saipan had been conquered.

Jim kept track of the *Spearfish*. She had a 40-day patrol doing lifeguard duty between Tinian and Japan proper. When she returned from her patrol Jim greeted his old shipmates. They would get together and have their "gab sessions" just like the old days. Janet was always glad for Jim to see his friends, as they seem to make him feel like he was still a part of the crew.

On June 6, 1944 the invasion in Normandy France took place. The advances in Europe and the Pacific made the United States and her allies feel they had gained the initiative in the war.

Guam was conquered on July 10, after two days of fighting. Tinian fell a few days before. The Marinas were now in the possession of the U.S.

Jim and Janet stayed busy during the summer. Most of their time was spent at work. They did go swimming at Waikiki Beach a couple of times. They would go see a movie about every week. Their favorite entertainment was going to the movies, listening to the radio and visiting friends.

Jim and Janet were faithful in writing their parents and others. They received letters and that always "cheered them up." Most of all they enjoyed one another. They were more than lovers they were good friends.

One evening Jim and Janet went to the movie. They saw *Dragon Seed*, which starred Katherine Hepburn. After the movie they went to the PX and ordered an ice cream soda. They sat in a booth, just like they did as teenagers back home.

Janet broke the spell, "Jim remember when we use to do this when we were teenagers? We really had a good time when we could see a movie and treat ourselves to an ice cream soda or malt."

Jim, "Yes I remember. That seems like a long time ago. A lot has happened since then Janet. For one thing really good came out of all this is that I married you."

Janet, "Yes, isn't it strange how things turned out? I guess it was fate Jim. We got together 4,000 miles from home. Each one of us was lonely, yet surrounded by hundreds of people. Our desires turned to love. I do love you Jim."

Jim, "And I love you Janet. My life is complete with you Janet. No matter what happens in the future remember I love you very much."

Jim and Janet walked back to their apartment holding hands, laughing, and talking.

The I & P office was informed to start using the designation of Planning and Intelligence Office. They were instructed to use the initials PIO. Normally PIO meant Public Information Office. That office was responsible for keeping the public informed about the men and women in the service. Among other things that office furnished the publicity about men and women to their hometown newspapers and radio stations.

Glen and his staff were informed that when asked where they worked they were to say in PIO. This way they could keep it a secret as to their branch. They were informed that if anyone ask detail questions about their work to notify the I G's office immediately.

The next day the PIO had received a communiqué from headquarters. Glen called a staff meeting.

Glen Harper, "I have some important news for you. This is a new assignment. First Jim and Ensign Paul Emery will fly to Guam and check it out for a new sub base. Seaman Eugene Slade will go with you. Your orders have been cut and here is a copy for you. You will leave tomorrow morning at 0600. Be here and we will get a jeep from the motor pool and drive you to the airfield. Seaman Slade knows short hand and types so you will be dictating your report as you go"

Glen continued, "While we have a team in the field, we in the office will be working on the problem. Hopefully we will have a solution shortly after our team in the field completes their work. Oh, Jim you guys will have to coordinate your work with the army. The army air corps wants to establish an air base at Tinian and maybe Saipan. They have not ruled out Guam. The Japs had a runway on Guam."

Jim was surprised by the assignment. He did not let on that he was surprise or disappointed. He only thought "I'll be away from Janet, but we knew the unexpected could occur."

Jim, "How long will we be gone, sir."

Glen, "Jim you don't have to sir me. We are working too close to be formal. I don't know for sure how long you will be gone. It will depend on what you find at Guam. Our office is to do a feasibility study about setting up a forward base on Guam. It could involve us moving our sub headquarters there. It will put up much closer to the action."

Jim, "Guam . . . we had a navy base there before the war. The Japs captured Guam just a few days after December 7th. The civilian population is mixed between natives and Japanese. I understand they remained loyal to us during the Jap occupation."

Glen, "You are right about your geography Jim. You were a navigator on the *Spearfish,* weren't you?"

Jim, "Yes, that is correct."

Glen, "How far is it from Pearl to Guam?"

Jim, "It is about 3,350 miles. That would put us that much closer to Tokyo."

Glen, "You are right Jim. I'll let you in on a secret. We will be checking this out for Admiral Nimitz also. He is thinking about moving the Naval Headquarters for the CINPAC to Guam.

Jim, "You mean they would move the whole central command to Guam?"

Glen, "I don't know how much of the Central Pacific Command they would move. It will depend on our report I imagine."

Jim, "Is there anything special I need to take?"

Glen, "No, Paul will have any equipment you may need. That is Seaman Slade and Paul. Just pack a few work cloths. Incidentally, I wanted to go but they wouldn't let me and I was to keep Tim here in the office. You will radio information to us by code and we can work on the plan while you are in the field.

Glen changed his speaking pace and said, "I know it is a little early in the day, but let's call it a day and I'll see you tomorrow morning bright and early."

Jim was anxious to get to the apartment to tell Janet the news. This separation is something they knew could happen. They did not know it would be so soon. They would not complain, because this came with the job. At least it was not a combat zone the island was secure, or was it?

CHAPTER 19
GUAM

JIM GOT TO the apartment early. He thought, "I'll surprise Janet and I will have supper ready. But what would he fix? He decided to clean up the apartment and take Janet out to eat. They could go to the officer's club."

When Janet arrived at the apartment she was surprised to see Jim there.

Jim, "What are you doing here early? Are you sick? Hey, you cleaned house. Thank you, but what are you doing off early?"

Jim, "First kiss me and I'll tell you."

The both laughed and Jim took Janet in his arms and kissed her. They held on to one another for a few minutes and kissed again.

Janet, "Okay now give me the news"

Jim, "The news is honey I'm taking you out to eat tonight at the officer's club. I didn't know what to fix for supper. The rest of the news is tomorrow they are sending me and a team to Guam."

Janet, "I knew something was up by you getting off early from work. Why Guam? What will you do? Oh I know it is all a secret and you can't tell me."

Jim, "You are right honey I can't really tell you much more than I already have. Oh honey, if anyone ask where I work just tell them PIO."

Janet, "Can you tell me how long you will be gone?"

Jim, "I really don't know."

Jim, "Janet I don't know how the mail is from Guam. Of course, I'll write you, but if you don't hear from me it will be because of poor mail service. Check with Glen at the office he can at least let you know how I am doing."

They went to the officer's club and ate. They went back to the apartment and went to bed early.

The next morning at 0600 Jim, Glen Harper, Paul Emery, and Eugene Slade all met at the PIO. Glen had already checked out a jeep and a driver to take them to the airport. To their surprise Ensign Tim Spencer showed up.

Tim to all, "I want to wish you all good luck and say that I wish I were going with you."

Jim, "Thanks Tim for getting out so early to wish us well."

The team was taken to the airport. For the first time they saw the type of aircraft to fly them to Guam. It was a Catalina. The Catalina was a twin-engine aircraft. It could fly long-range missions and was very reliable. A four engine PBY would have been more comfortable, but the team had to take what was provided.

They met the crew of the Catalina. The crew consisted of a pilot and co-pilot, a radioman, and two gunners. The radioman pulled double duty as he was also the navigator and if necessary could become a nose gunner. The Catalina crew was friendly and they appeared to know their jobs very well.

The flight time was going to be about 15 hours. They boarded the plane. Jim, Paul, and Eugene talked for a few minutes waiting for the take off.

Jim, "Eugene what kind of equipment did you bring for us to work with?"

Eugene, "I brought two pairs of binoculars, some note pads, pencils, a compass, a 100 foot tape measure, a portable typewriter, typing paper, and some rations."

Jim, "Very good, Paul what did you bring?"

Paul, yawning said, "I brought some maps, a camera, film, sun glasses, and my personal things. Supply put in a six-man wall tent, some flashlights, a couple of kerosene lamps, and some folding chairs and a table. We may have to rough it on Guam."

Jim, "You could be right Paul. We don't know what to expect when we get there. Now, let's sleep."

Jim said, "Fellas I'm going to get some sack time. I think I'll try to sleep. I didn't get a good nights sleep last night."

Paul, "That's a good idea Jim. I bet I could tell you why you didn't get eight hours of sleep last night. A newly married man leaving home for a while, it's not difficult to know why you didn't sleep."

Jim ignored Paul's remark and rolled out a sleeping bag and lay down.

Eugene said, "Good idea I think I'll sleep some but not right now. I did bring a deck of cards so I may play some solitary."

Jim and Paul fell asleep immediately. Eugene played a game of solitary and then fell asleep. Jim dreamed of Janet and their apartment.

A Catalina crewman woke Jim up. Jim looked at his watch. He had been asleep for about eight hours. This indicated to Jim that they should be about ½ way to Guam.

Crewman, "Sir, I was told to wake up. We are going to set down at Wake Island in a few minutes to refuel. Shall I wake the others?"

Jim, "Yes go ahead and wake them. Is Wake Island about half way?"

Crewman, "Wake is about 2/3rds of the way sir. We have had a good tail wind. We probably could make it to Guam without refueling, but the skipper wants to play it safe. It will give us a chance to stretch our legs and eat a bite of hot chow."

Jim, "That sounds good to me."

The Catalina landed at Wake and taxied up to a pier. Jim remembered, "The Catalina could land on water as well as land. It had a retractable landing gear."

All aboard the aircraft got off the plane and walked to a small building. The pilot checked with an officer in charge and they all went to a mess hall for a hot meal. While they were eating the aircraft was being serviced.

Jim to the others at the table in the mess hall, "You know Wake is in pretty good shape considering we haven't occupied it very long. I think somebody did a good job restoring the piers, docks, air stripe, and buildings."

The pilot, "You are right sir, I was through here about two weeks ago and it is amazing what the Seabees have done in that length of time."

They all sat and talked and got better acquainted. They exchanged information about their homes and families. Jim appreciated the airmen more after he got acquainted.

They ate their meal, walked around for a few minutes, and then took off for Guam. The men welcomed the "rest break" at Wake Island.

Jim, Paul, and Eugene fell asleep again and slept until they were about 100 miles from Guam. Again, a crewman woke Jim.

Jim woke the others and they began to get their things together. They were looking out the side blisters when they saw Guam. They had a good view. It was early morning so Paul took a picture of the island at about 2,000 feet.

They landed and as they were getting off the plane onto a pier the pilot wished Jim and his crew good luck.

The Pilot, "We will fly back to Pearl Harbor tomorrow morning. We will take a passenger or two and the mail. We may see you in two or three weeks. Good luck."

Jim, "Thanks, we appreciated you bring us to Guam. We wish you good luck."

Jim, Paul, and Eugene picked up there bags and started down the pier. They needed to check in with someone, but whom? Just then a rather ruddy looking 40-year old ensign dressed in a "fatigue jump suit" work outfit approached them.

The stranger, "Ahoy, do I have the right party? I was expecting an admiral or at least a commander from what my orders were. I am Vincent Spencer . . . you can call me Vince. As you can see I am not Navy. I am with the Seabees. Hell, I'm probably the oldest ensign in the navy."

Jim, "I am Lieutenant (j g) Jim Rush, this is Ensign Paul Emery, and this is Seaman Eugene Slade. We are here on a PIO assignment. We can go on a first name basis if you like."

Vince, "Uuhuh . . . I was told to cooperate with you guys and see that you got what ever you wanted. Humm . . . PIO with a camera and a typewriter. You guys gonna do a story on us?"

Jim with a smile, "We really can't tell you why we are here. You see it is top secret."

Vince, "Top secret, that's funny. Hey I am the foreman of this Seabee Battalion. We are here working to restore power, buildings, and anything else that needs to be repaired. We are also working on the landing strip."

Paul had kept quiet too long.

He said, "I have to know something, how come you are only an ensign. I don't mean any disrespect, but are you really 40 years old?"

Vince laughing, "Yeah I am really 40. You see I was a chief until about three months ago. They thought I needed a raise in salary since I was the foreman. The only way I could get a raise in pay was to become an ensign. I am really a civilian at heart. Hell I had my own construction company back in the states and wanted in this war, but I could only get in the Seabees because of my age."

Eugene said, "Where is you home?"

Vince, "I'm from Shreveport, Louisiana, but was born in Frankfort, Kentucky. We moved to Shreveport when I was six or seven years old."

Jim, "Vince can you show us our quarters? Also tell me where the headquarters building is located."

Vince, "Yeah sure thing. Follow me."

As they walked along, Jim thought that Vince was a real character but a lot smarter than he might appear.

Vince took them to a "tent city" and showed them their tent. It was an eight-men tent. A small table sat in the center of the tent. There was double bunk beds set up on along two walls of the tent. No other men occupied the tent. There were four wall lockers along the other side of the tent.

Vince, "Lieutenant get settled in and I'll be back in about 30 minutes to show you the headquarters building. By the way sir, there are not enough quarters for me to separate the officers and the enlisted men."

Jim, "We don't mind sharing quarters. We work together and we will be working nights. Vince before you leave do you know any Guam officials . . . you know like a major, governor, or what ever."

Vince, "Oh sure I know and work with all of the local wheels. If you are going to work nights I'll get you a gas generator with wiring for electric lights. That will be much better for night book work than the kerosene lanterns."

Vince left and Paul broke out laughing.

Paul, "Haw, haw, do you believe the character we just met. He is out of a Mark Twain novel. He is funny, but likable".

Eugene, "Yes, and he thinks we are here to take pictures and do publicity. I bet he can be a big help to us. He can direct us to the people and places we need to see."

Jim, "I think you are right Eugene. Now we had better get unpacked and ready to report to headquarters.

As promised Vince was back within 30 minutes with a small generator, electric extension cord and a can of gasoline. He had a jeep and drove them to the headquarters building. It was the old navy headquarters building. It had survived the Japanese invasion and the American bombing and shelling to retake the island.

Jim reported in at the A G's office. The officer on duty said they were expecting them and to give them anything thing they need. They had assigned an officer to be their guide and help them anyway he could. They agreed to report back tomorrow morning at 0700 and meet their guide and go to work.

As they left the HQ Jim ask Vince if he could show them around. Since that had a jeep and a man who knew his way around he wanted to take advantage. There was at least six hours of daylight left. Vince was a little surprised but glad.

Vince, "Hey I like you guys. You want to get to work right away. You know most guys would goof off the rest of the day."

Jim, "Well we just wanted to take advantage of your knowledge and see some of the sights. Can you direct us to any officials?"

Vince, "Oh, sure. Say let's drive out in the country I want to introduce you to one of the farmers I know. This guy is interesting and he hates Japs. He was captured once. The Japs tortured him and he has the scars to prove it. He was a civilian employee for our navy before the war."

Paul, "He sounds like a very interesting person."

They drove about five miles into the countryside. They passed several large coconut groves. They pulled off the main road and drove down a one-way country road and came to a modest house with a tin roof. They saw two or three out buildings or barns.

They went to the front door. Vince knocked and called the man's name.

Vince, "Flores . . . Philippe' Flores. You got company friend."

A man who looked about 50 years old came to the door. He walked stooped over slightly. He had a grin on his face.

Philippe', "Vince . . . come in, it is good to see you."

Vince, Jim, Paul, and Eugene went in. They were directed to a sofa and chairs to sit down. The furniture looked like it came out of a used furniture store. Vince introduced the three navy men to Philippe'

Philippe', "I am glad to met you naval officers. I worked for the navy before the war. I guess you have come for the file cabinet."

Jim and the others were surprised by his comment. They were bewildered.

Jim, "Mr. Flores or should I call you Philippe'?"

Philippe', "Please call me Philippe'. Let me call my wife and introduce her."

Philippe' called his wife in and introduced her. She was a very polite, humble person, and offered to get them something to drink. They decline the drink. Jim was anxious to hear what Philippe' had to say.

Jim, "Philippe' we did not know anything about a file cabinet. Please explain and we will certainly see that it gets to navel headquarters."

Philippe' continued, "The day Jap forces landed on Guam I was working in the headquarters building. The commander of the navy had us to burn a lot of papers. There was this one file cabinet he asked me to take it from headquarters and hide it. He wanted to keep this until the U.S. returned to Guam. He said it would help the navy and he said he would send for it."

Jim, "We have come on a secret mission Philippe' for the PIO. We would like to take the file cabinet. Do you remember the officer's name that was in command on December 12, 1941? That is the day that Guam surrendered."

Philippe', "Oh sure I remember his name. It was Commander Chester Windsor."

Jim, "Eugene are getting all this in your notes?"

Eugene, "Yes sir."

Jim, "Where is the file cabinet now? May we see it?"

Philippe', "Oh yes it was in the church for a long time, but when the Americans came I moved it to my barn. Come on out and I'll show you."

They all went outside to one of the buildings on Philippe' place. It was a building of corrugated sheet iron that was used to store coconuts. They went to one corner inside of the building and Philippe' pulled a canvas covering off and there was a four-drawer metal file cabinet.

Paul, "Oh gosh! This is amazing."

Paul was carrying his camera. He took his camera out and took a picture before anyone could move.

Vince, "I didn't know you had this Philippi'. I knew you were a part of the Guam underground during the war. I knew you had harassed the Japs, but this maybe the most heroic thing you did."

Jim, "I want a photo of Philippi' and Vince on either side of this cabinet. I bet Admiral Lockwood and maybe even Admiral Nimitz would like to have this picture."

At first Philippi' was reluctant to have his picture made, but was soon convinced that it was for only good. He wanted make sure there were no devious reasons involved in taking his photo.

Jim thought, "I think I'll write Philippe' up for a medal of some kind."

Jim, "Let's carry this out to the Jeep. Vince can we get this in the Jeep with all of us? Eugene, type me up a receipt and I'll sign and give it to Philippe'. That is just in case he needs to prove that he turned this cabinet over to the navy."

Vince and Paul loaded the file cabinet in the back of the Jeep. It might be a little crowded going back, but they could make it. Jim was not about to go off and leave the cabinet.

They spent another hour talking to Philippe'. Philippe' answered a number of questions and they wanted all the information they could get. He told them what the occupation was like under the Japanese. He told them about the people of Guam. Most could speak English, most knew U.S. History, and about 90% of the population was Catholic.

Jim and his friends found out more about Guam in one hour talking to Philippe' than they could have found out in a day reading books. They asked Philippe' several questions about the harbors around Guam.

They left Philippe's place with a promise to return and went back to their tent. Jim, Paul, and Eugene were excited about seeing what was in the cabinet. They carried the cabinet into the tent. Vince set up the generator and ran wiring for lights. There was one flap window in the tent and of course the flap door, but it was dark in the tent even in the daylight. The weather was moderate, but Vince set up a fan to cool them off.

Vince, "Jim I have to be going now. It is almost chow time at the mess hall. I have to check on my work crews. I'll probably be busy tomorrow, but I'll check back with you guys from time to time."

Jim, "Vince you have been very valuable to us. We appreciate your help. I think we can get a picture and a story about you in the Shreveport Newspaper. Eugene, make a note of that. Paul get another picture of Vince before he goes."

Vince left and immediately Jim, Paul, and Eugene started a systematic search of the documents in the file cabinet. They were so caught up in their work that they decided to send Eugene to the mess hall to bring back sandwiches and coffee. They were making notes and cataloging the contents of the cabinet.

Eugene returned after he had eaten a hot meal. He brought Jim and Paul four sandwiches, two pieces of apple pie, and a container of hot coffee. They ate while reviewing files.

After four hours of intensive work Jim made a decision.

Jim, "Paul, Eugene, do you know what we have to do? We need to write up a report and send it tomorrow morning to Pearl."

Paul, "I agree, but we may be working all night."

Eugene, "Remember, whatever you come up with I have to type it. Typing on a portable means I can't type but about 45 words a minutes. The word count gets slower after the first 30 minutes."

Jim, "If we can summarize what we have found, the report does not have to be long. Basically what we have found so far is a evaluation on every port on Guam. There is detailed diminutions and other data that can be used to decide which port would be best for unloading supplies, fuel, and personnel."

Paul, "You are right Jim, you made a pretty good summary. The information we have could tell which port would be best for submarines, tankers, cruisers, destroyers, carriers, etc. Just think the information we have was gathered in 1940 and 1941. We have historical documents. We will now have to find out what kind of shape the ports are in."

Jim, "Lets put together a report and see what we have."

Eugene, "Remember I have to type it, but also this has to be coded and transmitted. We don't know how good the communications center is here."

Jim, "We will rely on our coordinator officer to help us get this job done tomorrow."

All agreed and they set about to compose a report that would tell what type of information was in the file cabinet.

They finished with their report about midnight. All agreed the report was good and to the point. In the last paragraph of the report Jim recommended some kind of an civilian award or Medal of Honor for Philippe'. Eugene was happy because the report was only five type written pages long.

Jim, Paul, and Eugene slept soundly until revile time at 0600. They ate breakfast and hurried to headquarters with their report.

Jim reported to the A G's office. The clerk went to get the officer who was going to be their host or coordinator. An officer came out of an office and up to the counter where Jim was standing.

The Officer, "Hello sir, I am Lieutenant Samuel Vandergrift. You may call me Van."

Jim, "I am please to met you Van. I am Lieutenant. (j g) Jim Rush and I am with the PIO team and I understand you are to assist us."

Van, "Yes I am here to help. The orders came from HQ at Pearl that we are to give your team what ever they want. You guys must have friends in high places."

Jim, "You can call me Jim. We are rather informal when at work. Here are the other members of my team. This is Ensign Paul Emery, and this is Seaman 3rd Class Eugene Slade.

Van, "What is the first thing on your agenda?"

Jim, "We need to send a report to Pearl. Can your communications center code and send it for us."

Van, "Yes we can do that. Follow me we will go over to that building. It is at the top of the hill, but only about 100 yards away."

They entered the communications building. A Chief Petty Officer came to the entry counter.

Chief, "May I help you sir?"

Van, "Yes chief, we have a report to send. This team is from PIO, Pearl Harbor and wants it coded and transmitted."

Chief pulling out a pencil and pad says, "What's the message?"

Jim, "Here it is chief. We have already typed it out."

The chief looks at the stack of papers.

Chief, "Five pages sir?"

Jim, "Yes"

Van, "Say you guys just got here yesterday and you have a five page report already. You guys must have worked all night."

Jim, "Yes that's right, it is top priority. Can you code and send it Chief?"

Chief, "Yes sir we can. We will put our best operator on it and it should go out within the next hour."

Jim, "Thanks chief. Do you want one of my team to hang around just in case there is a question about something? Seaman Slade can wait and get confirmation that the message was received."

Chief, "Yes that might be a good idea."

Jim, Paul, and Van left. They made arrangement to pick Eugene up in about one hour. Jim had seen that the chief understood why Eugene was there. It was to really make sure that the message was sent promptly.

Within two hours a copy of the report was handed to Lt. Glen Harper in the PIO at Pearl Harbor. Glen looked at the file the report came in. The file was marked "TOP SECRET". A copy had been given to Headquarters. Glen called the staff together.

Glen, "Staff we have our first report from our team on Guam."

Tim, "A report all ready. I guess they wanted us to know they had got there okay."

Glen, "This is a five page report. I've just glanced over it, but I think it contains some very valuable information. Let's study it and see what we can learn. All I can say is those guys didn't waste any time. They are certainly earning their pay."

Tim, "We had better work hard they may send a 10 page report tomorrow. Ha, ha."

Glen went back to his office for a few minutes. He called Janet at the hospital and told her the crew made it safely to Guam.

Jim, Paul, and Eugene stayed busy the next four days. They visited several ports and/or harbors and interview dozens of people. They were trying to find out if anyone knew about the Japs laying mines in any of the harbors. They wanted to know if there were any harbor obstructions such as sunken vessels or wrecked aircraft.

The team learned something new and something they had not expected. They were talking to the Marine Commandant and learned that a small number of Japs had not surrendered and had fled to the hills. The small marine detachment was not going to chase them down. They would go after any that the locals reported.

Each morning they would send a report to Pearl. Most of their reports were three to six pages in length. The communications center had got use to seeing them each morning.

Jim decided that they had been very busy working. He thought it would be a good idea to take a day off, but wanted input from Paul and Eugene. That evening Jim brought up the subject.

Jim, "Paul, Eugene, what do you guys think about taking a day off tomorrow? We have hit it pretty hard and a break and rest would be useful. Besides tomorrow is Sunday. What do you think Paul?"

Paul, "I think it is a good idea. A rest would do us good. Jim I want to tell you that you are an excellent diplomat. I have seen your skill at work with Vince, Van, Philippe', and everyone else."

Eugene, "Mr. Rush I could use a break. I haven't had a full night's sleep since we have been here. Have you notice the number of good beaches with white sand? They look inviting. I didn't bring a bathing suit, but I would like to go swimming in my fatigues."

Jim, "Okay, then we will take tomorrow off and rest or swim or what ever you want to do"

The next day the PIO team rested. They did go to late morning chapel services. They slept, swam in the blue Pacific, went to the PX snack bar and ate hamburgers, wrote letters and generally loaf.

One of the reports that the team sent to Pearl contained a question Jim asked. He wanted to know if they could tell him the fate of Commander

Chester Windsor. He thought if he could fine out he would pass the information along to Philippi'.

Each day Jim or one of the team members checked with the communications center to see if they had any messages. If so they had to sign for them. Paul had checked on their "day off" and they had a communiqué from Pearl.

The message was addressed to Jim and it contained what information they had pertaining to Commander Windsor. He had been taken prisoner of war on Guam and apparently was in a POW camp in Japan. At least he was the last time his wife heard from him.

The message asked Jim and his team to obtain some additional information. It seemed minor to Jim and Paul, but they did not have the full picture of the operation and of course, would get the information.

Jim thought that Vince should be the one to carry the news to Philippi'. They would tell Vince which would probably be tomorrow.

Vince came by after breakfast. He was driving a ½ ton "carry all". He said he would take them to the capital of Guam. Agana is the capital with a population of about 1500. It was only ten miles away. The island of Guam is 30 miles long and from four to 10 miles wide. It has 78 miles of coastline. The largest city of Guam is Timoneng and its population if about 5,000.

Jim, Paul, Eugene, Van, and Vince met several Guamanian officials that day. They didn't learn much, but did establish some important future contacts.

After they departed Agana they drove north along the coast road. A large part of the island has coral reefs off the coast. They act as a barrier from high seas. They returned to Apra Harbor to examine it again. It is the biggest and best harbor in Guam. The Seabees had been busy around this harbor and it was open and going well.

Next they decided to pay Philippe' a visit. They told Van about Philippe' and he was really interested in meeting him. When they arrived at Philippe's he was in the yard talking to a man in white summer business suit. The man was just leaving.

Philippe' greeted the group. Vince introduced Van to Philippe'. They talked a few minutes outside. Philipee' explained that the man he was talking to was a coconut buyer for a syndicate.

Vince told Philipee' what they had learned about Commander Chester Windsor. He was glad to get the information. Eugene wanted more information about Philippe's resistance activities during the Japanese occupation of Guam. Eugene got Philipee to talk and he listened and took notes. Occasionally Vince would remind Philippe' of something. It seems that Vince knew a lot about the 'guerilla activities' during the occupation.

Rarely did Jim and his crew stop for lunch or supper. But today Philippe's wife insisted they stay for supper. They enjoyed the meal. They returned to their tent about 8 p.m. and set about preparing a report on the day's activities. They included Eugene's write up of Philippe's work for the underground during the occupation.

Two days later Van was briefing Jim, Paul, and Eugene.

Van, "Jim has anyone told you about Seaman George W. Tweed?"

Jim, "No I don't recall that name."

Paul, "No we have not run across anything on him. His name is not on my list."

Van, "Well he is someone you may want to interview. He probably has already been debriefed. He is no longer on Guam. He was probably given a leave to go home. Of course that was five or six weeks ago. He could be back on duty somewhere."

Van continued, "You see he was one of a five-man radio team that did not surrender when the Japs invade Guam. They hid out in the hills. One by one they were tracked down and kill, except Tweed survived with the help of the natives. He hid out until the navy and marines came back."

Jim, "Eugene did you get that? Did you get his name? Van are there any records in headquarters here of any of his interviews? Do you have his serial number?"

Van, "I don't know if we have anything or not. I'll put a couple of clerks looking through our files."

Eugene, "Mister Rush I got his name . . . George W. Tweed."

Van, "Let go for lunch right now and come back and maybe my men will have something for us."

After lunch Van and the team returned to headquarters. Van had five seamen searching their files. After two hours one of the seaman found something.

The Seaman, "Sir, I found something. Here is a file on Seaman George W. Tweed. It has his serial number on the file."

The file contained information that Tweed had provided the navy upon his being found. He was hiding out for two and one-half years on the island. He gave information on what he knew about the Jap defensive measures on Guam. He also gave names of those who helped him. He also gave names of those who helped the Japs.

Jim, "Van can we get a copy of this file? There are ten pages and it would save time if we could copy it so we would not have to get it typed."

Van, "We don't have a way to copy it. The army signal corps has a special camera. We could get them to take pictures and develop them. That would take a day or two. But I can get ten typists and each can type one page. That shouldn't take more than 30 minutes. That is the fastest way I have of getting it copied."

Jim, "Okay, let's get started with the typing. Eugene can help with the typing if you need him."

Van, "Shouldn't need him. I have plenty of helpers."

Van put all the clerk-typist in the headquarters on the project. Sure enough they completed their task within 30 minutes. Jim put the typewritten copies in a file and they went to a small conference room to prepare their report for the day and would include the report of Seaman Tweed.

After they had finished their report. Jim was wondering.

Jim to Paul and Eugene, "You know I am wondering why none of the Guam people we have talked to had not mention George Tweed to us. Surely it was known by a fairly large number of his hiding on the island."

Paul, "Jim, I have wondered the same thing, but come up with a blank."

Eugene, "Sir, I think the civilians had kept quiet about the Tweed business during the occupation for fear of reprisals. So maybe they just naturally continued to keep quiet about him."

Jim, "Umm . . . you could be right Eugene. Anyway we got the information now. If Pearl wants more info on Tweed let them get in touch with him."

The PIO crew slept well that night. After breakfast they made their daily morning journey to the communications center. They had a 20-page report including the 10 pages from the Tweed file.

The communications center crew thought this report was a record in length. There was a bet going with the coders and operators about the length of each day's report. Each man was to anti up a quarter and each page was worth a quarter. They would draw numbers between one and twenty. Each number represented a page. This took some of the dread off their job.

Eugene checked at the quartermaster. Each one of them had one or two letters. Jim had a letter from Janet and one that had been forwarded from his parents. The three men went to the 'day room' and read their mail. Their spirits seem to rise after hearing from the folks.

The PIO crew's work continued, but over the next week they decreased their daily work hours from ten or twelve to six or eight. They were getting more rest and some of the pressure was off. It was no longer necessary to send a report each day, but now they could send a report about every third day.

Lieutenant Glen Harper, head of the Pearl Harbor PIO, continued to get copies of the team's reports. He and his staff studied the reports and were formulating an opinion on its recommendation to headquarters and the admiral. Each Friday morning Glen held a conference with his staff. They would discuss what they had received. Every member of the staff was free to make comments.

Glen to staff, "Our team has been on Guam for three weeks now. I think they have gathered a lot of information. Does anyone know of any unanswered questions that we might have for Jim and his team?"

Glen went around the conference room table and asks each individual. No one had any other questions.

Glen, "Very well, with the admiral's permission I will call our team home. We might give them two or three more days."

Chief Petty Officer Ward Hendrex, "Sir, we need to tell the team to be sure to bring back that file cabinet. There could be a lot of valuable material in there and we need to examine it very close."

Glen, "You are right chief. I only hope the powers on Guam will let them take it off the island. But if anyone can do it I'll bet Jim can get the job done."

Walter Towers the top civilian in the office said, "Lt Harper I think you should write up a letter of commendation for the team. They have done an excellent job."

Glen, "I agree Walter. I'll assign that job to you."

Walter, "Serves me right for opening my mouth, Ha, ha."

Glen, "No Walter you are the best for the job. You can compose memos and letters better than anyone I know. You got the job because you are good at your job."

With Glen's compliment of Walter the staff gave applause. Walter took a bow with a grin on his face.

Glen called Larry at headquarters. They discussed ordering the team back to Pearl. Larry couldn't think of any reason for them to stay any longer. He agreed that they had enough information.

Orders were cut ordering Jim and his team back to Pearl. The message was sent the next day.

The next day Jim, Paul, and Eugene received the message ordering them back to Pearl. The message told them that an airplane would pick them up the next day at 0900. They told Van of their orders. Van ask if he could do anything for them.

Jim, "Van you have been a big help to us we appreciate it. We will see about getting you a commendation. Eugene get Van's picture and get the name of his hometown newspaper. Surely we can get a photo and a story to his home town."

Van, "Thanks for that Jim. Is there anything else I can do for you guys?"

Jim, "Well there is one thing Van. Just don't see us remove the file cabinet we have"

Van, "Oh that. I give you permission to take the file cabinet. After all it is property of the U.S. Navy. You guys are navy and you are going to our headquarters in the Central Pacific. I was told to give you guys what every you needed."

Jim, "Thanks Van, again you have been a big help in our mission."

Jim, Paul, and Eugene went back to their tent. They needed to pack. Vince dropped by to say his farewell. They didn't know how he knew they were leaving. Vince told them he would have a jeep by for them tomorrow morning at 0800.

Jim to Vince, "Vince could we get the ½ ton. You see we will be taking the filling cabinet in addition to our personal gear."

Vince laughing, "So you get the cabinet too. You guys are pretty good. I didn't think they let it off the island."

Paul, "Oh yes, we are part of the same navy. Their orders were to give us anything we needed."

Vince, "Hey, I got a letter from my mother. She sent me a copy of my picture and the article you guys had written up. It was in our newspaper. Thanks for the publicity."

The next morning Jim, Paul, and Eugene were on the pier at 0900. Their transportation was about one hour late. Their flight was in the same Catalina and the same crew that had flown them to Guam. It seems that they made the Pearl to Guam and return run once a week.

They boarded the plane while the pilot did an engine check. He said something about one of the magnetos was not functioning right. The PIO crew talked while waiting.

Paul, "Jim now how far is it to Pearl and what would be our ETA?"

Jim, "From Guam to Pearl it is about 3500 miles. If we stop over at Wake it is about 1200 miles from Guam to Wake. Flight time would be around six hours to Wake and from Wake to Pearl it would be about 9 hours"

Eugene, "Well I guess the mag checked out okay we are starting to move into a take off position. I'll be glad to get back to Pearl. I think of Pearl Harbor as home anymore."

The flight plan did call for a stop at Wake Island. They made it to Wake Island okay, but the pilot was experiencing some problem with the magneto on the number two engine. He requested that it be changed. The crew and the PIO team disembarked the plan while aircraft mechanics started to work.

The passengers of the Catalina ate a meal and lounged about a 'day room' while the aircraft was being worked on. It was almost dark before the work on the plane was finished and tested. They finally took off at 2100 hours (9 p.m.).

No one complained about the delay.

Eugene said, "We sure don't want to go down in the ocean. The Pacific is a big bunch of water. I prefer a 10 hour delay here as opposed to a 10 day float in the Pacific"

Paul agreed, "You are right Eugene. Remember we have a file cabinet to look after to boot."

The PIO crew soon fell asleep. Jim remembered thinking, "I can go to sleep anywhere at any time"

One of the aircraft crewmen woke Jim. Jim woke the others. They were approaching Pearl. It was daylight. Jim looked at his watch. It was 7:30. They had made good time.

The Catalina landed. Jim and his PIO crew where leaving the airplane. They had gotten two of the airplane crewmen to carry the file cabinet while they carried their personal luggage.

Waiting on the dock for them was Larry, Glen, and three or four people from PIO. And then Jim saw Janet just behind the group.

"How did Janet know?" Jim said.

Glen, "Good to see you Jim . . . you to Paul . . . and you to Eugene. You guys did a good job and we are glad to see you."

Before Jim could get to Janet, Larry stopped Jim momentarily.

Larry, "Jim take the rest of the day off and take Janet home. Report tomorrow morning at your office."

Jim, "Thank you sir. Does Janet have to go back to work today?"

Larry, "No, we arranged for her to have the rest of the day off. She had put in some extra hours at the hospital and has some leave coming."

Jim embraced Janet. They hung on to one another for a few seconds. Then they kissed and hugged some more. Jim thought that Janet look lovely. He thought she has never looked so good.

Jim, "Honey you look wonderful. I love you and I missed you. Even though we stayed very busy you were always on my mind. Oh, I do love you so."

Janet, "I thought of you too Jim. I love you and missed you. I am so glad you are home safe and sound.

Janet, "Jim you look like you lost a little weight. You really did not have any to spare. But you look good to me anyway."

Jim, "We kept a hectic schedule and we didn't always get to eat a regular meal."

Jim kissed Janet again and they walked off arm in arm heading toward their apartment.

CHAPTER 20
A TIME TO PLAN

JIM REPORTED TO work at the PIO the next morning. The whole staff was to drop everything else and work on the feasibility of moving the sub headquarters to Guam. They needed a forward base. Pearl would keep a sub base. This meant they had to come up with a very detailed plan.

The staff poured over all the material. After a week they came up with a report to submit to headquarters. They recommended moving the HQ, but keeping the machine and overhaul shops at Pearl.

One day Chief Ward Hendrex came out of his work cubical. He hurried to Jim's office.

Ward Hendrex, "Mister Rush we just got word that your buddies and the *Spearfish* are docking this afternoon. Also we have found out that the *Spearfish* will be sent to the east coast for overhaul or maybe dry dock."

Jim, "Does the communiqué say anything about what will happen to the crew?"

Ward, "The skipper, Commander Jackson, will get a 30-day rest leave back in the states. The other members of the crew get various leaves and/or assignments,"

Jim, "Let me see that message"

Ward hands Jim the sheet of paper with the information on it.

Jim, "Thanks Ward. hum . . . what does it say about Mac? Here it is . . . hey Mac is being reassigned right here on Pearl. Lets see what it says about Don. Don will get a 30-day leave home. Good for him. Al will get reassigned. Hey he will be promoted to a j.g. He deserves it. Richard will be reassigned."

Jim hands the paper back to Ward. He again thanks Ward for giving him the information. Jim goes into Glen's office.

Jim, "Glen, may I have the afternoon off to go see my old ship mates come in?"

Glen, "Sure, since we have the report finished and it has gone to headquarters. We will start on our next project tomorrow morning. Can you be back then?"

Jim, "Yes, sure thing. Thanks Glen for letting me to take off the afternoon."

Glen, "Hey you deserve it buddy. From what I hear you guys worked 10 to 12 hours a day while you were on Guam. Headquarters is really impressed with the file cabinet you guys brought back. They said to tell you 'well done'. I'll say it again your team did a good job."

Jim, "Well we did at first work 10 to 12 hours a day, but we tapered off after the first ten days. Glen I have written up Paul and Eugene for a citation and a promotion. They worked hard and they're both very intelligent. My appraisal is very good for both of them."

Glen, "I agree and I endorsed your recommendation and sent it up to Larry's office yesterday."

Jim, "Thanks Glen. Hey you deserve a commendation for the way you take expeditious action on your work."

Jim hurried over to the hospital he wanted to tell Janet about the *Spearfish* docking. He wanted her to know that he might be late for supper.

Jim saw Janet in the hall just outside of the nurse's station. They embraced and then kissed. They didn't seem to mind if anyone saw them. Every time Jim saw Janet he thought she looked more beautiful.

Jim, "Honey I just dropped by to see you and tell you I love you."

Janet, "I know you love me but, what else is on you mind?"

Jim, "Janet the Spearfish docks in about one hour and I am going to meet the crew. If we get too busy talking I may be a little late for supper."

Janet, "Okay, I am glad you told me. You could have called me on the phone."

Jim, "But in person is better and more friendly. Besides I can't hug a telephone"

Janet Laughs and gives Jim a goodbye kiss and he leaves the hospital to go meet the *Spearfish*.

Jim was on the dock to greet the officers and men as they came off the *Spearfish*. Things were somehow different this time. The crewmembers were carrying their duffle bags and carry on luggage and somehow seem sad.

Jim greeted the officers. They had a conversation on the pier. Mac, Don, Al, Richard, Jack, and Mike were all "worn looking" and their eyes looked like they were very tired. Suddenly Jim thought they looked older. They needed a rest.

Jim, "Mac how are you fellas. It's good to see you. Looks like you guys had a rough patrol."

Mac, "Hi Jim, it's good to see you. Yeah we had kinda rough patrol. Have you heard Jim that was the last patrol for the *Spearfish*?"

Jim, "Yes, I heard that the *Spearfish* was going to the east coast for a make over or to be scrapped. I guess they will decide which after she has been looked over.

Mac, "Jim, we are going to pick up our mail and then find our quarters in the BOQ. Why don't you drop by later?"

Jim, "Mac, why don't I let you guys read your mail and rest and drop by tomorrow or even better how about Saturday?"

Mac, "Okay by me."

Al, "Jim it is good to see you. Hey what's this we hear about you going on a dangerous secret mission?"

Jim, "Al, the mission was secret, but it was not dangerous. It was a PIO assignment. Oh, by the way in case you haven't heard Al you got a promotion."

Al, "I had heard something about becoming a (j g), but I'm so tired it didn't sink in."

Don, "Jim how is Janet?"

Jim, "She is fine Don. Thanks for asking. I hear that you will be getting a 30-day leave to go home. That's great and you need the break."

Don, "Yes, it sounds like you read the same orders we did."

Jack and Mike were the last to leave the *Spearfish*. Jack had the logbook under his arm and was carrying a brief case. Mike also had a box of material from the *Spearfish;* the shore crew was helping bring their personal gear ashore.

Jack, "Hello Jim. How are you? It's good to see you."

Jim, "Jack I'm fine. I hear that you will get a leave home for 30 days. You need the rest. It is well deserved. Jack you have been a first class skipper. Do you have any idea what you assignment will be after your leave?"

When Jim asked Jack that question all of the officers moved in close and were quiet. They seemed interested in his reply.

Jack, "No I don't know Jim. I am hoping they send me back to Pearl. I think Larry is working on that."

Jim, "Mike, what about you? I understand you will get some leave."

Mike, "Jim I will get a rest leave, but for only ten days plus three weekends. I'll fly home and then I report back here. I guess I'll be assigned to another sub."

Jim, "Jack, Don, and Mike, when does your leave start. Will I get to see you guys Saturday?"

Jack, "Yes we will still be here Saturday our leave doesn't start for a week yet."

Jim, "So long fellas. I'll see you later. I had better get back to work."

The officers of the Spearfish headed toward their quarters. Richard did head to the quartermaster to pick up their mail. Jim left and since there was about two hours of work time left he returned to the PIO.

As Jim entered the office he met Tim coming out.

Tim, "Jim, I thought you had the rest of the day off. Glen called a staff meeting for 0900 tomorrow. We get our new assignment. He gave the staff the rest of the day off. You can go home to Janet now."

Jim, "Okay Tim, but first I wanted to check my incoming mail"

Jim went to his office and checked his "IN" basket. He wanted to see if there was anything that needed his attention. It was still empty. Glen walked by about then and stopped at Jim's office door.

Glen, "Jim I thought I gave you the rest of the day off. What are you doing back here?"

Jim, "My buddies were tired so I thought they need rest more than to 'wool gather' with me. I told them I would see them Saturday."

Glen, "Well I gave the whole staff the rest of the day off. They got to leave two hours early. I told them to be here in the office by 0800 tomorrow and we would have a staff meeting at 0900. I have just received our next assignment. Now go on home to Janet."

Jim left and went to the apartment. He got there before Janet. He swept the floors and washed the dirty breakfast dishes. He then dried the dishes and put them away. He went in the bedroom and made the bed and picked up dirty laundry and put in the dirty clothes hamper in the bathroom. He had just finished cleaning the bathroom when Janet came home.

Janet, "Jim! I didn't expect you to be here"

Before Janet could say anything else Jim embraced her and kissed her. They held on to one another for what seemed like a hour, but in fact was just about two minutes.

Janet, "Didn't the *Spearfish* come in?"

Jim, "Yes, I got to see the boys, but they looked so beat that I told them we could get together Saturday. That was okay by them. So I came home to you."

Janet, "Well look at this apartment. You cleaned house . . . thank you honey. I appreciate it. How much will this maid service cost me?"

Jim, "Glad to help. You are enough reward for me. I'll collect tonight."

Janet laughed and said, "You crazy thing . . . I do love you. Now I had better cook supper."

After supper they went to a movie. They saw the movie *Laura* that starred Gene Tierney, Dana Andrews, and Clifton Webb. They saw the newsreel that showed highlights of the World Series. The St. Louis Cardinals beat the St. Louis Browns 3 to 1 in the 6th game of the World Series.

The same newsreel showed General MacArthur going ashore on Leyete in the Philippines. The invasion of the Philippines represented General MacArthur's fulfilling his promise to return. The newsreel showed the army advancing in France.

After the movie they decided to walk back to the apartment. It was only a mile. As they strolled along they held hands and talked about the movie. Jim commented about how beautiful Gene Tierney was and Janet thought that Clifton Webb acting was great. Jim did bring Janet to up date regarding the *Spearfish* and the crew.

Jim, "I enjoyed watching the newsreel tonight. Just think two St. Louis teams in the World Series. I doubt that the Browns will ever make it back to the series.

They continued walking and talking.

The next morning Glen chaired the staff meeting of the PIO. All staff members were present. Glen passed an agenda out to the staff members.

Glen, "We have a new assignment. We are to find areas that would make good sub patrols. They asked us to determine areas of Jap shipping and other suitable targets and recommend action."

Ensign Paul Emery asked, "Sir have you heard anything about what headquarters thinks of our Guam report?"

Glen, "I haven't heard a word yet. It may take them a while to review and decide."

Ensign Tim Spencer, "And they may never let us know anything until orders are cut transferring all of us to Guam, haw, haw."

Ensign Fred Lake spoke, "Sir, this new assignment. How specific should we get? I mean do they want us to give patrol routes and number of subs or just give the sea or straight areas?"

Glen, "Good questions Fred. I imagine all of the things you mentioned and maybe more"

Glen, "Jim you were a navigator. Just looking at the map of this part of the world how would you respond to headquarters?"

Jim, "M . . . m . . . well. Okinawa is the obvious next step. It is only about 300 miles from the Japanese Islands. I would set up a line of subs from Saipan to just off the Japanese coast for sinking shipping going and forth between Okanawa and Japan. The B-29 raids are getting more numerous so I would have my subs also doing lifeguard duty."

Glen, "Good thinking Jim. That will project us ahead about four or five months. I think something closer in time maybe Iwo Jima. The Army Air Corps would like to get a fighter plane base to escort our bomber to and from Japan."

Walter Towers, "Since we are thinking out loud what about the South China Sea area or the Formosa Straights? I know the Jap shipping is hurting, but there maybe two areas where the Japs are still shipping oil and freight."

Glen, "Yes those are two general areas we could think about. Kathy would you or Irene take notes and list these ideas?"

Kathy Holt, "Yes, certainly. I think Irene has already been doing that. Haven't you Irene?"

Irene Johnson, "Yes I have."

Jim, "We may want to go back to the Sea of Japan. We have not been there since the summer of 43'. I know it is a dangerous place to get in and out of. There are only three narrow routes in and out and the Japs have them mined and patrolled. But with the new sonar we have now mine fields can be detected with more accuracy."

Glen, "That's right Jim. You have been there and know the problem. Why don't you work on that part of the plan? Get Eugene and Kathy to help you. How did you know about the new sonar?"

Jim, "One of my buddies took me aboard one of the new subs that just came in. He showed me the new sonar equipment and other features the newer subs have."

Glen made other specific assignments. He gave each three person team one part of the overall things discussed. They would come up with a pliminary report by the next staff meeting. This meant they had a week to report their progress.

Saturday Janet had to pull duty at the hospital. Jim went to visit his buddies from the *Spearfish*. Since Janet was not going to be at the apartment Jim did not feel so bad. He really didn't want to leave her to see his friends.

Jim got to the *Spearfish* officers quarters at 1000. They were all there. Mac. Don, Al, and Richard were in one room. Jack and Mike were down the hall. It was a good opportunity to visit. Jim wanted to pick their brains about his next assignment without them knowing what he was after.

They talked for an hour on exchanging information about their families back home. The information exchanged came from letters. Then they talked about their work. Jim had to keep his talk about his work general. He let them think it was more publicity type work.

Jim to Mac, "Mac do you know where you are being reassigned?"

Mac, "No Jim I don't know where I will be assigned. I assume to another sub, but I'm sweating it out. I toured one of the new subs the other day. They are bigger than the *Spearfish*. They have a bigger crew, 70 or 75 men and 8 to 10 officers. Their sonar and radar is better than we had."

Jim, "Don, Al, Richard, do you guys have any idea what your assignments will be?"

Don, "I am to report back here to Pearl after my leave. I am assuming that Jack and Mike will report back here after their leave. I can't imagine headquarters letting the experience represented by those officers get way from them."

Jim, "I think you are right Don. There was some scuttlebutt about going back to the Sea of Japan. What do you guys think of that?"

Don, "That stands to reason because the Japs have been stopped in the Central Pacific. There is still enough Jap navy left to be dangerous to MacArthur in the Philippines. So the South China Sea and the Formosa Straights would still be good target areas."

Jim, "Don it sounds like you need to be in our office, PIO. I was wondering if Jack still has a copy of his report on the Sea of Japan patrol that we did in July of 43". What do you think Don or Mac or any of you?"

Don, "I'm sure Jack has his copy of that report. Jack is thorough and I bet he has a copy."

Mac, "I'll go down to his room and see. Do you want a copy Jim?"

Jim, "Hum . . . I guess so. Of course headquarters has all the reports and I could get it there, but I don't think it is worth the trouble."

Mac went down the hall. Jim acted like it was not all that important, but he really did want a copy of Jack's report. He could get a copy from headquarters, but they would have a lot of questions and it might take several days or weeks to get the report.

Jack came back with Mac. He was carrying his brief case.

Jack. "Jim how are you? I understand you would like a copy of my 'Sea of Japan' patrol report."

Jim, "Jack I'm doing fine. Jack this is confidential but I have been asked to work up a report on going back into the Sea of Japan. You and the *Spearfish* crew have the experience and I would appreciate your in-put."

Jim had decided to level with Jack. He knew Jack was smart enough to know the real reason as to why he was asking about the Sea of Japan patrol.

Jack, "I thought it might be something like that. You don't want to have to go through the red tape to get a copy from AG?"

Jim, "That's it exactly Jack."

Jack, "I tell you I have two copies of my report and I will give one to you. I also have two copies of Larry's report on the Sea of Japan patrol. You may have one of those."

Jack takes some papers from his brief case and hands a binder with several typewritten pages to Jim.

Jim, "Thanks a lot Jack. Have a good leave back home. Give our best to you spouse."

Jack, "Thanks Jim. I have to get back and finish packing. I understand my flight will leave tomorrow. They moved my leave start up a week. Oh, I do have orders to report back here at Pearl. I don't know what my duty will be, but I will get to see you guys again."

Jack leaves the room. The officers remained quiet for a while. Jim glanced over the reports Jack left.

Mac, "There goes one of the best guys in the world. He is a swell guy. I'm glad he gets 30 days at home."

Al, "Amen to that. He is a swell guy."

Richard, "You guys have known him a lot longer than me, but I agree with you 100%."

Jim, "Well fellas I have to be getting back to the apartment. Janet had hospital duty today, but she will be getting back about 4 o'clock. I'll check with you guys later. Say why don't you men come over tomorrow afternoon to the apartment. We haven't moved so you can find it."

Mac, "Okay Jim, we will drop over for a few minutes tomorrow afternoon. Tell Janet not to go to any trouble. We don't want to eat. We plan to go to the officer's club for supper."

Jim left and went back to the apartment.

When Janet came back to the apartment she had found that Jim had cleaned up the apartment.

Janet, "Jim you cleaned up again. Thanks darling. I love you. I am kinda tired, but give me a kiss and a hug."

Jim, "My pleasure sweetheart."

Janet and Jim wrapped themselves in an embrace and then kissed. With their arms around each other's waist they walked toward the bedroom.

The next afternoon Mac, Don, and Al visited Jim and Janet. Janet served beer to Al and Mac. Don and Jim had ice tea. They all talked for about one hour. Janet had baked some 'brownies' and served those. They had a very enjoyable time. It was like "old home week."

After the crew left Jim and Janet decided they would go to a movie on base. They saw the movie *Destination Tokyo* that starred Cary Grant and John Garfield. The film had been shown earlier that year, but Jim had missed it. Jim pointed out the technical errors in the film. Overall he liked the movie.

The newsreel showed combat films from the Leyte Gulf sea battle in which several Japanese ships were sunk. The news showed President Franklin D. Roosevelt election results on winning his 4th term. It showed the Vice President, Harry S. Truman. There was a short piece on Glenn Miller's plane missing. Glenn Miller was a master of swing. His music was very popular with the men in service.

After the movie they ate at the officer's club. Jim and Janet saw several people they knew at the club. Jim and Janet talked as they ate. They had coffee and pie for their desert.

Jim, "You know Janet as I watched the newsreel I realized that a lot of things are happening within a relative short time. I get the feeling that we have crammed 20 years worth of events into the last three or four."

Janet, "I feel the same way Jim. You know darling, I am glad we got married. At least we can kinda feel like we are not letting time pass us by. Maybe we are keeping up with events."

Jim, "Well put Janet."

They rode the bus back to their apartment. It was raining and they did not want to walk in the rain.

Sunday morning it was overcast and raining. Jim and Janet went to chapel services and heard a good Bible lesson given by Jack Hill. They talked to Jack after services and found out that his family back in Arkansas was doing fine. Jack was their favorite preacher in Hawaii.

Monday morning Jim asked Eugene and Kathy to come into his office. Since the three of them were going to work together on the Sea of Japan report he wanted them to help him compose a report.

They gathered around Jim's desk and he explained what he had in mind. They would use Larry and Jack's reports as a basis to explain how to get in and out of the Sea of Japan. They would tell what to look for in the way of targets. Tell them how to prepare the sub crews and the subs for evading Jap mine fields. Give information on how to avoid Jap patrols and getting out safely would be in their report.

Jim, "Larry and Jack's reports will contain many answers to the problems of going back to the Sea of Japan. Let's outline these reports and build our recommendations around the reports. We will use the reports as an outline."

Eugene, "These reports will be a big help. How did you get a copy of these so soon and over the weekend to boot?"

Kathy, "This report will help me outline and type a recommendation."

Jim, "I got these reports from the officer who wrote one of the reports, Lieutenant Commander Jack Jackson of the *U.S.S. Spearfish*. He also gave me a copy of Commander Larry Saxton's report. Larry was the skipper on that patrol to the Sea of Japan in '43."

The trio worked all day on an outline. They voluntarily increased their work day hours from eight hours to ten hours. The second day they discussed ideas. The third day they drafted a report. The fourth day they reviewed and revised their drafted report. By the fifth day they had a completed report and gave Glen a copy for his comments.

At the staff meeting time on Friday all teams had made progress on their reports. Jim's team was the only one with a completed report. Glen reviewed the progress made and asked for final reports by next Friday's conference.

After the staff meeting Glen met with Jim, Eugene, and Kathy.

Glen, "Jim I want to complement your team on the fine job you did on the report. I am approving it and will go ahead and send it up to headquarters. I'll also include it in our final report. Oh . . . incidentally I got orders promoting me to Lieutenant Commander. I want to say thanks to you and the rest of the staff that I got the promotion."

Jim, "Congratulations. You deserve the promotion and recognition"

Kathy, "I'm so glad for you sir. Jim's right you earned the promotion."

Eugene, "I'll echo what Jim and Kathy have said. Well done sir."

Jim, "Sir, let me announce your promotion to the rest of the staff."

Glen, "Okay, I guess they have to find out some how."

Jim picked up the intercom speaker and turned on the sound.

Jim into the microphone, "Attention staff . . . this is Lieutenant (j.g.) Jim Rush speaking, I have an important announcement. We have just learned that Lieutenant Glen Harper has been promoted to Lieutenant Commander"

The PIO building rocked with applause and whistles. The staff definitely approved of Glen's promotion.

The PIO staff completed their work on their assignment and was ready for another. It was nearing the Christmas season, but there was no let down in their work.

Reports came in on sub patrols and sinking of Japanese ships between the Philippines and Japan. Sub patrols around Okinawa were increased. Lifeguarding was an important duty as many downed airmen were being rescued.

Jim's biggest problem at this time was what to get Janet for Christmas. He had little opportunity to shop. He didn't like "shopping" anyway. He would try to decide what to buy her and then go hunt for it.

He finally got a couple of free hours and went into Honolulu to the Jewelry Store where he had purchased Janet's rings. He had an idea on buying a necklace, but instead bought her a nice jewelry box that played a tune when opened. The tune was Anchors Away.

Janet's folks had sent a box to be opened on Christmas Day. Jim' folks had sent him and Janet each a twenty dollar bill for Christmas. They appreciated the money. It seems they could always use cash.

Jim and Janet held a Christmas party in their apartment. Mac, Al, and Richard were there. Ginny and two other nurses from the hospital were there. A number of the PIO staff were there. In all the Rush's had 18 people in attendance. The little apartment was full. Janet had borrowed card tables and chairs from their neighbors. They had cake and punch. No gifts were exchanged, but the conversation made the Christmas very delightful.

After their company had left, Jim and Janet just sat down and rested.

Janet, "They seemed to enjoy themselves. I guess we are all very thankful for what we have. We did not have turkey and dressing and the trimmings, but we had each other and we are alive. And this was a tough of home."

Jim, "I agree honey. Shall we clean up or just call in the maid."

Janet, "You are very funny honey. I am afraid you and I are the maid."

Jim and Janet got quiet and just sat and looked at one another. Each was thinking, "This was a swell Christmas."

CHAPTER 21
A NEW YEAR

THE WEEK BETWEEN Christmas and New Year's Eve was a very busy one for the PIO staff. Glen called a staff meeting the day after Christmas. He had an important announcement to make.

Glen Harper, "I have just received word that Admiral Lockwood and his staff will be moving his headquarters to Guam something in January or February. We need to work out plans for billeting, feeding, and work quarters."

Walter Towers, "Commander does that mean our office will be moving too?"

Glen, "Yes it does Walter. Civilian Civil Service personnel will also make the move."

Ensign Fred Lake, "You said in January or February so that means no definite date yet. Jim and his Guam team can give us some information on housing."

Jim, "They are still building back the civilian housing. Navy Seabees, Army Engineers, and Marine Engineers are working to build living quarters, fuel storage tanks, dredging the harbors, and building warehouses. Guam was beginning to look like one big storage area. That was six weeks ago. I suspect they have made a lot of progress"

Ensign Paul Emery, "Mister Harper will CINPAC be moving also?"

Glen, "This is confidential, but the answer is yes. Admiral Nimitz thinks it is important for headquarters to be closer to the front. Pearl

Harbor is considered too far from the battlefield. Pearl Harbor will continue to be an important base."

Ensign Tim Spencer, "Does this mean we will have to send an advance team to Guam to line up some of the essentials?"

Jim, "Yauow, I can see it coming now. Paul and Eugene get your bags packed."

Glen, "Jim you and Paul and Eugene would be the logical ones for an advance team. You guys are experienced. Jim you are right your Guam team will be our advance team."

Eugene Slade, "Sir do you have any idea when the advance team might leave?"

Glen, "I don't know of an exact date, but I don't think it will be before the 15th. Sorry to mess you're New Year's Eve plans up, but I thought we need to get started planning this move now."

Irene Johnson, "Sir there are three civilian employees. Do they have to go or can we request a transfer?"

Glen, "If any of the civil service employees do not want to go you may request a transfer. I will approve any transfer request from the civil service employees. If there are no other questions I will let you go about your work. Work on details involving our move. Remember plan on only essential things to move."

The staff worked the remained of the week on plans to move. Most of the details had been worked out. It was decided that Jim's advance team would leave on January 15th.

Jim broke the news to Janet. Janet did not complain.

Jim to Janet, "I hate to be away from you darling, but maybe it will not be for long."

Janet, "We knew this could happen . . . that is we might be separated. Jim we took one another for better or worse. We are enjoying the better so the worse is yet to come."

Jim, "You are a real trooper. Gosh, I love you so."

During the week the PIO staff worked hard. The civilians met and decided they would not ask for a transfer, but go to Guam. They considered this a once in a lifetime adventure. They realized that some risk was involved.

Glen announced to the staff, "Other officers and I are throwing a big New Year's Eve party at the officer's club. You are all invited and that includes enlisted men and civilians. You may invite guest. I just need to know the number who plans to attend by the 29th. We will have music, food, and other entertainment."

Jim invited Mac, Al, and Richard. Jack, Mike, and Don were on leave. Janet invited Ginny and two other nurses, Cherry Mae Brown and Martha Thompson. She thought this would be a good match up for Mac, Al, and Richard.

The evening of the big party came. Those attending the party started gathering at 7 p.m. An orchestra was playing some Glenn Miller and Tommy Dorsey music. Several tables had been set up. Some early arrivals were Jim and Janet Rush.

Janet, "I like the way they decorated this room and the tables. It looks like we might as well pick out a table and sit down. They must be expecting 50 people to this party."

Jim, "I understand they will start feeding about 8 o'clock. It is almost 7:30 now. You are right let's find a table. Hey there are your nurse friends. Shall we invite them to sit at our table?"

Janet, "Sure, we can get 8 or 10 people around our table. Hey girls, Ginny, Cherry, Martha . . . over here."

The three nurses joined Jim and Janet. The women engaged in small talk, mainly about the hospital and what was going on there. About that time Jim saw Mac, Al, and Richard. Hey fellas over here."

The three sub officers joined Jim, Janet and the others. Jim introduced the men to the women. Ginny had met the officers before and reminded Jim that she already knew the "sailors."

Mac asks Ginny to dance and they went to the dance floor. Al asked Martha to dance and Richard felt obligated to ask Cherry to dance. Jim and Janet decided they would dance. They dance one dance and came back to their table. A waiter asked them if they were ready to be served. They said yes.

They all ordered some type of a drink. Most wanted ice tea, water, or coffee. Some wanted some 'mixed drinks' or wine. Their food was soon brought to them. Some had chicken, some had ham, and some had roast beef.

RUSH TO VICTORY

While the people at the Rush's table had been talking and eating the room filed up with people. Jim and the others saw many other people they knew. The whole PIO staff was there and Jim got to introduce them to his table guest.

The evening was spent dancing, talking, and drinking. Jim and Janet danced two more dances and then sat out the rest of the evening talking to friends.

About 11:30, the band stopped playing and a local comedian came out and told jokes and funny stories. Just before midnight the orchestra starting playing and everyone got on their feet as a clock ticked to midnight. At the stroke of midnight Jim embraced Janet and kissed her.

Jim, "Happy new year Janet. Here is hoping we have many more together."

Janet, "Happy 1945 to you Jim. Let's pray that this war will end soon. I hope we have at least 50 more years together."

Mac had kissed Ginny and they were laughing and seemed to be having a good time. The other couples seem to enjoy one another. Jim did remember that both Al and Richard were engaged. But Al and Richard were behaving themselves.

Jim and Janet slept late the next morning. It was a holiday and they both had the day off. The PIO and hospital had let ½ of their staff off. The other ½ had to work and would get a day off later . . . maybe. Janet fixed a big breakfast. This would be a late breakfast and as Jim would say a "two meal day."

Jim and Janet spent the day talking and loving one another.

The next two weeks went fast for Jim and Janet. Too fast because they knew Jim would leave on the 15th to go to Guam. Jim and Janet made the most of their time together. They hated to part but knew they would endure.

Jim, Paul, and Eugene were packed. Glen had ordered a jeep to take them to Wheeler Field. They learned that they were catching a ride in a B-29 to Guam. It seems that a new squadron of army air corps bombers where on their way to Guam and Tinian. They flew in from the States a couple days ago.

Wheeler Field was expecting Jim and his team. Special orders had been given to more or less give Jim's team what ever they needed. Jim carried a special letter signed by Admiral Nimitz stating that this team was on a special mission and was to be shown all possible cooperation.

Jim, Paul, and Eugene checked in at a flight building near the runway. Paul and Eugene went to a snack bar in the building. Jim stepped out to get a better look at one of the big bombers.

Jim had seen pictures of a B-29, but this is the first time he got to see one. He walked around the bomber. One of the crewmen was inspecting the aircraft and spoke to Jim,

Airman, "Hello, I'll bet you are one of our passengers?"

Jim, "Yes I am. This is the first time I have seen a 29. It's a magnificent looking airplane. I am Lieutenant (j.g.) Jim Rush, USN."

Airman, "Please to meet you. I am 2nd Lieutenant. Curtis McMurray. I am the co-pilot. Welcome aboard."

Jim, "I understand the B-29 can fly as height as 35,000 feet and as fast as 350 miles per hour."

Curtis McMurray, "Yes sir she can do all that and more. We have a sealed interior so we don't need individual oxygen mask and we have more freedom of movement inside. If you would like we can put your personal gear on and I'll show you in side."

Jim brought his carry-on bag and climbed into the bomber. He was shown the plane from nose to the tail. In the process he met the pilot, Captain Perry Harris.

At this time the remainder of the bomber crew came out and started boarding the aircraft. Some corporal brought Paul and Eugene out and showed them where to enter the B-29.

Jim and his crew would ride in the cabin just behind the bomb bay and at the end of the tunnel over the bomb bay area. They met two more of the crew. Sergeant Orbra Larch and Corporal Leo Wright. Both men were radar gun operators.

Soon they were airborne. They circled the field after they had taken off. As one of the airman explained they were waiting on the squadron to get airborne as they would fly in formation to Guam. Jim had not realized that there would be a squadron of B-29s, but this made him feel more secure.

Flight time from Pearl to Guam would be about 10 hours. Jim and the PIO crew slept most of the way. They really thought they had a comfortable ride.

When they landed on Guam Jim was surprised at the change since they had last been there. The Seabees and army engineers had been busy. They had accomplished a lot. Almost all the structures were of corrugated tin and shaped like a half oval.

Jim, Paul, and Eugene reported into the flight line control building. Within 20 minutes their transportation arrived. If was their old friend, Lieutenant (j.g.) Van Vandergrift. He was going to be their liaison officer again.

It was getting dark so Van took Jim and his team to their quarters. It was a Quonset hut, which accommodated eight officers. Jim and his crew were the only tenants. Van showed them the mess hall, the PX, the snack bar and the day room for this group of huts.

The next morning after breakfast Van came by with a Jeep to show them around. Van brought them up to date on the progress made on Guam. They would not have to stay in tents they would have a Quonset hut to stay in.

Jim, "Van they have built a city of Quonset buildings. There must be a hundred or more and of different sizes."

Van, "Yes this is a prefabricated shelter set on a foundation of bolted steel trusses and built of a semicircular aching roof of corrugated metal insulated with wood fiber. These are shipped ready to erect. I think a good crew can set one of these buildings, say a 20 by 40 feet structure in about sixteen hours."

Jim, "Have they built any permanent type buildings yet?"

Van, "No not yet. That will come later . . . maybe in three or four months."

Jim, "What about quarters for high ranking officers . . . say like an army general or a navy admiral?"

Van, "No not yet. They would have to stay in an officer's quarters housing six to ten officers."

Jim kept asking questions as Van drove them around showing them the base and this part of the island. They had requested a "look around" before going to headquarters. He wanted a workroom and a typewriter.

Van, "All of these structures look alike, but there are about five standard sizes. Two sizes for living quarters, one size for mess hall or galley, and one size for office buildings and the larger ones are storage or warehouse buildings."

Jim, "I assume these structures can be partitioned off?"

Van, "Oh yes, they can be partitioned. Some are for higher ranked officers quarters. Some are partitioned off for office space, such as for a CO's office, SPO' space, and a company work area."

Jim's conversation with Van gave him up to date on living quarters and work areas. Van drove them to the headquarters building. They were assigned a room with a desk, a file cabinet and a typewriter to the PIO team.

Van helped them get set up and was getting ready to leave.

Paul had a question, "Say Van what about our friend in the Seabees, Ensign Vince Spencer?'

Eugene chipped in, "Yes, and what about Philippe' Flores?"

Van, "Yes they are both around. Vince is still a foreman and Philippe' works on his crew now. They are working over on the other part of the base near the bay. We can go see them tomorrow."

Van asked, "Can you guys find your quarters from here?

Jim, "I think so Van. We know our street and building number. Thanks I guess we will see you tomorrow?"

Van, "I'll pick you up at your quarters about 0900."

Van left, and Jim, Paul, and Eugene set to work on their report. They wanted to send their first installment of the report tomorrow morning.

Jim, Paul, and Eugene went to their quarters they showed and shaved. They each had a footlocker and a wall locker. The head or latrine was located in the next building. Their living quarters had windows and electric lights and fans.

They went to the mess hall. The three stood out since they were in the khaki uniforms. Most of the personnel had work dungarees or fatigues.

After chow they went to the day room and looked at some magazines for a few minutes. They went back to their quarters and Jim set them to working on the report. He wanted to "polish it up."

Jim said, "The quicker we get this done the quicker we will get back to Pearl. And the quicker I'll get to see Janet."

Paul, "The thought occurred to me that it could mean the quicker we would get back to Guam."

Eugene, "You guys plan too far ahead. Let's take this one step at a time."

They decided to take a short break to clear their heads. The PIO crew went to the snack bar and drank a coke. They returned to finish the report on what they had learned today.

The next morning Van picked up the PIO team. They went to the communications building. The building was staffed with radio operators and decoders and coders. The communications building was larger than before and had a bigger staff. They had their message coded and sent.

Later Van took the team out to where Vince and his Seabees were working. They drove by two harbors and two bays.

Paul noticed, "The harbors seemed to be clear. Is that true of all the harbors on Guam?"

Van, "Yes the harbors in this area have been cleared. We have freighters and tankers coming and going now all the time. There are one or two small harbors on the east coast that they are still working on to clear."

Jim, "Van it looks like we are making Guam into a supply deport. Does headquarters here have any thing to say about that?"

Van, "Yeah, I guess it is no secret. I think Guam will be the big base for the Pacific Fleet before long."

Eugene, Paul, and Jim looked at one another with grins on their faces. Van was watching the road and did not see them. Their expressions would have confirmed his thoughts.

Van, "Yeah, Guam is becoming just one big supermarket."

They found Vince he was in the "foreman's shack" looking at some blueprints. He saw Van and his passengers when they drove up. He immediately rushed out of the shack with a big grin on his face.

Vince, "Well I be damn . . . if it isn't the three stooges. Jim, Paul, Eugene . . . how are you guys. What are you doing here?"

Jim, "Vince, we are doing fine. We are here to do a follow up story on you and Philippe' for the newspapers."

Eugene, "Yes see I have my camera. We'll get a photo for the press."

Paul, "I have my note book to take down some more of your adventures."

Vince, "What a bunch of liars. Van you have fallen in with bad company."

Vince laughed and they all shook hands. They talked for a while.

Eugene asked, "Vince where is Philippi'. We would like to see him."

Vince, "Oh sure. Renfro go get Philippi' and tell him there are some 'wheels' who want to see him."

Renfro who had been just outside of the foreman's shack hustled off. Within five minutes Refro was back with Philippi'. Philippi' had a big smile on his face and grabbed each one of the PIO men and gave them a hug.

Philippi', "It is good to see you my friends. I am grateful for what you did for me."

Jim, "What did we do?"

Vince, "Oh yeah, they awarded the civilian metal of honor to Philippi'. I forgot to tell you guys, but you are now looking at the oldest Lieutenant (j.g.) in the Seabees. All that publicity you gave Philippi' and me made us heroes. Philippi' got a metal and $200 and I got a promotion. The *Pacific Stars and Stripes* even had a article about us."

Paul, "Well we are glad. It couldn't have happened to two better men."

The PIO team asked Vince and Philippi' several questions about their work and what they were doing. They found out that a great number of Guam civilians were working with the Seabees and Engineers on construction jobs. They learned from Philippi' that some of the Guam men taken off the Island by the Japanese had been returned.

Philippi' said, "During the occupation of Guam the Japs took many of the Guamanian men and boys into forced labor camps. The men that had been taken to Tinian and Saipan have been returned. Others taken are still missing. I think that some may be in Japan and others dead."

Vince said, "Those fellas in the labor camps were worked hard. Some came back sick and crippled. But all are willing workers and they are grateful for a job."

The PIO team noticed that Philippi' had light duties. Despite his rough exterior Vince was a "good hearted" man. He assigned work based on skill and the physical strength to do the job. Maybe Vince was just smart at assigning work.

Jim, "Vince you guys have really been busy. I am amazed what you have built on this island. You obviously have been very busy with construction and cleaning up.

Vince, "Jim we have been very busy. We have worked hard with little regard for creative comforts. One officer has described the Seabees as they, 'smelled like goats, lived liked dogs, and worked like horses.' I was not that officer."

Jim, "Well my hats off to you guys."

Vince, "Yeah and you know what? The Secretary of the Navy said, 'The Seabees carried the war in the Pacific on their backs'. No wonder my back hurts. Ha. Ha."

Jim, "Vince and Philippi' we have to go now, but we are inviting you guys over to our quarters for more talking. Come any evening. Paul give them out street and quarters numbers."

Paul wrote the numbers down on a slip of paper and gave one to each of them. The PIO team and Van got into the jeep and continued on their reconnaissance, they wanted to see what other areas of the island looked like.

The PIO team was very busy the next week. They surveyed the island. They made daily reports but only sent a report every other day. They gave factual information and clearly indicated opinion where it was used.

They were making their final report and they were recommending moving the headquarters to Guam. They did not have to make the decision about relocating the submarine headquarters, but did give their opinion that it was feasible and the move should be made.

Jim knew that their recommendation was not necessary and that they ran a risk of inviting the higher-ups anger. Jim, Paul, and Eugene discussed their recommendation and decided to do it because they honestly felt that having a base closer to the front was best. Glen would get a copy of their report, but he could do nothing to alter it.

Jim, "We know that the final push will have to be against Japan proper. It will not be easy. We are sure the Japs will fight to the last man."

Paul, "From the reports of the fighting on Saipan they may fight to the last woman and child."

Eugene, "I saw one top secret report saying that our casualties for invading the Japanese Islands could run as height as 100,000 killed and maybe twice that number wounded."

Jim, "Then we all agree on the final report and our recommendation?"

Eugene, "Yes."

Paul, "Definitely yes."

The next morning Jim sent the report. They waited for a message. All they received was an acknowledgement that Pearl had received their report. They returned to their quarters and packed. Van would pick them up and take them to the airstrip for the trip back to Pearl.

The PIO team flew back to Pearl. This time they flew in an army C-54. The big four-engine army air corps cargo plane was fairly comfortable. They would all be glad to get back to Pearl. Jim would be especially pleased. Their ETA was 0230. That early of the morning there would be no one to meet them.

Jim was sitting next to a window. As he looked out into the night sky he wondered what the future held and thinking of Janet.

CHAPTER 22
A NEW STATION

THE C-54 LANDED on time at Wheeler Field, Hawaii at 0200. Jim, Paul, and Eugene got off the plane with the other passengers. They went into the flight shack, as it was the only building around with lights on this early of a morning.

As Jim and his team entered the small building a sergeant greeted them.

Sergeant, "Sir are you Lieutenant Rush?"

Jim, "Yes I am."

Sergeant, "I have a message for you and your men."

Jim, "Oh,"

Sergeant, "The message is from Commander Harper and he said to tell you to go on to your quarters and you have the day off to rest. He said he would see you Thursday at 0800."

Jim, "Thanks sergeant. Can you help us about getting transpiration?"

Sergeant, "Oh yes sir, I have a jeep and a driver to take you to your quarters. All the other passengers will have to wait on a base bus which will be here in 20 minutes."

Jim was dropped off at his apartment and he was glad he had his key with him. He did not intend to wake Janet. He opened the door and quietly stepped into their living room. A light was immediately turned on in their bedroom.

Janet came out of the bedroom. She stood in the bedroom doorway rubbing her eyes. She had on her short nightgown. The light behind Janet showed her figure through the flimsy negligee. Jim thought how good Janet looked, what a beautiful figure.

Jim, "Janet, honey I didn't mean to wake you. You look lovely and very desirable."

Janet, "Daring, you did not wake me. Glen had told me about what time you would be arriving. I had set my alarm."

Jim took Janet in his arms and kissed her. They embraced and kissed for several minutes. Jim could feel Janet soft skin as he ran his hands over her body.

Jim, "Oh Janet I love you so and want you. I'll clean up and let's go to bed"

Janet came out of the bedroom and stood in the doorway.

Janet, "Let's go to bed, and we both can clean up later."

The next morning Jim found out that Janet had traded a Wednesday off with a fellow nurse. She would work that Sunday. Jim was glad Janet had got the day off. They wanted to be together.

Thursday morning Jim reported to work. Glen met with Jim, Paul, and Eugene. He reviewed their report with them.

Glen, "Confidentially, the admiral had already decided to move our headquarters to Guam. Your report gave him what they need to know about living and working quarters. I understand that Admiral Nimitz thought your report was good. Your recommendations agreed with what he wanted to do."

Jim, "Then we didn't make headquarters angry?"

Glen, "No, on the contraire you guys are smart because you agreed with Admiral Nimitz. I understand that when a subordinate said some (j.g). has a nerve to recommend we move to Guam. Admiral Nimitz was alleged to say, 'that (j.g.) should be promoted.' That's what he said"

The next day during the staff meeting Glen assigned the PIO staff to follow up on find suitable target areas. Jim and his team had already completed that part of the assignment. Jim's team was given the remainder of the day off.

Jim looked up his buddies from the *Spearfish*. He went to their quarters Mac and Don were the only one's there. Jim, Don, and Mac talked for one hour. They were catching up on the news.

Jim learned that Jack and Mike were back at Pearl after their leave. Both had been assigned as a commander of a sub. They were the new subs, so both were in school at this time on the modifications of the new submarines. Al and Richard were attending a school to learn about the new subs. Don and Mac had not been assigned to a sub crew yet, but expected orders to be cut any day.

Jim reported on his Guam trip. He tried to play down their trip there as a PIO assignment. But Don and Mac were not buying it.

Mac, "Come on Jim level with you buddies. What's in the cards about us moving to Guam?"

Jim, "Fellas, I would like to tell you, but the move to Guam is top secret."

Don, "Thanks for not telling us Jim."

The following Monday morning Glen called a meeting of the PIO staff.

Glen, "Staff, this is official, we are moving our base of operations to Guam on or about the first of March. The invasion of Iwo Jima started yesterday. Admiral Lockwood's main headquarters will be on the Tender *Holland*. Our office will be on shore in the Agana Bay area. We will have sub pins or docks at Agana Bay, Port Apra, and Tumon Bay. There will be a dry dock for major repair work at Tumon."

Glen, "Start packing our files, equipment, and office machines for the trip. Our working gear will be moved by ship. Personnel will fly. I'll give complete details later. Are there any questions?"

Jim, "Sir, there is a navy hospital on Guam. It is small. With all this moving do they have plans to increase the hospital size and staff?"

Glen, "I really don't know Jim, but I would assume they will have to increase the size of the hospital to accommodate the increase in population to the island. I wouldn't tell Janet to pack her bags yet. I am afraid you and she will be apart for a short time."

The staff laughed and some kidded Jim. They were all good-natured about their ribbing of Jim. With that the staff meeting broke up. Since they only had about one week they started packing and getting their equipment, machines, files, and office furniture ready for shipment.

That evening Jim broke the news to Janet. As usual she took it in stride. Jim did not mention the hospital, because Janet might prefer to stay at Pearl. He really did not believe that, but he still did not tell her about the hospital on Guam.

Janet, "Jim do they have quarters on Guam for married couples?"

Jim, "No not yet, why do you ask?"

Janet, "I hear they are going to need additional personnel at the Guam Navy Hospital when they get their new building constructed."

Jim, "I did not know they were building a new hospital on Guam. How did you find out about a new hospital?"

Janet, "That is a military secret Jim. But I know some people in high places. One or two are only secretaries, but they know what's going on,"

Jim did not want to pursue the subject any longer. He changed the subject.

Jim and Janet spent as much time as they could together. The days passed rapidly and it was soon time for Jim to report to the embarkation station for a plane ride to Guam. By this time Iwo Jima had been secured and the Seabees and army engineers were already rebuilding the runways.

The PIO staff would breakup into two groups to fly to Guam. As Glen said this way if there was a mishap at least some of the staff would survive. The group that Jim was traveling with boarded a navy PBY for Guam.

Many of the headquarters personnel would go with their office in tact on the ship the U.S.S. Holland. There would be a fleet of submarines and ships making the trip to Guam. They would sail together and would have escorts. They should arrive in about one week.

So the move to Guam was made and there was plenty of work to set up the new operations. At the same time their jobs had to be accomplished.

The PIO staff moved into a Quonset Building. Its size was 30 feet by 50 feet and office space had been petitioned off. There were three small offices, a file room, a conference room, a small break room, and a big open work area for most of the staff. Glen, Jim, and Walter Towers, the top civilian, had an office. Each office was about a 10 by 10 feet in size.

Glen called a special meeting after they had 'settled in' and got organized.

Glen to staff: "Generally sub targets are now scarce. The B-29s and the bombing of Japan gets top priority. Many of our war patrols mounted from Guam will look for targets in the Sea of Japan as our staff had planned and recommended. They will use the Tsushima Strait to enter and exit using the La Perouse Straights as we recommended."

Jim, "Sir, when will this patrol start. Will they modify the subs as we suggested?"

Glen, "They will depart next week Jim. There will be three sets of three in the wolf pack making nine subs. This group is really three wolf packs. Their code name is 'Hell Cats.' The three packs are known as Bob Cat, Hep Cat, and Pole Cat. The modifications are being done this week."

Fred Lake asked, "Sir forgive an ignorant ensign, but what modifications?"

Glen, "Fred, you and most of the staff where not in on this planning so there is no way you would know. That's a good question. I am going to call on the officer who planned this to explain the modifications we are talking about. Jim inform the staff please."

Jim, "Aye, aye sir. The straights of the Sea of Japan are narrow. They are heavily mined and patrolled. To navigate the mine fields the newer subs have better sonar equipment for detecting mines. The subs are having cables installed down the port and starboard sides to move mine cables."

Paul joins in, "You see mines are attached to cables and anchored on the ocean floor. The cables hold the mines at various depths for surface ships. But the mine cables can snag on a sub. The cables being installed will let the cables holding mines slide along without catching of the sub. At least that's the theory."

Chief Petty Officer Ward Hendrex ask, "Sir, did your team come up with this idea? If you did I commend you and think you guys deserve special recognition."

Jim, "This idea was that of Commander Jack Jackson. He was the executive officer of the first subs into the Sea of Japan back in the summer of '43. He and Commander Saxton had a number of suggestions that we used."

Ensign Paul Emery again, "Jim is modest. He was also on that same patrol and he knew the men to talk to in planning this."

Ensign Tim Spencer, "Sir what about our recommendation on the lifeguard patrols?"

Glen, "Good question Tim. Our plan was adopted and is being followed. There are 12 submarines stationed on lifeguard duty. They have pulled 36 airman out of the drink since this started."

Chief Petty Office Eugene Slade ask, "Sir what about the plans we had for Iwo and Okanawa?"

Glen, "Well as you know Iwo Jima is now ours. The subs carried out their assignments, but they played only a minor roll. Now, and this is Top Secret, 'Operation Ice Berg' will begin soon. That is the code name for the invasion of Okanawa. As you know Okanawa is only 300 miles from the Japanese mainland. They expect a major battle. Again the submarine warfare will be minor here."

Paul asked, "Sir what about our plans for the patrols in the Luzon Strait and the East China Yellow sea?"

Glen, "Both of those areas are being patrolled. Most of the subs are out of Brisbane."

Kathy Holt, "Sir, our living quarters are rather cramped. Do you know when we will get bigger quarters?"

Irene Johnson, "Amen! And we could use some furniture."

Kathy's questions broke the ice and the staff laughed and some even applauded and whistled.

The next day Jim had a visitor. Irene, who was receptionist that day, came to Jim's office. She told him he had a visitor.

Jim, "Okay, show him in Irene."

Irene escorted Vincent "Vince" Spencer, Lieutenant (j.g.) of the Seabees to Jim's office.

Jim, "Come in Vince. It's good to see you. How are things going?"

Vince, "Hi Jimbo. I heard you guys had moved here. They said the neighborhood was going to the dogs. Ha, ha. Thought I would drop by to see if you needed anything. We are staying busy building dry docks right now. I saw some of your submarines."

Jim, "How is Philippi'?"

Vince, "Oh, he is fine. I should have brought him along. You guys made a friend for life in Philippi'. He would do anything for you."

Jim, "I've been so busy since we got here I have not had a chance to get out of the office. What about Van?"

Vince, "Oh Van is still around. He has been staying pretty busy."

Jim, "Vince, what do you know about a new navy hospital?"

Vince, "I am not working on that project, but it is coming along. They are really building a permanent type building. It may take a few more weeks yet."

Jim, "Vince do you know anything about any quarters for married men?"

Vince, "There are no such plans in the immediate future that I know about Jim. I would imagine those are in the long range plans."

Jim, "What about better and bigger quarters for our civilian female personnel? They were use to better quarters on Pearl."

Vince, "I think it will be awhile before we have bigger quarters. If they need better furnishings now I may be able to help."

Jim, "Well that cute young thing that showed you in is Irene. She and her roommate could use some furniture."

Vince, "Well call them in and let me take their request."

Jim picked up his phone and paged Kathy and Irene. Within minutes they were standing in his office.

Jim, "Kathy and Irene I would like you to meet Lieutenant (j.g.) Vincent Spencer. We call him Vince. He was a big help to my team when we were here before. He can help you with getting better furnishings."

Vince, "Ladies I am please to meet you. We don't get to see many good ole' American girls. We can't get you bigger quarters right now, but I can help get you better furnishings. Give me your list."

Kathy, "Thank you sir. We have it written out. Irene give him our list."

Vince, "You don't have to call me sir. Rank in the Seabees doesn't require the same respect as rank in the navy. Or at least I don't. You see you are looking at the oldest Lieutenant (j.g.) in the Seabees or the navy."

Irene, "Here is out list . . . . Vince. We would appreciate your help."

Vince laughed, "Jim keep these two young girls lockup. There are 5,000 horny men on this island."

Jim dismissed Kathy and Irene. He and Vince talked a few more minutes. Vince left, as he had to get back "on the job."

Jim stayed busy the next two weeks. He did visit Philippi'. He went down to the sub pins to see the submarines and crews, but didn't see any of his old buddies. He wrote Janet a letter about every three days. He got mail from Janet and his folks.

Jim thought of Janet constantly, but staying busy with his work helped pass the time. One day Jim was at his desk, when Eugene came running in the PIO building with news.

"Okanawa had been invaded!" Eugene shouted.

The PIO staff followed the news close. It seems that the initial landings were made with few casualties. But within about three days Japanese sent Kamikaze and conventional aircraft. Over 300 enemy aircraft were shot down, but six U.S. ships were sunk and 24 damaged. About 5,000 of our sailors and marines had been killed. The casualties continued to increase.

Glen called a staff meeting to give them a new assignment.

CHAPTER 23
THE LAST BATTLE

GLEN, "IT APPEARS that Okanawa is a preview of what it will be like to invade Japan. Staff we will help with invasions plans. Our job is to plan how to best use submarines to invade Japan."

Jim, "Sir, what kind of a dead-line are we under?"

Glen, "The ET for the invasion of Japan is set for September 1. It is subject to change, but they need our report within ten days."

Paul, "We had better get started then. The real problem will be how can submarines be used in the invasion of Japan?"

Glen, "Paul, you hit 'the nail on the head.' You have stated the problem very well. Let's get started. We will have a staff meeting tomorrow morning to start throwing out ideas."

The next day Eugene came into the PIO building excited and yelling, "Turn on the radio. There is news about President Roosevelt dieing."

The staff gathered around the radio and there was an announcement about the president's death yesterday April 12, 1945. The Vice President, Harry Truman, was sworn in as president. The new president said that all plans and policies would continue as is.

Jim was stunned. FDR had been president for three and one-fourth terms. Jim knew they would continue to do their jobs. Even the president's death would not keep events from occurring.

Within a few days news reached the PIO staff that Mussolini was captured near the Swiss border and killed by partisans. A few days later news was released that Hitler was dead.

Glen and Jim were talking over a cup of coffee one morning.

Glen, "Well at least two of the three Axis leaders are dead. Now if we can get Tojo and Hirohito it will be a grand slam."

Jim, "Japan is going to be a 'tough nut to crack.' I hear that the invasion forces will be the biggest invasion force ever gathered when we go into Japan."

Glen, "Yes that is true. The master plan is to land in three or four places at once with a million men.

A few days later Germany surrendered. Field Marshall Jodl signed the unconditional surrender agreement at Eisenhower's headquarter at Rheims, France. On May 8th President Truman and Prime Minister Churchill declared V.E. Day (Victory in Europe).

Vince delivered new furniture to Kathy and Irene's quarters. The girls were glad for the furniture. Jim and Vince were talking during a coffee break after Vince had made the delivery.

Jim, "Thanks for the furniture Vince. Did you hear? President Truman declared V.E. Day. Great news. Things seemed to get happening a faster pace."

Vince, "You are right Jim. Remember how slow and infrequent war news was during 1942 and 43'? Now we are living in a faster paced war. Now if only the Japs would surrender maybe we could go home."

Jim, "Yes events are occurring more often and the news, for the most part is good for us. The B-29s are fire bombing the Jap cities and other targets. A few days ago our decoders found out that the Japanese had closed their schools and ordered all over six years of age to war service."

Vince, "Yeah I heard that. That is hard to believe, but it will be costly when we do invade Japan. Jim, I enjoyed talking to you, but I have to get back to work so long buddy."

Jim, "Thanks again for the new furniture. I enjoyed talking to you Vince. See you later."

Glen called Jim into his office. Jim was wondering what Glen wanted. Had he fowled up?

Glen, "Jim, I have good news for you. Your promotion to lieutenant came through. Congratulations. Now you are a full Lieutenant equal to a captain in the army or marines."

Jim, "Thank you sir. I appreciate it."

Glen, "It is well deserved. You have done an outstanding job on every assignment you have had. This was supposed to have come through last month, but it seems only combatants made the list last month."

Jim, "Glen I appreciate this. You know it takes us all to do the job. Paul and Eugene deserve a lot of credit."

Glen, "Well Paul and Eugene are on the promotion list. Paul is now a (j.g). and Eugene is now a Master CPO. I plan to announce your promotion to the staff Jim. I'll call Paul and Eugene in now and let you give them the news."

Glen paged Paul and Eugene to come to his office. Within five minutes both were standing before Glen.

Glen, "Paul, Eugene, . . . Jim has some news for you."

Jim, "Paul you have been promoted to lieutenant (j.g.) and Eugene you have been promoted to Master Chief Petty Officer. The promotions were effective the first of this month. Congratulations, you both earned it."

Paul, "Thank you sir. I appreciate it. But what about you Jim?"

Eugene, "Yes sir, you led our team. Surely you deserve a promotion?"

Jim with a low laugh, "Thanks fellows, but I'm on the same promotion list."

Glen picked up his intercom speaker, "Attention staff. I have good news. The following named personnel are on this month's promotion list: Lieutenant (j.g.) James Rush to lieutenant, Ensign Paul Emery to Lieutenant (j.g.), and Chief Petty Officer Eugene Slade to Master CPO. In honor of these men we will close the office one hour early and adjourn to the PX for a beer. The drinks are on me."

The PIO staff clapped and whistled. Some even whooped and hooted.

Eugene with a smile, "The staff is really happy about getting off an hour early and getting free beer too."

Eugene said, "I know they are glad for the promotions in the office. It is recognition that they think we did a good job. Actually I think the entire office has done a good job."

Glen, "Oh Jim, you may be interested in this message. Your buddy, George MacDonald is coming in on the sub, *Sea Dog*. They are coming in from Pearl. I imagine they will get lifeguard patrol duty between Iwo and Japan."

Jim, "I glad to get that news sir. Do you have an estimated TOA?"

Glen, "They are scheduled to arrive at 1300. Jim take the afternoon off and meet that sub."

Jim, "Aye, aye, sir. Thanks for letting me off."

Glen dismissed the team and they went back to their work. Jim did leave to go meet Mac at 1300. He would be glad to see Mac. Jim wondered if Mac had news from Janet. Oh well he would soon know.

The U.S.S. *Sea Dog* was on time. That surprised Jim. He was waiting for the crew to disembark. They soon started out. Jim knew the officers would be among the last. After about 15 minutes he saw Mac coming down the gangplank.

Jim yelled, "Mac, over here."

Mac came running over to Jim and gave Jim a big handshake and pat on the back.

Mac, "Gosh it is good to see you Jim. I was hoping you would be here. We just came over from Pearl. I guess we will work out of Guam, but some of our subs will work out of Pearl."

Jim, "Mac, did you get to see Janet before you left?"

Mac, "I sure did Jim. I went to the hospital and talked to Janet the day before we sailed. She sends her love. Jim I think that girl is crazy about you."

Jim, "Well how did she look? Was she well?"

Mac, "She looked well and fit Jim. How did you manage to land such a good-looking girl? It couldn't have been you charm or personality."

Jim, "Very funny. What happened to Don, Al, and Richard?"

Mac, "Don got lucky. He was assigned to headquarters working for Larry. Al and Richard were assigned to the *Shark*. Oh yeah, Al was promoted to (j.g.) last month. Say can you tell me where the BOQs are?"

Jim, "Yes I can direct you. Let's hitch a ride."

About that time Lieutenant Samuel "Van" Vandergrift drove by in a jeep.

Jim, "Hey Van . . . how about a lift."

Van, "Jim you old son of a gun. I have been meaning to look you up, but have been busy. It's good to see you. Hop in,"

Jim and Mac get in the jeep with Van. Van slowly drives Jim and Mac to their destination.

Jim, "Van this is my good buddy George "Mac" MacDonald. Everyone calls him Mac. He just came in on the submarine *Sea Dog*."

Van, "Glad to meet you Mac. Did you come in from Pearl?"

Mac, "Yes I did. It's good to meet you Van. Jim how do you know Van?"

Jim, "Well it's a long story, but Van was the liaison officer when I was here on an assignment two or three months ago."

Van, "Congratulations Jim on the promotion. Where are the new bars"?

Jim, "How did you know Van? I just found out today."

Van, "Remember I work at headquarters and know people in the management. Did you know even Philippi' was pulling for you. He gave headquarters a glowing report of you activities. You know that you and your team are heroes."

Before Jim could ask about Philippi' Mac could not stay quite any longer.

Mac, "You got promoted Jim? Why didn't you tell me? What was the mission you were on and who is Philippi'?"

Jim, "I'll explain all that later. Right now we are at the BOQ?"

Mac, "It looks like a prefab tin building to me."

Jim, "Mac I will have you to know that this is a Quonset building. It is the latest thing in architect on Guam."

Mac carried his duffle bag in and checked in at a desk just inside the door. The 'clerk' gave him a key and a room number. It seems that he would be sharing a room with two other officers.

Mac and Jim went down the hall to his room. Mac unlocked the door and they went in. There were three bunks and it was obvious that two were all ready taken. Mac took the third one and sat down on his bunk.

Mac, "Jim sit down and let's talk. Oh I almost forgot I have a letter for you from Janet and she forwarded a letter from your folks."

While Mac went to the head to clean up Jim read the letter from Janet. He was so glad to get the letter he read it over and over.

Janet had pretty handwriting Jim thought as he read her letter. She told Jim how much she missed him. She wrote about her work at the hospital. Ginny and Dr. Hubbard sent their best regards. She told Jim the news from her parents.

Jim felt upbeat and good after reading Janet's letter.

Mac soon returned and he and Jim continued to talk. They exchanged information and Jim brought Mac up to day on his job activities regarding Guam. Mac told Jim of his last two patrols. Both patrols involved lifeguard duties.

Mac, "Oh Jim, have you heard that Simon Lake died? Do you know who he was?"

Jim, "He was the father of the modern submarine. Remember we learned that in sub school. He lived in Bridgeport, Connecticut. Let me see . . . he invented the modern sub in 1894."

Mac, "You have a good memory Jim. I might have known I couldn't fool you."

Jim, "Mac things are happening all over the Pacific. It won't be long until we invade Japan itself. We have just secured Okinawa. It took 83 days. It took the 7th and 96th army divisions and two marine divisions to take that island. Our casualty rate was high."

Mac, "Say I heard on the radio that President Truman will ask the Senate to ratify the United Nations Charter."

Jim, "I hadn't heard that. The last I heard was they were meeting to form a United Nations in SanFranscio."

Jim and Mac continued their discussion of world events. Jim had asked Mac to join him at the PX as the PIO office was meeting there to celebrate. Mac was tired and said he would rest up. Jim left and went to the PX.

The PIO staff sat around in the snack bar drinking beer, cokes, or other soft drinks for an hour. They talked and broke up and went to their quarters. Jim had almost forgot about the letter from his folks. He was anxious to read it.

Jim read his folks letter after he got to his quarters. He found out that his sister, Shirley, had graduated from high school with honors. She had a scholarship at Southwestern State. She wanted to be a schoolteacher. She had taken a summer job at *Sears* to earn some school spending money.

Jim learned that his brother Joel would be a sophomore in high school next school year and was playing summer baseball. His brother Noel had finished the 7th grade. Mom and Dad were well.

Jim muttered to himself, "I still think of Shirley and the boys as they were four years ago. Gosh they are growing up. I won't know them when I get home."

Jim missed his folks and home. He missed Janet even more.

Jim said to himself, "I'll be glad when this war is over."

Jim in a prayerful attitude out loud said, "Lord, after this is over, if I complain just let me remember this war and then I'll realize I will not have a legitimate complaint. And if that won't do it let me remember the Great Depression. Help me to try to make this world a better one for people who need help."

Jim, "Thank you Lord for our nation and letting me live during these historical times. Thank you for Janet, thank you for my family and friends. Be with us and bless us. Forgive me for my sins. I pray in Jesus name. Amen."

Jim usually prayed after he got ready for bed and just before he went to sleep. The training of his childhood had stayed with him. Jim remembered that we just don't pray when times are bad, but prayer is appropriate all the time. He was convinced that God had a hand in the United States and her allies winning the war.

All of a sudden the stillness was shattered as an air raid siren sounded. Jim immediately ran outside. An enlisted man was running by and yelled that a bunch of Jap Kamikaze planes were spotted a few miles out. Jim felt that the Kamikaze planes would be after the navy vessels and not land targets, but he headed toward the bomb shelter to play it safe. He stopped at the shelter door to see what was going to happen.

Jim remembered that there was an air force base on Guam now. A squadron of B-29s was stationed there. The Kamikazes could be after that airfield. He could now see several Jap planes about 10 miles away. U.S. fighter planes were in the air engaging the enemy planes. By the time the

Jap planes made it to Guam there was just four left. The anti air craft fire from the ships and the land opened up hitting at lease three of the planes. The remaining plane had been damaged and it crashed on to a roadway.

The next day Glen called a staff meeting. As usual the PIO staff met in the conference room. Glen had the usual place at the head.

Glen, "Good morning staff. I have some news for you. We have no new assignments as far as submarine patrols. They will use subs to blockade Japan and to do lifeguard duty."

Jim, "That sounds like we may be out of a job."

Glen, "No, not quite yet Jim. Staff, here are your jobs for now: Jim, Paul, and I will sit in on the skipper's reports of action on their patrols in the Japanese Inland Sea. I want every one else to work on a plan as to how to best deploy our submarines around Japan."

Paul, "They are back—the subs that went to the Sea of Japan? How successful were they? Did we lose any subs?"

Glen, "Paul, I do not know. We will find the answers to your questions at that meeting. It will be at 1000 hours tomorrow."

The next day Glen, Jim, and Paul went to the headquarters building. They were ushered into a very large room. There were table's set up in a 'U' shape. Officers started filing in within a few minutes.

Jim noticed that submarine officers were easily identified. Their faces looked pale and tired. The emotional strain had been heavy and its effects were evident. The last two officers came into the room and were seated at the head table. They were Admiral Lockwood and Commander Larry Saxton. The admiral opened the meeting.

Admiral Lockwood, "Good morning gentlemen."

"Good morning sir," came the group reply.

Admiral, "We are here this morning to hear reports from our skippers and others about their patrol in the Sea of Japan. Before we get into that I think it is fitting for each of us to introduce our selves. You know who I am. Incidentally I will be leaving to attend to another matter is about 20 minutes. Lets start with you Commander Saxton"

Larry, "I am Commander Larry Saxton, head of the planning."

As they started around the table Jim counted eight sub skippers and eight XOs. There had been nine subs. Two officer times nine would be 18 Jim thought. One sub did not make it Jim thought. There were four other officers from headquarters beside Jim, Glen, and Paul. There were three other officers sitting along one wall. They were other officers from the submarines.

After the introductions were made Admiral Lockwood rose to his feet. The room got very quiet.

Admiral, "Congratulations to the Hell Cats. You have just turned out one of the most successful submarine operations of the war. I am saddened by the loss of the *Bonefish*. Unfortunately she and all hands were lost. I have personally read all the skipper's reports and know every sub sunk at least one enemy vessel. I know one sub sunk as many as six ships in 10 days. You are invited to a celebration at the officer's club at 2100 hours tomorrow. I am proud of you. Thanks for doing a good job."

The Admiral left and Larry rose and spoke.

Larry, "Now we will ask the sub skippers to give their reports. We will start with Joe."

Jim listened closely. He wanted to know if the PIOs suggestions worked. He learned that the boats went through the straight in packs of threes. Some boats stayed deep—below 150 feet to avoid the mines. Some of the boats had the FM sound head mounted near the keel. They reported no FM contacts were made which could possibly mines.

The sub skippers continued reporting. They told about sinking the enemy ships. The fairing cables leading from the hull to the edge of the stern plans worked very well. Several skippers reported that mine cables slid off and past the stern planes.

It seems that the only mistake made was the sinking of a Russian ship of 12,000 tons. Many of the skippers reported barreling thru the straight at 18 knots on the surface at night when coming out.

Jim looked at Larry and winked. Larry smiled at Jim. Both knew that Larry and Jack had recommended this maneuver in coming out of the straight.

After three hours of reporting the meeting adjourned. Glen, Jim, and Paul stayed around talking to various individuals. Jim was happy to see Larry and asked Larry about his family. They all soon parted. Glen, Jim, and Paul decided to go the mess hall and eat lunch.

After Glen, Jim, and Paul returned to the office Walter Towers met them and requested he meet with them in Jim's office. Walter was acting very mysterious.

Walter, "Glen I have just been delivered a TOP SECRET message. I signed for it and read it, but it is really for you."

Glen, "That's okay Walter. We are all cleared for Top Secret. Let me read this.

Glen reads the message and after a minute he looks up at the group.

Glen, "This is good news. I don't know why we would want to keep this a secret unless we don't want the Japs to know."

Jim, "Well what is the news Glen?"

Glen, "Navy carrier planes have hit navel targets at Nagasaki, Kure, Kobe, and Tokyo. They have destroyed at least 500 enemy planes. Army air force bombers have hit several major Japanese cities on Honshu. Within two days time over 100 enemy ships have been sunk. They believe we have destroyed the Japanese navy."

Glen, "I am authorized to let 50% of my staff take a five to ten day leave if I deem it necessary."

Walter, "What would we do with five to ten days? That's not enough time to go home to the states."

Paul laughed and said, "Well we could always take a day or two to see the sights on Guam."

Glen, "Aw I don't know. Jim would have plenty of time to go the Pearl and see Janet."

CHAPTER 24
BACK TO PEAR

JIM, "THAT WOULD be great to go see Janet. But I don't want to go unless you really want me to and I wouldn't want to knock someone else out of going on leave."

Glen, "Very noble Jim, but you heard what Walter said, who really wants to use their leave if they don't have a good reason? I will authorize up to ten days leave for you Jim. Go send a message to Pearl. I'll check and see what air transportation is available."

Jim went to the communications building and had a message sent to the Navy Hospital at Pearl Harbor for Janet. In the meantime Glen had found out that a navy PBY was leaving in four hours for Pearl.

Jim rushed to his quarters and packed a carry on bag. Paul checked out a jeep and a driver drove him to the dock area where a PBY was going to take off. Within another hour Jim was airborne on his way to see Janet.

Jim estimated that their flying time would be about 12 hours. As usual he slept most of the way. It seems like the only time Jim could catch up on his sleep is when flying. He dreamed of Janet and how good it would be to see her. After about eight hours one of the crewmen came back and woke Jim.

He said, "Sir the pilot wanted me to wake all passengers. We are experiencing some engine trouble and may have to ditch."

Jim rubbing his eyes asked, "Huh, what . . . how far are we from Pearl? What is your name?"

Crewman, "Sir my name is Zach Hamilton, airman 2nd class."

Jim, "Thanks Airman Hamilton. I am Lieutenant Jim Rush"

Zach, "I think we are about 1,000 miles from Pearl sir. I'll double check with the navigator if you wish."

Jim, "No, that's okay. How serious is the engine trouble?"

Zach, "I think it's number three engine. It keeps missing and once and a while it back fires."

Zach alerted two other passengers in Jim's compartment and left to warn others.

Jim thought, "This is a heck of a note. I get leave to see Janet and on the way crash in the sea. Gosh a guy could get killed."

Jim tried not to think of crashing into the sea, but think of Janet and home.

They continued flying, but at a slower speed. Jim thought maybe the pilot had feathered number three. He looked out a cabin window, but could not see anything in the night sky.

There were two other passengers in this part of the plane with Jim. One of the passengers was navy and one marine. Both were enlisted men. Jim thought that maybe they should talk and get their minds off the engine trouble.

Jim introduced himself to the two men. They told their names and he asked where they were from. They talked about their families and home. This did help pass the time and took their minds off the engine trouble.

Zach came back and reported to Jim and his traveling companions that the radioman had notified air/sea rescue of their location and would report their position every 30 minutes.

The Marine, "Well, this is a sea plane ain't it? It could land on the water and we wouldn't have to crash. As big as our navy is there is bound to be a ship nearby."

The Sailor, "Yeah this is a sea plane, but it isn't that simple. The sea could be too rough or a big wave could hit us or there may be a rain squall or we might catch on fire before he could set us down."

The Marine, "Gosh you are just full of good news."

Jim laughed, "Okay fellows let's change the subject. Why are you guys going to Pearl?"

Jim directed their thoughts to something beside the problem at hand. The time droned on. The time seem to pass so slowly. But Jim reasoned that with each minute passing they were getting that much closer to Hawaii. He wish now that he had not sent the message to Janet. Maybe she would not get it until tomorrow.

Then Jim thought of something. "Janet's birthday was one day next week. Anyway maybe I could still get her a birthday present. Crossing the inter-national date line messed up the dates when you were moving back and forth across the Pacific."

Zach came back into the compartment. He motioned for Jim and his traveling companions to put their headsets on.

Zach said, "Put you ear phones on. The pilot wants to make an announcement."

Jim and his two fellow-passengers put their head sets on as directed.

The pilot, "This is Lieutenant Craig Sikes, your pilot. Because of engine trouble we are going to set down on the sea. The sea is relative calm. Please brace yourselves and take the crash positions. The good news is that we are only about 200 miles from Pearl so we should be rescued shortly."

Many thoughts went through Jim's head as he took a crash position.

Jim said to his fellow passengers, "If the sea is calm and if this pilot is good we should have a fairly smooth landing. If we crash take what you can to help us survive. One of you grab that first aid kit on the bulk head and the other one grab that flare gun and I'll get a canteen of water."

Marine, "Yes sir, I think we are ready for the landing."

As the big plane hit the water things seemed pretty smooth to Jim. He thought that two of the engines were out. It was still dark outside. After the pilot landed he came on the inter radio.

Lieutenant Craig Sikes, "This is your pilot. We had a safe landing, but I don't know how long this airplane will float. Let's all breakout the life rafts and be ready to abandon the plane."

Jim looked out a window and said, "It looks calm, but the waves can be calm and still be big enough to capsize this plane."

The Sailor, "Sir I can't swim."

Jim, "That's okay, you have on a life jacket and it will hold you up in the water."

Marine, "What! You're in the navy and you can't swim. Didn't they teach that in boot camp? I guess you were never a boy scout?"

Jim thought this would all be very funny if it was not so serious. He guessed that the pilot would make the decision on abandoning the plane. He thought of Janet and hoped that they did not report that his plane went down.

Craig came back though the fuselage of the plane checking his passengers and giving them information.

Lieutenant Craig Sikes said, "We are going to leave the plane. Water has started to some in. Do not panic, we have plenty of time. We will break out three rubber rafts. Each raft will hold six to eight men. We have a total of 11 people on board. One raft is in your compartment."

Zach pulled the raft out of its storage area. He started toward the outside hatch for this compartment.

Airman 2nd Class Zach Hamilton said, "Follow me. We will inflate this once we are out of the hatch."

Jim to his fellow travelers, "Men be sure to get the first aid kit, the flare gun, and I'll get a canteen of water. Pick up anything else that we might need."

Zach, "That's a good idea sir. I have a knife, matches, and a compass. There is an emergency kit in the raft."

Zach opened the hatch and held the raft out side and pulled the ring to inflate the raft. Within a few seconds the raft was inflated and the men were scrambling out of the PBY to get into the raft. Water was already six to ten inches deep in the plane.

The other two rafts were launched from the front of the plane. The pilot, copilot, navigator, radioman, and three crewmen were in the two rafts. The pilot instructed all the rafts to paddle out a few feet and attached to one another.

Craig said, "There are some short pieces of cord in the raft. Latch all three rafts together. We do not want to separate. Now lets paddle out away from the plane so that when it sinks it will not capsize out rafts."

They paddled east toward Hawaii. The sun was just coming up and it gave a glow in the east. Jim could see a rainsquall. Within 20 minutes the PBY sank. It was sad to see their lifeline go under. Now they were all alone on the ocean. They began to take inventory of their supplies.

Four hours later and 3400 miles away on Guam the next morning Glen was reading a dispatch that the PIO had just received.

Glen, "Attention staff we just got word that Lieutenant Rush's plane crashed. We don't have any other details at this time."

Paul, "Gosh I hope Jim is okay."

Glen, "I am going over to headquarters and see if I can get more news. Paul take over and I'll return as soon as possible."

Glen knew that if anyone would know what was going on it would be Larry. Larry was in headquarters for the subs on the ship *Holland*. He took a whaleboat out to the *Holland*. He went to the Admirals office area. He found Larry and asked him about the PBY that Jim was in.

Larry, "I have been following this closely. The PBY radioed in last night that one of its engines was giving trouble, but they would feather the prop and continue on."

Glen, "About where were they then sir?"

Larry, "They were just a little over ½ way. They were ordered to continue on. They were given a choice to divert to Wake Island. The pilot opted not to do that saying that would put them out of their way and Pearl was just as close."

Glen, "Any other news sir?"

Larry, "The PBY radioman gave a navigation check about every 30 minutes. Then about eight hours ago the PBY reported that a second engine was heating up and missing. They travel about another 100 miles and had to feather that engine. They were afraid it might catch fire. It was at this point that they started losing altitude and the Pilot decided to put her down on the sea."

Glen, "Then they didn't crash?"

Larry, "The last communicate we had said they had landed, but were going to take to life rafts and ask for a rescue. They reported no casualties."

Glen, "What about rescue? Will they send a plane or a ship?"

Larry, "I can't say, because Pearl is in charge of the rescue. But I would think they should be rescued within a few hours. I sure they will send the nearest ship"

Glen, "Thank you sir. I appreciate the information. I had better get back and give the news to my staff. They were all concerned.

Jim, Zach, the sailor, and the marine, were in one raft. The sun was hot and it reflected off the ocean. The rainsquall that Jim had spotted earlier had dissipated. The sea was fairly calm although once and a while a big wave would hit them.

Craig had a pair of binoculars and kept a lookout toward the east. The hours seemed to go by so slow. About noon they passed some C-rations around. Jim was not hungry but did eat a little anyway. He took four or five big gulps of water.

Time was going so slow and it was boring time. Jim laid back and thought about Janet. He wondered what she was doing. He said a silent prayer and fell asleep. He could not get a deep sleep, but just cat napped. He felt his face burning from the sun and wet his handkerchief and put it over his face.

Craig yelled, "I see a ship! Hey I see a ship, it's a submarine and it's coming our way. Give me the flare gun."

Craig shot the flare gun. The sub answered with a flare. All the men in the life rafts cheered.

Jim said, "The first day of my leave was spent on the sea being rescued by a sub."

Within in an hour the men in the rafts were being helped aboard the submarine. Just as Jim was being helped on board he hear a familiar voice.

The voice, "Hey Jim. Jim Rush what are you doing in a raft."

Jim looked up and there was Mike Moreland coming to give him a big hug.

Jim, "Mike I am so glad to see you. Now I can tell you how important that lifeguard duty was. Thanks for saving us. So you are the skipper of this boat?"

Mike, "Yes. You are now aboard the *USS Stingray*. Look her over. This is one of the later models."

Jim went below and the others survivors followed him. They figured he knew his way around a sub since he had been in the sub service. They went to the galley and were served coffee and a ham and cheese sandwiches.

Mike soon joined them and asked them about their "crash" and how long they had to wait to be rescued. Mike told the others of some of Jim's sub service. Mike left and said they would radio Pearl that all were safe.

Mike, "We should be back at Pearl within about four hours. Welcome aboard men"

Craig, "Captain we thank you and your crew. We appreciate what you did."

Mike, "You are welcome. See you later."

Mike left and the crash survivors had a lot to talk about. As one of the airman said "We experience something we will never forget."

The *Stingray* and her passengers reached Pearl Harbor in the mid afternoon. The air-crew and the passengers were told to report to a certain office for a debriefing. Jim and the other passengers were soon dismissed, but the aircrew stayed to give additional details of the flight and the crash.

It donned on Jim that he lost his carry on luggage. He discovered that the aircrew had saved the mail and other items, but not their luggage. He would need a change of clothing. He stopped at the quartermaster and signed for some clothing. He needed two pair of kakis (shirts and trousers), a tie, some underwear, socks, a cap, and shoes.

Jim said to himself, "Janet will be getting off work soon and will be at the apartment in about one hour."

Jim got a ride to the apartment. He went in and took a good bath and shaved. He had just finished cleaning up and was sitting on the sofa when the front door opened. It was Janet and she was startled.

Janet, "Jim you are here already."

Jim jump up from the sofa and took Janet in his arms. He gave her a big hug and then they kissed one another. Jim could feel her body against his. They kissed and sat on the divan, continuing to kiss.

After a while they just sat looking at one another.

Janet, "Oh, Jim I am so glad to see you. I just got your message today that you were coming to Pearl on leave. I am glad you got leave. I have missed you so."

Jim, "I just got to the apartment and cleaned up. I did not have time to come to the hospital to see you. Oh honey, I've missed you too."

Janet, "Gosh Jim, I need to fix supper."

Jim, "Forget that honey. I tell you what let's adjourn to the bedroom and then I'll take you to the officer's club for supper. We need to celebrate.

That night Jim and Janet just sat on the sofa listening to music and holding one another close. They talked in low voices as though they did not want anyone to hear them.

The next day Janet had to work. Jim slept and spent most of the day resting. He had not realized how tired he had been. Janet always made him feel good and seemed to give him energy. That afternoon he did clean up the apartment. It did not need much cleaning as Janet had it in good shape.

Janet came in about 5:30 p.m. She looked tired to Jim. He realized that she was under a strain—trying to be with him, keep the apartment, and work.

Jim, "Janet you are quite a gal you know. You have put together work, marriage, and loving me in a winning way. I love you honey. You look bushed. Why don't you go lie down for a few minutes and then I'll take you out for supper?"

Janet, "Thanks Jim, but can we afford to eat out?"

Jim, "Oh sure, I got paid just before my leave started. You are now looking at a full Lieutenant and with the increase in pay we will celebrate."

Janet, "You got promoted! Why didn't you let me know?"

Jim, "I told you in my last letter. I guess you haven't got it yet."

Janet rested and cleaned up. She looks great Jim thought.

Jim, "Janet you look beautiful, honey. No wonder I married you. You have beauty, charm, personality, and brains. It is all package so wonderful."

Janet, "How you do go on, but I like it. You're not bad yourself."

They went to the officer's club for supper. As they were eating Jim looked up and saw Mike Moreland. He thought Mike was on patrol duty, but he guessed Mike was in and out of Pearl.

Mike saw Jim and Janet. He came over to their table.

Mike, "Jim and Janet good to see you. How is my favorite couple? Janet did Jim tell you about us pulling him out of the drink?"

Janet, "No, Mike he didn't"

Mike, "Maybe I'm talking out of school, but Jim's plane crashed in the sea and we rescued him and the crew and the other passengers."

Jim, "I hadn't got around to telling Janet about our trip stop-over."

Mike, "Well I see that my table is ready I had better be on my way. I wish you two the best of everything."

Mike walked off and Jim and Janet sat looking at one another.

Janet, "You weren't going to tell me about the crash were you?"

Jim, "Yes, I was Janet, but I was waiting for the right moment. Besides we didn't crash. Honey, don't ever think I will keep any secrets from you. I love you too much."

Janet, "I am glad you were not hurt and that you are here now safe and sound. Thank the good Lord."

Jim, "Janet tomorrow is Saturday. Do you have to work tomorrow or Sunday?"

Janet, "No thank goodness. I have the weekend off. When I told the Director of Nurses that you had leave she worked the schedule to give me the weekend off plus Monday through Wednesday."

Jim, "I am glad. You can rest up and we can enjoy our time together."

Jim got up early on Saturday morning. Janet was still asleep. He let her sleep and he slipped out to go to the commissary. He wanted to buy Janet a birthday present. But he did not know what to buy her. Janet was one year and six months younger than Jim so that meant she would be 21 on August 8th. This would be a special birthday.

Jim purchased a necklace and matching earrings. He knew she couldn't wear the jewelry with her uniform at work, but there would be special occasions. He had the present gift-wrapped. He hurried back to the apartment. He was hoping Janet was not up yet.

Janet was up, but was in the bathroom. This gave Jim the opportunity to hide her present. He put the gift on the top shelf in the bedroom closet.

The next few days seem to past fast for Jim and Janet. They had a swim at Wakhii Beach, a picnic, a movie, a drive around Oahu, and attended two parties with friends. There were still enough reminders of war that the topic was never off their minds.

The day before her birthday Janet went to the commissary to buy some groceries. Jim stayed at the apartment resting in an "easy chair."

Janet rushed into the apartment carrying a sack of groceries. She was very exited.

Janet yelled, "Jim turn on the radio. I just heard that we dropped one bomb on Hiroshima wiping out the whole city."

Jim turned the radio on. The local station carried NBC news. There was an announcement on the radio.

Radio announcer, "President Truman has just released a statement that a lone U.S. B-29 dropped an atomic bomb on Hiroshima yesterday, August 6, 1945. The one bomb was as powerful as 30,000 tons of TNT. That is all we know now, but stay tuned for more news later."

Jim, "An atomic bomb? I don't think I ever heard of it before. It is hard to believe that one bomb wiped out a city? Surely the Japs will surrender after this. We have their ports blockaded and we are fire bombing their cities. How can they keep fighting?"

Jim kept his ear to the radio.

Jim, "If I could talk to the guys at PIO I bet I could get more details."

Janet, "I don't know. If the PIO did not know about an atomic bomb it was TOP SECRET and not even navy headquarters knew I doubt that they know any more than you do."

Jim, "You are right of course. I guess I wish some of the fellas were around so we could discuss things."

Janet, "Are you saying they would be better company than me?"

Jim, "Oh no! Of course not honey. It just that this could be the end of the war and I am on leave. But loving every minute of being with you."

The next day Jim sang 'happy birthday' to Janet. He gave her the gift he bought.

Janet, "Oh Jim, you remembered my birthday. You hadn't let on so I thought maybe you had forgotten. Thank you for the necklace and ear rings. Now I have more jewelry to put in my jewelry music box you got me for Christmas. I'll always remember this birthday."

Jim, "If I ever forget your birthday it will be because I have 'lost my mind.' Besides we must remember that the first atomic bomb was dropped two days before you birthday. Happy birthday honey."

Jim took Janet in his arms and kissed her. Janet and Jim clung to one another for several minutes. Later that day they went to a movie on station. Jim was more interested in the newsreel than the feature film.

The next day Jim and Janet decided to clean the apartment. They were busy doing that when there was a knock at the door. Janet went to the door and there stood Mac.

Janet, "Mac, come in. What are you doing here?"

Jim, "Mac, its good to see you buddy, how are you?"

Mac, "I am fine Jim. I was in the neighborhood and thought I would drop in"

Janet, "Mac let me fix you something to drink. Would you care for ice tea, lemonade, or coke? Sit down and make yourself comfortable."

Janet served Mac a coke. She brought one for Jim and herself.

Jim, "Mac bring me up to date on the news about yourself."

Mac, "Well the *Sea Dog* was detached to Pearl. We were doing lifeguard duty between the Marinas and Japan. We developed some kind of a problem with our sonar and they sent us to Pearl to get it repaired."

Jim, "Mac what do you think about the atomic bomb on Hiroshima? Think the Japs will surrender now?"

Mac, "I hope it will keep us from having to invade Japan proper. But haven't you heard the news today?"

Jim, "No we haven't had the radio on or even been out of the apartment."

Mac, "Just a few minutes ago it was announced that a second atomic bomb was dropped on Nagasaki."

Janet, "No we hadn't heard. Jim why don't you see if you can get some news on the radio?"

Jim turned the radio on and was turning the dial knob to see if he could get some news. He found a news program in progress. They heard the announcement, but there wasn't mush more than a short one about a single plane dropping an atomic bomb on Nagasaki. The city was completely destroyed.

Jim, "Well Janet we will always remember that the nation celebrated your 21st birthday by dropping an atomic bomb two days day before and one day after your birthday."

Mac, "Happy birthday Janet . . . a belated happy birthday. Say I will treat you two to lunch . . . if you haven't already eaten."

Janet, "No we have not had lunch. We had a late breakfast so we were going to have a late lunch."

Mac treated Jim and Janet to lunch. He brought them up to date on the news from his family. After lunch they returned to the apartment. They continued talking and after awhile thought a short nap would be in order.

After a short, but restful nap they woke up.

Mac, "Janet I hope you don't mind but I invited Ginny over when she gets off at the hospital."

Janet, "Why of course I don't mind. After all Ginny and I are friends, but why would she what to see you Mac? Ha, ha, just funning."

Jim, "Maybe we could go out on the town."

Janet, "I don't know about that because Ginny and I have to work tomorrow. So we have to get up early. You two sailors can loaf and sleep late."

Mac, "Yeah you are right. We need to get you girls home early."

About 5:30 p.m. Ginny knocked at the apartment door. Mac let her in. They embraced and kissed. Jim and Janet sat looking bewildered.

Janet, "Come in Ginny. Say is there something going on between you two that we need to know about?"

Ginny, "Mac and I are just very good friends. When he is in town we try to get together. Did you hear the latest news? They are saying several thousand people were killed at Nagasaki. Washington has been in communication with Tokyo"

Mac, "Surely the Japs will surrender after this."

Jim, "The Japanese will never surrender they may accept the cease fire or peace terms, but they will not use the word "surrender'. They really don't believe in surrendering. They have proven that by the way they have abused our POW's. It is estimated that they have killed or let die 30 % of our POWs. In their eyes it is a disgrace to surrender"

Mac, "Hey let's forget the war and go get dinner at the officer's club"

Jim, "Okay Mac, but we will go Dutch. You got our lunch, but not our dinner. Incidentally we call it supper in Oklahoma."

All laughed. The girls 'freshened up' and they all went to the "O" club.

After supper they all attended a USO dance. Jim and Janet danced two or three waltzes and Ginny and Mac danced a couple of fast rumba dances.

Jim and Janet returned to their apartment. Mac took Ginny to her quarters.

Jim to Janet, "Honey do you think Ginny and Mac are serious?"

Janet, "I doubt it. Ginny told me once she would not get engaged again until the war is over. I think you knew that she had a fiancée who was killed."

Jim, "Yes I do remember that, but sometimes love and a hot romance can make a person change their mind."

Janet, "I guess so. Well we need to get to bed. I have to get up at 6 a.m. and go to work."

Jim, "Janet, tomorrow I will check in with the AG office and see about a flight to Guam next Monday. My leave is up Tuesday so I'll need to leave Monday or maybe even Sunday."

Janet, "Oh that is right. I did not want to think about your leaving."

Jim embraced Janet and they kissed. They partly disrobed as they made their way to the bedroom.

The next morning Jim fixed breakfast while Janet was getting ready for work. He fried bacon, scrabbled eggs, and had toast and jelly on the table when Janet came into the kitchen. Jim was sitting at the table drinking his coffee and reading the morning newspaper.

Janet, "Jim that looks good. You deserve a big kiss for that."

That was all the prodding Jim needed. He grabbed Janet and kissed her and fondled her breast.

Janet, "Careful honey, don't get my uniform wrinkled or dirty. There is always tonight. I had better eat and be on my way."

Jim, "Yes I guess so."

Jim released his embrace of Janet. They sat down and ate their breakfast chatting about the latest letters from their folks.

After Janet left to go to the hospital Jim showered and shaved. He did not have his navy blue dress uniform, but thought, "I'll wear my khaki's after all that is the summer dress uniform."

Jim said to himself, "I'll go see what the Adjunct General's Office has in the way of transportation back to Guam.

Jim checked in at the officers records division at the AG office.

A CPO at the desk said, "Yes sir, may I help you?"

Jim, "Yes I am Lieutenant James Rush. Here is a copy of my orders. I need transportation back to my unit on Guam."

CPO, "Yes sir. Let me check with air operations."

The CIO left and came back within a few minutes.

CPO, "Sir, we have a PBY flying out at 1000 hours on Sunday and we have a Catalina flying out on Monday at 1100 hours. The Catalina flight will stop over at Wake Island.

Jim, "Book me on the PBY Sunday. I have flown in both planes and they are both okay, but I like the shorter flight time of the PBY."

CPO, "Yes sir. Let me take down all the info from your orders."

The CPO completed a form and gave Jim a copy. It gave Jim information where to go for his departure and gave as EDT and other information.

Jim returned to the apartment and turned on his radio for the latest news.

The news reported that a U. S. Naval task force was going up and down the Japanese Coast with out any opposition. The news report stated that U. S. bombers were bombing military targets in Japan and that submarines have sunk a number of Japanese ships.

Jim said to himself, "It sounds like we are pouring it on."

Jim and Janet spent the next three days clinging to one another like there was not going to be a tomorrow. They slept late every morning that Janet did not have to work. Finally Sunday came. Jim kissed Janet goodbye and left to catch his plane.

After Jim left Janet couldn't stop thinking about the plane crash that had occurred when he was on his way to see her. She prayed that he would have a safe trip to Guam.

CHAPTER 25
FINAL ASSIGNMENT

JIM CAUGHT HIS plane ride to Guam. He had a safe trip arriving about midnight at his destination. By the time Jim settled into his quarters it was about 0200 (2 a.m.). His two room-mates were asleep so he did not turn any lights on or unpack. He had slept about six hours on the plane, but was tired.

Jim remembered, "I got back a day early. Actually I am a day early with one day of my leave left so I can sleep in tomorrow morning."

The next morning Jim awoke at reveille. Although it was 0600 Jim decided to get up. His two roommates welcomed him back and they hurriedly dressed to go to the galley for breakfast. Jim decided to join them for breakfast. He was anxious to hear all the latest news.

After breakfast Jim decided to check in at the office. He caught a ride and was among the first to get to the PIO. The first person Jim saw as he entered the office was Kathy Holt.

Kathy, "Mister Rush it is good to see you sir."

Kathy threw her arms around Jim and hugged his neck.

Jim, "Thanks Kathy it is good to see you. How is everyone?"

Kathy, "Oh just fine Mister Rush. We have really missed you. We were really worried when we heard that your plane had crashed. We were so relieve when you were rescued. I hope you had a good leave."

Jim, "I did Kathy, a very good leave. Is Glen in his office?"

Kathy, "No sir, Mister Harper hasn't come in yet. Mister Emery and Mister Spencer are here."

Jim, "Okay, thanks. I'll check in with them. I guess they are in the break room?"

Kathy, "Yes they are."

Jim went to the break room. Paul and Tim were drinking coffee and talking. Paul was the first one to see Jim.

Paul, "Jim, good to see you fella. What are you doing here today? You are not scheduled back until tomorrow. How is Janet?"

Tim, "Hi Jim."

Jim, "Hello fellas. The transportation I choose got me back a day early. Janet is fine. It was difficult to leave her. But I just had to get back to see my old buddies and find out how the war was going."

Paul, "Yeah I'll bet. You probably know about what is going on better than we do."

Glen stuck his head in the door about that time.

Glen, "Welcome back Jim. Kathy told me you were here. After you guys finish your coffee we will have a meeting in the conference room."

All the PIO staff was present for the meeting. Glen called the meeting to order and circulated a copy of the agenda.

Glen, "Good morning staff"

Staff in unison, "Good morning sir."

Glen, "I will bring you up to date on events. We have a copy of a TOP SECRET message from Washington that President Truman has asked the Swiss and the Swedish ambassadors to deliver surrender term to government of Japan today or tomorrow."

Paul, "Sir do we know any of the details of the terms?'

Glen, "No, we don't know the details. We know that the Japanese considers the Emperor of Japan as a God. What they are trying to work out is how to leave him in place with no power."

Jim, "I suspect many of our military leaders are for executing Hirohito and tell the Jap army to kiss off."

Glen, "The Jap army is the big problem. Apparently they want to continue to fight. It is believed that the civilian officials and the navy are ready to give up."

Walter, "The U.S. Secretary of State has been very busy. He has kept the trial hot to various capitols of the Allies. I know there is a strong feeling that Russia should not have a say in the peace treaty."

Tim, "Yeah keep the Russians out. They jumped in after two atomic bombs were dropped and declared war on Japan. They just want to carve up some of the turkey."

Several staff members gave their opinion. There was a lively discussion.

Finally Glen announced, "I will give you a new assignment some time this week. We are waiting on headquarters to send a new assignment any day now. You are dismissed."

Later that day on Monday, August 13, 1945 the PIO learned that the Japanese had responded to the surrender message. They accepted the unconditional surrender demands by the allies, 'provided the allies would not dethrone or charge the Emperor with war crimes.'

The allies replied that these terms were acceptable, provided the Emperor submit to the authority of a Supreme Allied Commander and give the Japanese people the right to decide his ultimate status through free elections.

The next day on August 14, 1945 President Truman announced on the radio that he deemed the Japanese reply to be an acceptance to the terms of the unconditional surrender.

At fifty-six minutes to midnight, August 14, 1945 Admiral Nimitz sent a message to all navel units:

"CEASE OFFENSIVE OPERATIONS AGAINST JAPANESE FORCES. CONTINUE SEARCH AND PATROLS. MAINTAIN DEFENSIVE AND INTERNAL SECURITY MEASURES AT HIGHEST LEVEL AND BEWARE OF TREACHERY OR LAST MOMENT ATTACKS BY ENEMY FORCES OR INDIVIDUALS."

On August 15, the President announced, "This is V-J Day."

Glen called the PIO staff together, "I am pleased to announce that the Japanese have surrendered. All offensive action is to cease. We need to celebrate this occasion. I have ordered that a ration of medicinal brandy be mixed with pineapple juice and that each staff member can have one drink."

Kathy, "Irene and I have mixed and poured the drinks and each one of you can take a small paper cup and drink it. And the drinks are not real strong."

Walter Towers, "I propose a toast to our great nation and all that it stands for."

Eugene Slade, "Here, here, I second that and add what a privilege it has been to work with this bunch of people."

Jim, "Let's not forget to thank God in our prayers. I am so thankful and can hardly wait to be with Janet again."

Celebrations were occurring all over the world. The final surrender documents would be signed on September 2, 1945 on the deck of the battleship *Missouri*.

Jim and Janet would soon be going home.

CHAPTER 26
THE ANNIVERSARY

"WAKE UP MISTER Rush," the stewardess said.

The Stewardess, "You asked me to make sure to wake you when we were about one hour out of Hawaii."

Jim, "Yes, thanks."

Jim looked out the airplane window and the sun was just coming up. The Pacific looked blue and calm from 30,000 feet. He glanced over at Janet who was still asleep in the seat next to him.

Jim thought that Janet is as beautiful as ever. He debated whether to wake her or not. About that time Janet opened her eyes.

Janet, "Are we there yet?"

Jim, "No we are about one hour out."

Janet, "I wonder how much Pearl and Honolulu have changed?"

Jim, "Quite a bit I imagine."

Janet, "Happy anniversary dear. Just think we have been married 50 years this month."

Jim, "Happy anniversary darling. I love you. Married 50 years. Where did the time go Janet? I am glad we decided to return to Pearl for our 50th anniversary. I am glad the kids suggested this anniversary trip."

Janet, "I love you Jim and I am glad we took this anniversary trip. The kids suggested and we pay."

Jim, "It is worth it. We both have so many fond memories of Pearl and our life here during the war."

Janet, "Jim I think I'll go back to sleep. Wake me when we get there."

Jim, "Sure thing."

Jim looked at Janet and thought, "Today in 1994 Janet is 70 and I am 71. I still love Janet—it is a different love than the one on our honeymoon. Janet's hair is still its natural color, but my hair is gray. Thank goodness I have not lost too much hair. Janet still has a good figure for a woman of 70. She carries herself very well and even though she weighs a few more pounds than when we married it is proportioned right. Of course, I have put on a few more pounds, but neither of us is fat."

Jim thoughts continued, "I have put on a few more pounds. Jim thought of their three children and their five grandchildren. We were lucky to have raised a good family. The family had changed as they had lost Janet's and his parents. Jim's sister and brothers were still living."

Jim's thoughts were interrupted.

Virgil Sears the tour director of Jim and Janet's travel group of twenty people came by and sat down in an empty seat next to the aisle and Janet. Virgil looked past Janet to Jim.

Virgil, "Jim I am glad that you and Janet got to come on this trip. We have a good group on this tour and I think you will all have a good time. I understand that you were stationed here during the war Jim?"

Jim, "Yes that is right. Both Janet and I were stationed here, I was here in '42 to '45. Janet was here in '43 to '45. We got married here 50 years ago this month. We wanted to come and see Honolulu, Pearl Harbor and all the other locations of historical value. We especially wanted to see the Arizona Memorial and visit the National Memorial Cemetery."

Virgil, "I didn't know this was an anniversary trip for you two. Congratulations. When we land I will inform the rest of the group . . . if that is all right? We will make sure you and Janet get to visit all the places you want to."

Jim, "No we don't mind if our group knows this is our anniversary. We are proud to have been married so many years."

Virgil, "We will be spending the first four nights at the Sheraton Princess Kairulani Hotel in Honolulu. I'll arrange for us to have an anniversary party for you and Janet. Is this your first trip back since the war?"

Jim, "An anniversary party would be great Virgil. This is our first trip back since the war. We are anxious to see what changes have been made. Plenty I bet."

Virgil, "No trouble, glad to do it. I had better check on some of the other members of our group Jim. I'll see you later."

Jim sat daydreaming, "It had been a good life. Oh there have been ups and downs, but over all it has been a good life. You have to take the bad with the good. How lucky that I have Janet as a mate. I remember she continued her nursing work except for about 12 years or so to tend to the children when they were small. Janet retired at age 61, but I continued on until age 67 before I retired."

Jim muttered to himself, "I think of my navy days in Pearl and Guam. I wondered what every happened to Mac, Don, Larry, Jack, Ginny, Linda, and all the others. I haven't heard from Linda. I did write her that last letter in '44."

Jim's muttering continued, "With the exception of Mac and Don, the last I had heard from any of the others was when the *Spearfish* crew had a 10th anniversary get together in 1954. I had just got home from the Korean War. I had been called back to duty in 1952. I had six years of reserve service when I was released from active duty in 1946, but discharged in 1954. I still think about Mac, Don, Larry, Jack, Ginny, Linda, and the others. What good people they all were."

Jim thoughts continued, "I do know that Don, Larry, and Jack stayed in the navy. They made a career in the navy. I remember that Larry did make admiral. I not sure about the others.

Jim said, "Well I guessed that each has gone their own way and carved out a life. I guess that is another story that I probably will never know. I know that Janet and I have had a wonderful life."